A NEW LIFE...

My head was whirling. There was something wrong. There had to be something wrong. Or was I really Catherine Alice Amber, that lucky girl who belonged to someone, on my way to an estate in a tropical world of glamor and mystery? What a thing it would be, to be surrounded by my own people, my own flesh and blood, and never alone again!

My horoscope had been right. This was the opportunity promised me. I would go warily, but I would be daring. I was almost afraid to breathe, for fear I should awaken.

Something nagged at the back of my mind —not a coherent memory, but a sensation of dampness and corruption and inexplicable fear. I had known this creeping terror before.

Was it only in a dream?

A LANCER ORIGINAL

CURSE
OF THE
ISLAND
POOL

VIRGINIA COFFMAN

LANCER BOOKS • NEW YORK

A LANCER BOOK • 1965

For my producers with love,
Edythe DeuVaul Coffman
and
William Milo Coffman

CURSE OF THE ISLAND POOL

LANCER BOOKS, INC. • 185 MADISON AVENUE • NEW YORK 16, N.Y.

ONE

It was the nightmare again.

In my recurrent dream giant ferns enclosed the path everywhere, their moist prickle spurring me on in my headlong flight. There was the same blood-red sky far above the interlaced greenery with its treacherous appearance of peace. There were the fiery waters that lay ahead of me somewhere in the murky dawn, and into whose depths one misstep would send me. Above all, there was myself, running . . . running. . . . From what danger I never knew. The exotic scene was unknown to my conscious city-bred mind. It was all vague and misty. All but the terror.

I had lived through the same nightmare a dozen times in my life, and it was as much a mystery on that last April morning in a New York hotel room as it had been in San Francisco on my fifth birthday, twenty years before.

I awakened with a start. The telephone on the nightstand beside the bed jangled insistently, ending my nightmare just where the nightmare always ended, as I stood on the brink of discovering the face of the terror from which I fled. One minute more, I thought, as I fumbled for the hotel phone. One instant—and I would have known my enemy.

"Hello. Hello—Catherine?" asked the voice over the phone, a well-modulated female voice, entirely strange to me. So it was not Brett Caldwell, after all. My uneasiness subsided. I was running away from him and from the snobbery of his aunt and uncle, who had reared him and whom I had yet to meet. But perversely enough, now that my relief set in and I knew Brett wasn't going to pursue me, I felt a distinct depression. He might at least have called me from the Coast and made some pretense of caring.

I said, "Yes. Cathy Blake speaking. Who is this?" What elderly woman in New York knew me by my first name? It was curious.

I had a sudden clutch of hope and panic. Suppose this was Brett's aunt, come up from South Carolina to inspect me. I wasn't absolutely sure, even yet, that I wanted to marry Brett; it seemed a shame to take such a delightfully devil-may-care bachelor out of circulation. But I did want to make a good impression on Mr. and Mrs. Caldwell, if only for my dead mother's sake. Mother had been very secretive about her family, and I knew nothing of my father, or if I even had one, legally. I will never forget the letter Brett showed me, in his joking way, in which both his aunt and uncle made impertinent inquiries about Mama's background and father's family. Since I could not answer the letter, and since Brett was laughing at my sudden access of pride, I threw the letter at him indignantly.

Two days later I advertised on the Coast and in a New York paper for any information as to Mama's or my background. I even enclosed an old picture of my mother and me. That was a month ago. Of course, the only replies came from idiotic pranksters, one of whom offered to "adopt" me. I hadn't really expected any sensible answer. And the cost was too prohibitive for a repetition in other papers.

But I wasn't going to allow Brett and his family to be ashamed of me. As soon as I could get a leave of absence from my secretarial job in San Francisco, I came East on my vacation, with a stopover in Chicago, about which Brett knew nothing. This would give him a chance to find another steady date, or to show me that he cared as much as he pretended, by the time I reached New York. Now it looked as though he'd found the steady date—and she wasn't me.

"I do hope you are ready, dear," said the mysterious, unidentifiable voice on the telephone. "We shall be sailing in four hours, and Michael will be so cross with me if there is a delay. I tried all yesterday to reach you. . . . Are you still there, Catherine? . . . Cathy Amber?"

Like other lonely visitors to New York, I had spent the previous day at a museum, then window-shopping along Fifth Avenue, and finally at the Music Hall. Meanwhile, I was not this woman's "Cathy."

"You have the wrong number; I'm sorry," I said politely. "There is no Cathy Amber here. My name is Blake. Catherine Blake." And I hung up.

The telephone rang again immediately, but I was too depressed and lonely to answer, since it had proved to be none of the Caldwells after all.

Though it was still early, I couldn't get back to sleep. Outside my eighteenth-floor window the golden morning sun glinted off the skyscrapers everywhere, and the city appeared in one of its rare beautiful moods. As my feet shifted under the covers, they knocked the morning paper off the bed. I had bought it the night before in the lobby. I had an idiotic obsession, and still have it: I always read the three-line horoscopes printed for superstitious people—like me. I picked up the paper, turning the pages quickly, and reread my horoscope for today:

Tremendous opportunities. Tread carefully.
You are at a turning point. Be daring. But
be wary.

What on earth did that mean? Like the Delphic oracle, each phrase denied the one before. I had to smile at my own gullibility. Besides, the one opportunity I had to change my dull life—an inspection by Mrs. Caldwell with its attendant proof that someone in the world actually loved me—had come to nothing. The only opportunity so far was a well-spoken lady looking for a mysterious Cathy Amber. Lucky Cathy Amber. She sailed in four hours. For a minute or two I wondered where. If only *I* were Cathy Amber, sailing somewhere! Anywhere.

Meanwhile, I was wasting my precious leave of absence. There was Rockefeller Center to be seen, with the ice rink still intact and the RCA Building. Many a gin-and-tonic I had drunk there in the RCA Bar with Mother during the years before she died. In those days, we had taken our vacations together and had made New York our goal. Mother had been the Women's Buyer for the finest department store in San Francisco. She had all sorts of background knowledge and often seemed curiously unlike other Americans we knew. But it had only been since her death, and the snobbish curiosity of the Caldwells had intruded, that I had become concerned over Mother's background and her secrecy.

I showered and dressed quickly, and as I did so, I caught myself wondering with absurd irrelevance what that lucky Cathy Amber was like and where she might be sailing four hours from now. The morning sun, filtering between the open venetian blinds, cut a pattern of light and shadows across the small desk portrait of Brett that I had opened and placed on the dresser during a lonesome moment last night. His big grin was engaging, his black hair and eyes just as good-looking as though he hadn't "jilted" me. (Or had I technically jilted him?) I couldn't help feeling a pang of regret at what I had lost.

For no reason except to give me a badly needed lift, I got out my new pumps, whose stiletto-blade heels and almost total lack of covering gave me the self-confidence I needed at this point. I had one shoe on when I heard the chambermaid in the hall say plainly, "That's it, sir. Room 1836. She's still in, all right. Chain's on."

Brett! No wonder he hadn't written or phoned. He had made the trip himself. Bless him! How good it is, I thought, to have someone in the world who cares about you! Shakily, I waited for the knock on the door. When it came, a brisk, masculine rap, I told myself not to be too eager. I must remember that to enjoy someone's company and to love a man were two different things. But it was so dear of Brett to come all this way.

With an effort I managed to open the door and still retain a cool dignity, a casual interest.

"Well, hello, Br——"

It was not Brett. The man did not even look like Brett, whose easy Southern charm and lazy stance, which did not conceal his height, set him apart in a crowd.

This man was slightly older, probably in his middle

8

thirties, with very deep-set hazel eyes, broad and prominent cheekbones, and the most stubborn mouth I had ever seen. When he spoke, I changed my mind about his mouth; for his voice was beautiful. He spoke with an accent, perhaps English; yet he did not look English, and even while I adjusted my mind to the fact that he was not Brett, I wondered what he really was.

For one thing, he was a man in a bad humor. A strong, powerful-looking man, whose anger might be frightening to watch. Although his features appeared sombre, he added a frown to clinch the impression.

"What the devil did you do to your cousin Isobel?" he asked me directly, as though we had only just parted an hour before. "She said you rang off when she called you."

He had obviously mistaken me for that lucky but tiresome Cathy Amber. I told him so. "I hung up—rang off—because I'm afraid she mistook me for a Catherine Amber, sir. I didn't mean to upset her. But my name happens to be Blake. And, frankly, this mistake is getting a little boring. I expected someone else."

"Undoubtedly," he said, glancing down at my hand. The strange and exotic planes of his face were highlighted by a sudden smile.

Puzzled, I followed his glance, saw that my left shoe was still dangling between my fingers, and felt strongly tempted to hit him with it. "I'm not Cathy Amber!" I repeated loudly, for the benefit of anyone who might be loitering in the hall. "I was born Catherine Alice Blake, in San Francisco. . . ."

"On July 28th, 1939," he finished easily. He did not look nearly so formidable or strange now, with that curious smile. "Your mother was Catherine Frances Blake, so far as you know. Your father was—ah, but that puzzled you."

Suddenly, the whole thing came to me, and I was angry with myself for not having suspected it sooner. I didn't know the purpose of this man and his precious "Cousin Isobel," but I realized where he had got his information about me.

"You read the advertisement I sent out a month ago; didn't you?"

"Of course. And thought the picture of you quite

charming. It also served to identify you, or I'm afraid we should have been a good deal longer in finding you. For you are Catherine Alice Amber, you know. And your father . . ."

"Never mind my father," I said heatedly, not wanting to go into my fears on that score.

". . . was Richard Ainsley Amber. Quite respectable," he assured me with such a sudden access of gravity that I knew he was teasing. "Background unexceptionable. Or at least I consider it so, since it is my own. I am your late father's cousin, Michael Amber."

He held out his hand, and although I very much wanted to let him take my own hand, all my caution was up in arms, and I retreated, avoiding him. He was apparently not used to defiance, for he reached out, closing his fingers around my wrist to stop my retreat. As I had suspected, the grip of his hand, with its single ornament, a stately signet ring, was enough to make me wince. It was as though he knew exactly what he wanted and never let it go. His hands were very different from Brett's hands, with their long, lean fingers that flipped away from me instantly when I frowned. Brett was so much easier, more gay; he was never difficult at all. I had a notion that this man, who might or might not be my cousin, would prove to be extremely difficult to those who knew him well. Also, I recalled something the elderly lady had said to me on the telephone earlier:

". . . Michael will be so cross with me. . . ."

Yes. This man could inspire terror. But for a few moments he brought into my life an excitement that was not altogether unpleasant. He said now, "Am I to understand that you received none of our communications in San Francisco? When I made a call there, your office informed me you would be stopping here. Why else would you be in New York at this precise time?"

"I happen to be here on vacation. I left San Francisco two weeks ago and spent a week in Chicago. I suppose that is why I never heard of you before."

He sighed with strong impatience. "We must talk then. Shall it be in your room?" He appeared to think this an ideal solution, and he started to pilot me into the room.

I said quickly, "I don't entertain strangers in hotels.

I'll go downstairs, if you like. I haven't had breakfast yet."

He seemed to find my prim concern for the proprieties rather amusing, but he agreed that if I did not dawdle over my food, we might transact our business at breakfast. "You sail in a little over three hours," he reminded me as he turned away.

I was so nervous I forgot to ask him where. I put on my shoe, dashed a lipstick on without a brush, twirled mascara over my eyelashes, and was out in the elevator within ten minutes. I knew as well as I knew I was not Catherine Amber that all this man told me would be lies, or mistaken identity, but still . . . To think I just might be that lucky Cathy Amber! Where was she going? And why?

In the lobby I looked around, feeling that the Halloween masquerade was over when I did not catch sight of the man who called himself Michael Amber. Then I was accosted by a small lady who might have been in her fifties, but whose sculptured face had been so well-cared-for that she seemed ageless. From the tiny pill-box hat perched on the crown of her head, to the tip of her extremely fashionable toes, she had a look of remarkable chic.

"Dear Cathy," she said as she tucked her arm into mine, "I should have known you anywhere. There is something about you so like your lovely mother." This was absurd, as Mother had been tall and darkly beautiful, and I was quite the contrary. We were not in the least alike, except for a certain family cast of countenance.

"I am Isobel Amber, my dear. How confusing to unravel the whole skein in such a short time; for Michael is frightfully impatient to get you back to Saint Cloud, you know."

"But I don't know," I said. "Is that in France?"

"Heavens, no. Much nearer. The Antilles. That's in the Caribbean. But our windward shores face on the Atlantic."

I felt like informing her that I knew where the Antilles were, but there were more immediate matters. Was I an heiress, perhaps? And then I thought of Brett's relations. I pictured their faces when they discovered that my mother was actually a great lady.

11

"What makes you think I am Cathy Amber, ma'am?"

"Child, we have all the evidence. There can be no doubt of it. The marriage certificate of your mother and my cousin Richard. She was his second wife, you understand. And any number of pictures of dear Catherine and Richard, taken on their honeymoon. You will recognize your father's picture at once. You have his eyes. Much lovelier than his, I'm afraid. Come. The dining room is this way."

The lobby was very dark at this hour, and I felt the morning chill of the great, empty place with its marble pillars and Grand Central elegance.

"Did mother divorce your—Mr. Amber?"

"Not that we can discover. But there were many bitter quarrels. Your mother was a very headstrong girl, and the Ambers were—well, my dear, they are accustomed to ruling their little world. Richard was a quiet sort. Despised attracting attention to himself. It was only a matter of time, however. They even had words over you, Cathy, before you were born. Or at least Catherine had words. Richard, poor soul, scarcely raised his voice. But he was determined you would be a boy. There was already your half-sister, Ellen, of course. The next child had to be a male, to manage the estate, you understand. One night your mother disappeared after one of her quarrels. Of course, we traced her from island to island, but at last the trail was gone. We guessed she had returned to the States, but we could find no trace."

It sounded plausible, but there would be a flaw in it somewhere. "And now my father is dead, and I am the only one left?" I asked.

"To be exact, my dear, your elder sister, Ellen, is dead. She died last October. Quite suddenly. Your father passed away some eighteen months before. He left everything to Ellen with the proviso that if she had no immediate heirs, her own will should name her stepmother, Catherine, or in the event of Catherine's death, her child. Yourself. Michael was executor of the will, which is appropriate, you will allow, since Saint Cloud's economic welfare depends, for the most part, on dear Michael. We must be very careful not to offend him, you see. Unfortunately, Amber—your poor sister's estate—has been allowed to go to ruin since your father's illness began, three years ago."

Ah! This sounded like something I could believe—that I was still a pauper. "You mean I am not the heiress to a great fortune?"

She laughed, a cool, elegant laugh with no feeling in it. "More probably a great debt. Michael has ideas about reviving your plantation, rotating crops, experimenting with pineapples, and I don't know what all. But, of course, nothing could be done while poor Ellen remained."

I wondered why. How odd it seemed to have had a half-sister I never knew in life or in death! The knowledge of a lost companionship was so painful that I scarcely realized we were entering the big hotel dining room, which looked depressingly ordinary with only half the old-fashioned crystal lusters lighted at this hour.

"Then my half-sister is dead?"

"*Exceedingl*y dead, if I may . . . Here we are, dear. Michael will join us as soon as he gets some of the documents from his room. You see, we sent off our best ones to you in San Francisco. What a pity! Copies of your mama's marriage license and Ellen's will, some photographs, that sort of thing."

My head was whirling. There was something wrong. There had to be something wrong. Or was I really Catherine Alice Amber, that lucky girl who belonged to someone, on my way to an estate in a tropical world of glamor and mystery? What a thing it would be, to be surrounded by my own people, my own flesh and blood, and never alone again!

My horoscope had been right. This was the opportunity promised me. I would go warily, but I would be daring. I was almost afraid to breathe, for fear I should awaken.

The hotel dining room was cold, and the heavy, old-fashioned silverware was chill to my touch. Something nagged at the back of my mind—not a coherent memory, but a sensation of dampness and corruption and inexplicable fear. I had known this creeping terror before.

Was it only in a dream?

TWO

I CAME OUT of my flurry of tangled doubts to surprise Isobel Amber's eyes, like two little deep-set blue marbles, fixed on me with a look of cold and inhuman brightness. There was no liking, no warmth, in that look nor even the tepid heat of dislike. It was as though I were a bolt of goods, and she, with sharp-bladed shears upraised in those jewelled hands, was about to cut a pattern to her measure. When I intercepted her calculating stare, the expression broke so quickly into a smile that I nearly convinced myself I had imagined that other—that peculiarly inhuman look.

"Dear child," she murmured in her soft, beautifully modulated voice.

Without intending to, I shivered at this sudden warmth that seemed so false.

The waiter arrived, and while I was ordering, I was startled and oddly reassured of my sanity by the voice of a young bellman paging:

"Miss Catherine Blake. Call for Miss Catherine Blake."

Thank heaven I was still myself to someone. Perhaps this was a call from Brett in San Francisco. He would bring me back to reality, to plain Cathy Blake, father unknown. Fortune? Two hundred dollars in traveler's checks! I began to rise and was detained by Miss Amber's quickly outthrust hand.

"How provoking! So ill-timed. Cathy dear, why not ignore it? That part of your life is over." Her face beamed gently. "Only think of what lies ahead for you!

14

A lady of property. The First Lady of Saint Cloud. Throw away these tiresome tidbits of your poor little past . . . Cathy!"

I pulled away from her tenacious, curling fingers and went to the bellman. My call was at the Registration Desk, he told me, and I crossed the dark lobby, which was coming to life with the breakfast meetings of various businessmen. I asked one of the clerks at the desk if he had called me. He looked prim, his lips pursed, with the faintest effort at a smile, but he did not answer. I felt myself assailed from behind by two hands which covered my eyes, in the well-worn tradition of the American cry "Guess who?" I knew at once. Only Brett would try such a collegiate trick before half of sophisticated New York, and although I was pleased, I was embarrassed too. Then I scolded myself mentally for false pride and turned to face him. It wasn't Brett's fault that I had twice expected and been disappointed in him this morning. How could he know? Besides, he had come clear across the country to see me, bless him!

His friendly, lean face looked playful and mischievous, and he winked elaborately at the desk clerk as I presented my cheek to him a little shyly. I had not known just how far he wanted to go. We were only friends, more or less, after all. It was awkward, not being sure.

"Well, hon, is that all I get after three thousand gruelling miles by dog team, mushing all the way?"

I kissed him again, trying to concentrate, but half my mind was buried in plantations, unknown dead fathers, and half-sisters *"exceedingly"* dead. (What did that mean?) Then I saw Isobel Amber, her stunning, chic little figure outlined against the shadow of the dining room corridor, across the lobby. She had come out of the dining room to watch us.

Pretending I hadn't seen her, I said to Brett, "I'm so glad to see you. What are you doing here, for goodness sake?"

He grinned and took my arm. "Silly question. See my best girl, of course. Missed you like the devil. I think I'm getting serious. Heinous thought."

I couldn't help agreeing, much as I liked him. He was not cut out to be serious. "Yes. When I think what that

15

would do to all the girls you would leave scattered over the universe . . ."

"Now, hon, I was taught to spread a little cheer wherever possible. And that reminds me, how'd you like to pop down to visit Auntie? Likewise, the Honorable Unkie? Thought it might soften them up to . . ." He saw my frown and added quickly, ". . . to things, I mean."

Always before, when he joked about his relations, calling them the nicknames so ridiculous in his broad and easy accent, I had been half scared. But this morning, for the first time, I could smile at their disapproval.

"I'm afraid I couldn't go, quite yet. You see . . ." Oh, the glorious pride in it! His aunt and uncle would never sneer at Mother again. "I've got to go and inspect my estate."

"Your . . . what?" Brett's large black eyes looked so ludicrously surprised I had to laugh. He made an ungallant stab at laughing it off too. "Doll, you've been out in the midday sun!"

So I pulled at his coat sleeve, got him away from the inquisitive desk clerk, and briefly told him about the Ambers. He began by dropping his whole six feet-four noisily onto a lobby sofa and almost pulling me down too. I had a weather-eye out for Isobel Amber and, without knowing why, felt uneasy to see that she was gone again. I kept having the feeling that she might pop up right at my back, or rubbing shoulders with me, her little blue marble eyes burning brightly, inhumanly, as she eavesdropped.

Brett looked up at me, all the fun and idiotic clowning gone from his face. "Cathy, it just isn't possible. These things don't happen to ordinary people. They only happen to people in . . ."

This hurt me, because in my hypersensitive concern over his family's wealth, I thought he was thinking of that difference between us. "What makes you think I'm so ordinary?" I asked, my voice shaking with anger. "I'm just as extraordinary as your old—auntie, and your unkie too!"

"Simmer down, sugar. You didn't let me finish. I was going to say, 'these things don't happen to *real* people.' What do you know about this woman and her cousin? Have you ever heard of them before? For all you know, they may be white slavers."

This was so funny it put me in good humor again.

"Brett, for heaven's sake! . . . Michael Amber, a white slaver? Preposterous. He was much too . . ." Or was he? Doubts crept back. "Oh, Brett, what do you think I ought to do?"

But Brett had been thinking the problem over and came to my rescue in his best sensible manner. "That's easy. While this fellow is collecting your evidence—such as it is—we'll call Saint Cloud and check on *his* evidence. Auntie knows the manager at Cross and Bingham. They handle cargo for our firm throughout the British West Indies Federation. If the Ambers are what they claim, Joel Bingham will know all about them."

How easy it sounded! When Brett got up, I could not help hugging him, which he seemed to like, for he returned a bear hug that left me breathless. We walked over to the row of telephone booths around the corner of the lobby. On the way, I saw no sign of the Ambers. The morning had been so fantastic, I wondered if Michael and Isobel Amber really existed.

Brett fished around for his credit card, got the operator, and before I would believe it possible, he was explaining the situation to an exceedingly English voice on the line. "Yes. Yes. Joel? This is Brett Caldwell. No, Brett! The no-good nephew. Uncle's fine. No problems. Why should there be problems?" He grinned and motioned me closer to the finger-stained black receiver. I could hear the voice at Saint Cloud saying airily,

"What else am I to think, old chap? Your family never calls me unless there's a ruddy slipup in the manifest somewhere."

"Not this time, Joel. Just want to check on a suspicious character floating around here in New York. Ever hear of a— What's her name, honey?" I told him. "That's it. Isobel Amber. You know her? Middle-aged and handsome. Well-dressed. You did say well-dressed, honey?" I agreed.

The plaintive voice of Joel Bingham came to us then. "I wish you'd speak a little more plainly, man. I keep fancying I hear you call me 'honey.' "

This made us laugh and relieved my tension. Brett explained that I was his girlfriend.

"I see," said Joel Bingham. "I must say, I did wonder there, for a bit. Now, about the well-dressed middle-aged female. She may be a member of the Amber family here on the island. Then again, she may not. There are several of them. Keep to themselves, for the most part."

Brett wrinkled his nose at me. We hadn't got far. Brett went on. "And there's a man involved. Calls himself Michael Amber. Fellow's in his . . ."

"Thirties," I said into the phone.

The rest was cataclysmic. "Not *the* Michael Amber! But good Lord, old chap! You haven't offended him by any chance?"

"Not so far. What's your Amber like?"

Joel ticked off phrases as he visualized them. "Deep-set eyes? Cheekbones broad as a Jivaro? Odd sort. Makes one think he doesn't quite 'belong,' if you follow me. Maybe a wee dram of the tar-barrel in the blood. But don't offend him. Ever notice how fierce the beggar is when he's bested?"

"I wouldn't know. I've never bested him." Brett turned to me. "Does that sound like him, doll?"

"Doll?" Joel repeated.

"Girlfriend."

"Oh," Joel paused. "Well?"

There was no question. I would have recognized that description anywhere.

"Dear boy," said Joel. "If you've made an enemy of Michael Amber, you've got a tiger by the tail. He *is* Saint Cloud. Why, I'd sooner jump into La Soufriere —that's our local volcano—than get that bloke down on me."

I spoke into the phone.

"Is there an old plantation called Amber? And did the owner, a young woman, recently die?"

"Quite. Oh, quite! Ellen Amber. Heaps of excitement. They couldn't locate the next of kin. Michael Amber himself took the trail to find the heiress. . . . Don't tell me, ma'am, that you're—well, by jove!"

"I—I don't know," I answered faintly. I wanted to sit down. It was a shaky notion to find there really was an Ellen Amber. For in that case, I might well be Catherine Alice Amber. I had been embarrassed over poor Brett's exuberance—now I wanted to laugh—and laugh! Partly at Brett's family, partly because I would at last "belong" to my own family, and partly, too, at the sheer adventure of it. If I really was Cathy Amber, there would be no more living alone all year in wretched little single apartments. No more wondering if I should relieve the loneliness by marrying someone I liked but wasn't quite sure I loved.

I tried hard to look sober, but Brett, hanging up on his friend at Saint Cloud, cuffed me under the chin and complained, "You needn't look so happy, doll. The prospect of getting away from me sure peps you up."

I was so happy I kissed him on the cheek, and he beamed and said he forgave me. I had often envied him his cheerful disposition. Maybe, with his advantages in great wealth, I could salt down my own uncertain temper and be jolly all the time too.

Breathing deeply, I said, "Well . . . let's go and beard the lion."

Brett grinned. "Or twist the tiger's tail."

The lobby was no longer clammy and silent. Everywhere I noticed the buzz of conversation, the exciting heartbeat of a big hotel. I was somewhat surprised when we reached the dining room to find Michael Amber seated opposite Miss Amber at the table, leaning forward, his head lowered toward her, as he discussed something brusquely, with a certain amount of what seemed to me flamboyant gesture.

Isobel Amber, who was facing us, saw us first and made a quick motion to him. He looked around with his familiar scowl and stood up. In spite of his scowl, he gave me a penetrating, not ungentle look, which I found interesting. How different he was to the cold, bright, bubbling Cousin Isobel!

While I tried to make introductions as I sat down, Michael Amber drew out my chair for me and inched me closer to the table before Brett could do so. I don't think Brett liked it, but he made a funny expression to me which Michael Amber intercepted with raised eyebrows and a glint of humor in his strange, foreign-looking eyes.

I felt I had been caught doing something underhanded and reached for my water glass, that savior of awkward situations, but Brett immediately plunged into a demand to know what the Amber intentions were toward me.

19

Pretending to sip ice water, I furtively studied Brett and Michael Amber over the rim of my glass. It was like watching a tennis match in which I was not only the spectator but the tennis ball!

"For all we know," Brett went on, "You two might be kidnapping Cathy for some . . ."

"Brett!" I cut in quickly, to keep him from going into his "white slave" speech.

"What could be more absurd?" asked Isobel Amber in a shocked voice of righteousness.

Brett was undaunted. "There might even be danger."

Michael Amber surprised me by nodding agreement. He had a long, stiff manila folder about six inches wide in his hand, and he began to untie the frayed cord which bound it.

"I quite agree. And in return for my proofs, may I inquire as to your precise interest in the affairs of Miss Amber?"

"I happen to be Miss *Blake's* closest friend," said Brett loftily.

"I happen to be Miss *Amber's* closest relative," Michael Amber reminded him, with a note of finality like the closing of a book. It was not strictly true; for surely "Cousin" Isobel was just as closely related to me, but I suppose Michael felt, as I did, that she didn't count.

Even Brett was silenced for a moment or two, while Mr. Amber passed me the folder. The legal documents I expected were in the folder along with cuttings from old yellowed newspapers and a photostatic copy of a marriage certificate, naming Richard Ainsley Amber and Catherine Frances Blake, but these did not seem to me very powerful proofs of my own connection with the family. Then came the pictures, most of them old, dogeared, black-and-white snapshots, not too well focused.

"Dear Catherine never was mechanically minded," Isobel Amber explained brightly. "She took snaps any old way. See? Heads off, feet off—all hobbledehoy."

Yes. That would be mother's temperament, as I remembered her. When an electric iron, or a sewing machine, or a toaster failed to function, out it was thrown. We did without the appliance until mother or I could afford a new one.

When I finally saw a snapshot that included mother it gave me a queer, painful sensation; for she looked so young, her dark hair parted on the side and almost straight, in the style of the time, with funny "spit curls" and a horrid dress like a sack with a fringe.

But the important thing was—I recognized mother. There could be no mistaking her lovely broad forehead or her wide, generous mouth, which I'd seen with that wry little twist to it when I behaved badly.

"She looks unhappy," I told myself. But I had spoken aloud, and Isobel Amber said quickly, "I told you so, dear. You remember . . . I did tell you."

"For God's sake, Isobel! Don't rattle on so," Michael Amber cut in, much to Brett's and my surprise.

Isobel merely beamed graciously and replied, "Of course, dear."

There were so many proofs, a dozen documents, pictures I could not deny. I shuffled them back together like playing cards. They didn't matter so much as something much smaller.

"Why was she unhappy?" I wanted to know. I began to study the man in the snapshot. Richard Amber didn't look cruel or beastly. He looked, on the contrary, rather nice in a quiet, forgettable sort of way. And he was obviously fond of mother. His arm was around her waist, and he was waving at the camera, the gesture of a plain, serious man trying hard to be lively.

"Who took the picture?" Brett asked as he looked over at my "evidence." I, too, was curious to know the person my father was waving at. It must be someone with whom he felt free; for the more I studied his stiff, lean figure, looking awkward in knee-length khaki shorts, the more I was convinced that he was normally reserved and shy. I liked him for this feeble attempt at flippancy.

As though she had been primed and waiting, Isobel Amber recalled, "Your poor half-sister, Ellen, took the snap. Such a quiet little thing! Only ten at the time. But for a child, she was clever with a camera. Don't you think so, Michael dear?"

Before Michael could answer I burst out with something that had both troubled and annoyed me. "Is it necessary to speak of her always as 'poor Ellen'? She was an heiress. She lived well. Why is she so pitiable?"

Michael laughed abruptly. "I've no doubt that behind my back I am 'poor Michael' to Isobel," he said. "And in no time, your—er—friend here will be 'poor whatever-his-name-is.' "

Brett grinned at this bad-mannered reference to him, but it was Isobel, after all, who had the last word.

"My dear! One simply wouldn't *dare* call you 'poor Michael.' One wouldn't dare!"

I waited uneasily to see his reaction, but to my surprise his face reddened a little and he glanced at me and then shifted his gaze, as though embarrassed. So this inscrutable and all-powerful man was vulnerable. It made him more human, I thought. Perhaps, deep down, he wasn't so sure of himself as he pretended.

Isobel appeared happily oblivious. She said, "Poor Ellen was virtually housekeeper and companion to Richard all those years after Catherine left. Ellen never married. Though there were rumors." Michael looked at her, but she only called attention to this by underscoring it. "Well, you know there were rumors, among the servants. About her secret trips to the inner islands. Perhaps that's why she . . ."

"Ellen was drowned," Michael explained flatly, interrupting all this bubbly malice. "She was returning across the Amber fern forest one evening from a local native ceremony. Some sort of jingoism that they called voodoo—for the sake of the tourist trade, I imagine. It blew up a rain suddenly. She lost her footing and stumbled into a pool."

"The Tangerine Pool," said Isobel.

"But couldn't she swim?" A woman living more than thirty years on an island and she could not swim?

Michael hesitated. He pretended the arrival of the waiters had interrupted him, but I felt sure he was choosing his words.

"The Tangerine Pool is a natural body of water in a lava basin. Through the years the sides have been covered by slippery vines, ferns, and the mud and slime of centuries. Without help from soneone on the path above, it would be nearly impossible for any but an athlete to find a firm hold and climb out."

My nightmare! The curious sense of tropical danger that had haunted my life . . . had it foretold the death of my half-sister? I felt very close to this unknown woman, as though, in that dream, she had tried to reach me, to tell me . . . what? Perhaps my recurrent nightmare could be explained by something mother had told me when I was too young to remember the tale, and only the horror, the ferns and monstrous jungle growths remained.

Brett watched my expression. He must have read more than my horror at Ellen's death; for when the first shock of it passed, I knew that I was destined to go to Saint Cloud. The singularly persistent dream that drew me to Saint Cloud even while it warned me was something I had to exorcize forever.

Brett knew me well enough to guess. "Now, honey, it's all wrong. It's not even safe. That's no place for you."

"On the contrary," Michael Amber said and added with a gentle note in his beautiful voice that completely won my agreement, "That is the place for you. Come home, Cathy Amber, to your family and your loved ones."

He did not touch me, but I was aware of his hand, with the peculiarly golden flesh of his coloring, beside my own hand on the table. I wondered at the tingle of my fingers as though there had been a physical contact between us.

"Well, that does it," Brett grumbled. "Before you're through, Cathy, you're going to wish to God you'd listened to me." He stood up, shoving his chair back noisily. "You have my address, hon. Send me a cable and I'll be down there so fast it'll curl your hair."

I tried to protest, to keep him a little longer, because he was my last link with "Cathy Blake" and the old familiar days.

"Please, Brett, couldn't you—couldn't he visit me at Saint Cloud?" I asked Michael.

Brett forestalled him. "Thanks for nothing, hon." Then he surprised me by leaning down and kissing me on the forehead. "Okay, sweet. I'm not angry. Not at you. But see that you don't go wandering beside pools in the rain. That's my girl. Write to me; won't you, doll?"

I agreed, feeling sad, as if I had betrayed him.

No one said anything until Brett was gone. I was full of fears and doubts, nervous over the fascination

23

of my strange "Cousin" Michael, always aware of the lovely words that had made my decision for me: "Come home . . . to your family."

Yet the closest members of my family were buried. There was mother in California. And the tragic, pitiful Ellen. I could not bear to dwell on the long horror that must have been her death. And my father was dead. I might have liked him. How had he died, poor lonely man? "Was my father ill for long?" I asked.

For once, Isobel said nothing. She sat looking at Michael with her vacant smile.

"Quite long," he told me without hesitation. "He had a bad heart."

Isobel agreed in a pleased way. "Overexertion. Or so that wretched native Doctor Torri said. But really, Catherine, I should have thought even Richard knew that one does not race madly through acres of fern forest as if the devil were after one. Not at his age, and with a bad heart!"

THREE

AT DAWN, two days later, Cousin Isobel and I had hurried out on a forward deck of the big British liner, hoping to be the first passengers to catch sight of Saint Cloud. As we waited, I asked her, "Why do they call it the Tangerine Pool?"

I was reminded of this by the action of Cousin Isobel, who had brought a mandarin orange up on deck from the basket in her cabin and was peeling it with a nail scissors while we watched the smudge of land that was Saint Cloud grow larger on the Eastern horizon. My question apparently did not interest her; for after I asked it, she sucked plaintively at her thumb before replying.

"Oh, the deuce! Stabbed myself. I do hope the blades were sterile. Well, dear, speaking of the Tangerine Pool, do you see the color of the sunrise off there to the north of that volcanic peak? Just where the mountain slopes down into the sea."

I saw the point she mentioned, the lofty, rugged peak of La Soufriere, the quiescent volcano of Saint Cloud, and then, below the precipitous slope, I could see the first little swatch of blazing tangerine-colored sun between the sea and the mountain. As I watched, the little swatch of color became round as a ball, but its peculiar, dazzling hue did not change. It completely overwhelmed the exquisite blue waters of the Caribbean tumbling at the shores of the volcanic pile, so that the sea around us became, under that eery glow, an amber color.

Cousin Isobel popped an orange segment into her mouth and licked her fingers daintily. "The pool catches that frightfully gaudy sunrise," she said. "The natives—dear me—I must call them 'the locals'—say the voodoo god of death lurks there at sunrise and sunset; for the light can blind one, you know, and then a slight misstep among all those rainsoaked ferns may be the last."

"How jolly!" I said, thinking that in her perversely humorous way, she meant to frighten me. "If the Tangerine Pool belongs to me, I've a good notion to have it filled in, or whatever they do to such places."

"You won't," said Isobel sagely. "Richard used to say the same thing, poor boy. But he couldn't bring himself to destroy it. Enticing, he called it, in spite of Ellen's silly, superstitious attitude. Once she had the voodoo man in to remove the 'curse.' It was the only time I ever saw Richard literally white with fury. He loathed anything to do with voodoo. Really, one wonders if that Ellen was altogether sane. Probably too much native superstition in her childhood. As though Miss Nell were not enough of a fright."

Cousin Isobel did love to startle people into attention and then dismiss the whole subject. It was a game with her; I was now sure of that.

"Who was Miss Nell?" I asked, but with pretended indifference.

"Nobody, dear. Just Ellen's nurse. She's lived at Amber for nearly forty years. Really part of the scenery. One can't remove her any more than one can destroy the Tangerine Pool." She laughed her brittle, sarcastic laugh. "They are very much alike, in some ways, Nell and the pool. The plantation boys call her 'balmy.' Just a joke, dear. I'm sure she's harmless—in her horrid way."

This annoyed me so much I refused to be further drawn out, and, staring across the sparkling Caribbean waters, I thought of my half-sister, close to me in blood and perhaps in spirit, whom I could never meet. "I wish I had known Ellen," I said. Even now, I found it difficult to call her by her name. I was completely unused to the intimacy of family ties.

Isobel threw curls of orange peel over the rail of the liner and slapped her hands together. She said, "I think not, Cathy. Poor Ellen was very bitter against any child of your mother's. She'd have set her voodoo to destroy you, as near as makes no matter. . . . Such a charming girl, too!" I looked surprised at her belated praise of Ellen, but she added innocently, "Of course, Michael said that the first day he saw you."

I was secretly but extravagantly pleased. I could thank my mother's firm training and her access to the latest fashion trends for my ability to present a good appearance. Yet, had Michael really made that remark, or was this one of Cousin Isobel's delightful little lies "to make the day go," as she had explained to me once?

I had expected that Michael Amber would accompany us on the ship and was a good deal surprised to find that he was flying down to Saint Cloud, leaving me in the hands of Cousin Isobel, who was most entertaining but hardly inspired my confidence. She talked a great deal but always in half-phrases and innuendoes so that I was never sure afterward whether she had actually said something important or was merely rambling on in her unconscious way. I began to suspect she was not as "unconscious" as she sounded. After two days in her company I still knew very little about Saint Cloud, or my inheritance, or, especially, about Michael Amber. I did not even know if the estate had as many mysterious pitfalls as Isobel had hinted at so far. It seemed sometimes as though she would like to frighten me off completely, make me turn about and go back to New York again. But, of course, she was too awed by Michael Amber to take any drastic action, so she could only rely on hints and veiled suggestions of danger.

Whatever her attitude toward my coming to Saint Cloud, her own interest was even greater than mine in the distant smudge of charcoal-colored mountain slopes, which grew larger and greener as the great ship inched its way along the shallow Saint Cloud Channel between these busy West Indian islands. The peak of La Soufriere loomed up, swallowing the sunrise and reaching into clumps of rainclouds as we moved, but the rest of the island took on a deep, verdant green hue, and Cousin Isobel sighed.

"How good it is to be home again! My bougainvillea will be looking its best."

I wondered if I would ever feel this way about Saint Cloud, because at the moment my anticipation made me so nervous I nearly wished myself back in New York, waiting for Brett's long-distance call. Brett's cable to me a day at sea hadn't helped matters:

DOLL, LOOK OUT BEHIND YOU. LOOK OUT FOR PATHS, BRIDGES AND POOLS. IF NEEDED, MARINES TO THE RESCUE.
                                LOVE, MARINE BRETT.

The harbor of Port Anne, the capital city, became visible between jutting prongs of deep green, rain-washed land that ran down to the sea leaving only a hilly little hollow for the town and a long, twisting canal, which bisected the town and was the island's careenage for sailing vessels. A curious, skeletal iron finger dominated the Port Anne skyline, but I had used the ship's library to good advantage and realized that this iron finger was the church steeple, which had been built in the last century, when Saint Cloud still had remnants of the French culture that left its mark on the island.

As our liner dropped anchor out in the bay beyond the narrow careenage of the harbor, I could see the quayside buildings in the distance, with their balconies and jalousies, and faded pastel buildings where I had expected the cool, English-type landscape I associated with the other islands of the British West Indies Federation.

"Pink buildings?" I asked incredulously.

Cousin Isobel peered into the sunrise and defended her island with more vigor than I would have given her credit for.

"And charming they are, too. Very soothing to the eyes in this sunlight." She looked over the ship's side, far down to the water, where a launch from Saint Cloud was pulling in, and a local official stepped briskly from his rocking little boat to the rope ladder of the great ship. "Oh. I thought it might be Michael. His boat will come alongside presently, I expect."

The volcano was further off now, one of its spurs separating the fern forests of Amber and the windward coast from our view. Once, long ago, when pirates had infested Saint Cloud, it had erupted and destroyed an entire harbor on the windward side of the island; even in the last century it had erupted and done considerable damage. But those times were gone now, or so the books said, and present eruptions were small and were publicized as tourist attractions. Staring at the great, ominous black thing which shadowed the whole north of the island, I wasn't so sure.

Cousin Isobel was enthusing over the courtesy Port Flag which had just gone up, so I was the first to see another launch that approached the ship and was received on excellent terms by the crewmen of the liner. I did not have to ask Cousin Isobel who the white man standing in the bow of that launch was. Michael Amber wore tropical whites, but his head was bare, and his hair gleamed with that peculiar bronze brightness that I had noticed in his skin on our first meeting. With him were two half-naked West Indians who looked like the coin divers of the other islands and one West Indian who was also dressed in whites that did not quite conceal one of the most magnificent physiques I have ever seen. He and Michael bandied a few jokes back and forth with the ship's crew, who were leaning out over the rope ladder, and presently I could see Michael's white shoes take a quick foothold on the swinging ladder, while his magnificent West Indian companion held the little launch to a steady dip and rise on the blue waters.

I rather hoped that Michael would look up and see me, but he did not. He mounted rapidly and disappeared somewhere inside the ship. I pretended not to have seen him, and when the ship's rail became crowded with the later risers, interested in their first view of Saint Cloud, I soon became "engrossed" in the conversation of one of the men I had danced with the night before.

With reluctance, seeing me occupied, Isobel stepped back a few feet, toward the open entrance to the Promenade Deck, where she waited irresolutely, looking from her watch to the sky and then out over the bay. While my companion talked to me and I pretended to listen, I watched Isobel out of the corner of my eye. It seemed to me that her nervousness arose, not so much from wondering why Michael Amber was late, as from

29

fear that he would catch me with another man. Was this her object in accompanying me to Saint Cloud? But if so, why hadn't Michael come along himself or made accommodations for us to fly down? I supposed he had flown down ahead of time for reasons of his own, either to attend his urgent business affairs or to arrange Ellen's plantation house for my arrival. Now I began to wonder. Surely, it would have been more polite and considerate to allow me to help in these matters. Just how many things and how many people must be prepared for my arrival? And how were they to be prepared? The idea was troubling. I glanced over at the island, wondering what lay in wait for me behind the face of the old pirate haunt. How many blood-curdling crimes had occurred in the shadow of fern forests and volcanic slopes, while the dusty, tropic eyes of Port Anne winked and then looked the other way?

In the middle of my companion's small talk, I heard Isobel, behind me, choke off an exclamation. What attracted my attention was her clearly spoken, "Oh, no!"

She was silenced by the voice I remembered so well from the few hours I had heard Michael Amber speak in New York. "It won't matter in the least. She cannot have got far. I have half the plantation out searching for her. However, it is best if you and Cathy do not wander off alone in the town. Stay together."

I did not look around, but I listened.

Isobel recovered quickly. "How tiresome!" she said. "And Alain's Boutique has a fantastic bargain on perfumes this month! You simply must give us a few moments to shop. I'm so seldom able to come into town."

"You know there may be trouble if . . ."

"Besides," Isobel went on in her wheedling way, "dear Cathy would love to buy some perfumes, I feel sure."

I could not have remembered what my own companion was saying if my life had depended on it, but I went on smiling to him, while I listened for the effect of my name on Michael. I felt a quickened pulsebeat in my throat as he hesitated and then gave in. Had he given in because of Isobel's mention of me?

"Well then! But you had best take one of the Amber boys with you from the boat. And don't go beyond the Carrefour."

"Thank you, dear. And I may use your account? Last time I was in Alain's they were dreadfully rude about a tiny, tiny check of mine that hadn't quite cleared."

"Yes, yes. And put to my account anything Cathy buys."

My companion had either finished speaking or paused for breath, and I took this opportunity to turn and discover Michael's presence. He greeted me with a handshake and that steady gaze which I found far from unattractive, though it at once made me wonder if my makeup was on straight and think other self-critical thoughts. Also, he was no fool, as I soon found out.

"You must have overheard your cousin and me. There is nothing to be concerned about, but your sister's nurse and companion has wandered off the plantation. She took Ellen's death very hard. Miss Nell is not young, and we don't want her to come to any harm."

"I'm so sorry," I murmured, feeling that I owed my loyalty to anyone who had befriended my poor half-sister. "I hope she may become my friend, as well."

He did not reply. I could not mistake his intention to draw me away from the ship's rail, so I went along dutifully with him and Isobel.

As we descended the liner's side by the passenger steps, I felt that by doing so I was taking one more step from the known into the unknown. I only hoped that each step back to the known would be as easy. In the Amber boat Michael introduced me to the massive West Indian in white, who was the overseer of Michael's enterprises.

"Cathy, you will find that nothing on the island moves without David Earle's hand behind it. If ever you have any problem or are in any difficulty and you cannot reach me, come to David."

The big man grinned at me as we shook hands, and his gentle, deep voice gave me confidence that I could count upon him. "A pleasure to see you, Miss Cathy. It'll be good having real Ambers setting up the house again. Anybody may see you are not one of those imitation Ambers."

I thought he was joking until Isobel followed her light laugh with another item I had not known. "Oh, dear, David! Weren't they dreadful, those others? You are not the first Cathy Amber to claim the plantation, you know. During the first few weeks after Ellen's death, we were besieged by horrid people claiming to be Ellen's and Catherine's heirs. Two of them actually stayed at Amber, one after the other. But we soon got to the bottom of it. The man claimed to be Catherine's son. He was there only two nights, and off he went, taking a little fishing schooner out of Saint Cloud. Haunted by his own fakery, I daresay. And then there was a crude young woman—between Soochi, the house-keeper, and Miss Nell, they got the truth out of her. The creature was glad enough to depart. Didn't even wait for her own belongings. Soochi had to ship them to her."

"Amber knows when it's an Amber come to stay," said David Earle, as he stood at the tiller guiding our little launch into the twisting, picturesque careenage of Port Anne. This channel was lined with schooners of all shapes and sizes, some actually careened, so that I saw their red-painted bottoms high out of the water, with the mud and barnacles drying in the tropic sun. I had never seen so many little sailing vessels before, and I felt once again that Saint Cloud was not too far removed from its old buccaneering days.

Michael helped Isobel and me to step up to the Amber dock, and then turned back to discuss some business with David Earle.

"My dear," said Isobel, "I've made Michael promise I might take you to Alain's. That's our local bazaar for perfumes. Very nearly as good bargains as our neighbor Martinique. And we are to use his account."

"I'm afraid I couldn't . . ." I began, not wanting to be obligated financially any more than I had to, for I could not rid myself of the feeling that the Amber affair was temporary, and that I might be leaving one of these days like the girl Isobel mentioned, who hadn't even waited for her belongings.

Michael looked up at us on the dock. "Please don't hesitate, Cathy. It merely saves bookkeeping. Ellen always had access to my accounts in Port Anne."

"Pity she wouldn't use them. It would have improved her no end," Isobel remarked, apropos of nothing. Why had Ellen disliked Michael so much? Couldn't she appreciate his attractions and what he did for the island?

We started along the cobbled path beside the careenage. The overseer said something to Michael in his low voice, and Michael called to us. "Isobel, remember what I told you. Not beyond the square." He looked at me. "Alain's is the large, two-story shop on the left as you enter the town. Don't leave that street."

He said nothing about one of the launch's crewmen following us, but presently, when we reached the pink stucco building opposite a dusty little palm-fringed park, I looked back and saw that one of the boys had left the Amber launch and was walking at a slow pace behind us. Isobel seemed so used to this that she paid no attention. She was too interested in the perfume displays of the open-air shop. In spite of Michael's offer, I had no intention of using his account for anything, and while Isobel gossiped with the dark young beauties behind the counters, I stood on the cobbled sidewalk under the metal awning and watched the foot traffic on the street. Crowds of every degree of color wound back and forth between the fast little foreign cars, with apparently no casualties. I had read about the rare good looks of the Martiniquaise, and discovered that Saint Cloud, too, could boast of the beauty of its people, their colorful costumes of bright red- or blue-flowered prints, and their grace. Among them, the hot, dusty, sweating tourists (including myself, no doubt) made a painful comparison.

I took out my compact and powdered my nose, and was just putting the compact away when a Saint Cloud boy ran out of Alain's shop and nudged my arm. "Missy . . . Missy?"

I had not yet assimilated the differences in the features of these boys, and for a moment I could not place him. Then I realized that he must be the Amber boy who had followed us from the launch. "Yes?"

"Mister Michael says you follow me."

"Yes, but Miss Isobel . . ."

"She knows. I told her. He says you follow me. Mister Michael wants to show you the town, he says. You follow me."

I looked into the shop and dimly made out Cousin

Isobel among the swarm of tourists and other bargain seekers. I waved to her and pointed to the boy. She raised a large, embroidered straw bag and swung it up in reply, nodding and smiling. I wondered if she intended to fill the entire bag with perfumes. She must be quite a drain on Michael Amber's resources. I pointed again to the boy beside me and saw her nod her head vigorously before her smile turned to a frown as she lost her place in the line and began to edge back to the glass counter. I assumed this nodding of her head was her way of identifying the boy beside me.

The boy started down the street toward what I could see was probably the town's main square, the *carrefour* of old French days. He took big strides in his dusty brown sandals, and I had a difficult time keeping him in sight, especially as I was jostled at every step on the narrow sidewalk.

At the square, he turned and slipped into a dingy little sidewalk cafe. I followed him with some hesitation. I knew my way back to the shop where I had left Isobel, so there was no danger of my becoming lost, but the cafe did not look like Michael Amber's choice of a meeting place. I began to wonder if this was a rather public attempt to rob me. Only one customer was in the cafe, a very fat, dark man who sat reading a Trinidad newspaper and sipping espresso. Even the proprietor did not seem to be on the premises. I saw the West Indian boy slip up a narrow flight of wooden stairs at the back of the cafe, but this time I knew I was not going to follow him. I stood there in the middle of the cafe by an empty table, trying to decide whether I should watch the fat man in case he tried to take my purse, or whether I should simply turn and hurry back down the street to Alain's.

From the dark staircase where the boy had disappeared, I heard a woman's voice, calling to me. The sound was not in the least alarming.

"Miss Amber? Will you come this way, please? Mr. Amber is busy at the moment, but he has asked me to meet you."

Exceedingly curious, I took a step in that direction and saw a tall, elderly woman, her grey hair pulled loose from its confining bun, so that it raggedly framed her thin, austere face as she stood on the top stair looking down at me. There was something wrong about her clothing. Then I realized she was not wearing a full-skirted dress, as I had supposed at first, but a negligee. I was close enough now, at the foot of the stairs, to see the acute misery in her face.

"Please be patient with me for deceiving you. You see, I had to. I am your sister's nurse, Jessica Nell."

She saw my quick, instinctive withdrawal, even though I had suspected her identity, and she added apologetically, "I do hope you are not afraid of me. I have been in seclusion for so long, I hardly know how to conduct myself in public. . . ."

Her dignified manner, in spite of the tears that lay close under the surface, moved me deeply. I wanted to comfort her, yet did not like to go so directly against Michael's wishes. But he had said she was harmless. I put one foot on the lowest stair, tentatively.

Miss Nell beckoned to me. "It is good of you. Come nearer—nearer, please. My eyes trouble me lately. I can't quite see if you look like my dear Ellen."

I did not want to offend the poor soul, but I was still hesitant as I moved up barely within reach of her. I could see that her face was mottled and pink with weeping. Yet suddenly, as we met, she smiled, an incongruous split in that grim face, and I saw her eyes for the first time.

In their depths as she reached for me was naked, glaring hatred.

FOUR

"LIAR! CHEAT!" cried the terrible old woman, her voice choked with awful righteousness.

I moved quickly, but not quickly enough to avoid a ringing slap across the side of the head. She tried another slap but missed me, as, in a daze of shock and anger at my own gullibility, I retreated backward down the stairs.

Miss Nell followed me, stumbling like a sick person unused to exercise, but valiantly shouting at me. "Don't deny it! You are another cheat. You aren't the least like my Ellen that they put to the wet, dark ground as if she was dead!"

I tried to soothe her until I could at least get out of this dreadful little cafe. "No, Miss Nell. I'm Ellen's friend. And yours, if you'll let me. Do you understand? Your friend." I repeated this once or twice, and it finally penetrated. She stared at me, completely ignoring the fat man whose coffee she had spilled as she pursued me around a cafe table. The fat man sighed, paid no attention to us, and presently, while I was still trying to pacify her, I could hear him drawing fresh coffee from the espresso machine.

"If you are our friend, why did you take Amber from poor Ellen? Do you know they keep me locked up in her house?" She seemed to calm down a trifle, but this return to her senses only called horrid attention to her dishevelled night clothing in the muggy heat of daylight.

"I won't let them keep you prisoner," I promised

quickly. "I'm sure they don't mean to. Perhaps its because you were . . . ill."

"Ill? I've never had a sick day, until they got to me," she said with a dry little laugh that was half a sob. She sank into a wire-backed chair, burying her ravaged face against her crossed forearms. "But I will go out of my mind if they lock me in there again, where she lay—after they took her out of that hideous forest pool."

"No, no. Of course not!" I exclaimed, shocked at the thoughtless cruelty of the Ambers. I could no longer be frightened of this pitiful woman, who was so loyal to Ellen's memory. And besides, what if she were telling the truth? I reached across the table and furtively patted the crown of her head.

She murmured almost to herself, "Ellen was right. They are evil, the Ambers." Then she raised her head and looked at me. "If I don't get off the island, he'll track me down like those fugitive slaves in the old days. Nothing leaves this island without Michael Amber's knowledge. They've taken my money, my clothes . . . there's no one to help. That poor boy who led you here only did so out of spite. David Earle dismissed him yesterday for theft. Don't you see? If they catch me, they will lock me up again." She caught my hand before I could withdraw it. "Look at me. Do you think I was always like this? Whatever you see is their doing. If I am mad, they made me so."

I was bewildered, and embarrassed, too.

"But why?"

"Because I know they wanted Ellen dead. He wants Amber for himself, and Ellen wouldn't let him touch the plantation. When they told me she was dead—when they brought me a dreadful thing all sheeted in white and said it was Ellen—I insisted on inquiries. Just as I was told to do."

"Told? Who told you?"

"Ellen, of course. She was afraid . . ."

As I stared at her, her gaze shifted from me to a point behind me, and I saw fear leap into her eyes.

"I don't know," she finished lamely, and added with a pitiful little attempt at a white-lipped smile, "Good morning, Mr. Amber. I—I thought I'd stay in town a few days. I hope I haven't given you any trouble."

"Not at all," said Michael Amber courteously, coming in from the sidewalk. He did not appear to notice her desperate withdrawal from him as he approached. "You look tired, Miss Nell. You've been overdoing, and in all this heat, too."

She stiffened with dignity. "I warn you, you can't silence me with your tricks. I won't be locked in her room again. I absolutely refuse to go back until I have your promise."

"Don't be absurd. Come along!"

Not liking to interfere, I said in a stifled voice, "Please, won't you do as she asks?"

Michael looked annoyed but showed no further signs of monster tendencies. He reached for her. She was very nearly his height and in her lean way appeared exceedingly strong, but she shrank from him. He took her firmly around the waist, assuring her, "When you are rested, Miss Nell, you may stay anywhere you like. In the meanwhile, perhaps my cousin will be good enough to look after you."

"Oh, yes, I will!" I cried eagerly, hoping to end this painful scene. I was touched by the change in her at this. The poor thing grew quite submissive and tried to smile at me.

"In that case," she said regally, "I have no objection."

Between us, we got her to the sidewalk, where I was relieved that big David Earle had a car waiting at the curb. It was all done so quickly that not too large a crowd had gathered yet, and Miss Nell was seated at close quarters in the back seat between Michael and me. The last thing I saw at the dingy little cafe was the fat man still drinking his coffee and reading his Trinidad paper. I wondered what he was thinking about the painful episode. Or was this an average scene in the life of Saint Cloud?

Meanwhile, Jessica Nell closed her eyes and let her head fall back, but I don't think she got much rest. The little car bumped and jumped over every cobblestone in the street. David drove rapidly with the breathtaking skill at missing pedestrians that I had already noticed in the town, and in a few minutes he had circled around the long block and come past the waterfront, up to the dusty pink building that houses Alain's Bazaar.

Isobel Amber was waiting, happy as a lark over her heavily weighted tote basket. She twittered so much while David Earle helped her into the front seat that I sympathized with Michael when he said, "For God's sake, don't rattle! Miss Nell is tired. And I'm sure the rest of us ought to be."

I said not a word. I was seething with questions about Miss Nell, about her true situation at Amber, and, incidentally, how Michael had happened to find Miss Nell and me. But I wasn't at all sure where to go for the answers. I could hardly ask Michael Amber to his face: "Is Miss Nell correct? Are you a monster?"

On the other hand, I had given my word to Miss Nell, and from that moment I felt a responsibility toward her. No one was going to lock her into any Bluebeard room in my house! Michael Amber and I might even come to blows over it, figuratively speaking. The prospect was dangerous, yet oddly alluring. I sat forward, watching the dingy remnants of Port Anne speed past as we took the hot, barren road up over a spur of La Soufriere and saw the Caribbean foaming against the rocks far below. But though my mind unconsciously registered the view, I was busy marshalling up courage for the coming battle with Michael Amber.

There was no use in telling myself that every minute this car climbed higher, leaving the dry leeward cliffs of Saint Cloud and the azure Caribbean behind us, so that our flushed faces were slapped by the invigorating air of the mountains, I came closer to the fulfilment of my horoscope—my destiny, as my superstitious mind told me. There was no turning back. It was in my stars. I wondered if Michael Amber were in my stars too. The dangerous one predicted in my newspaper horoscope? The menace of which I should be wary?

But when I thought of what I had left behind me, the flip Brett Caldwell, with his hidden but very definite concern with what "Auntie and Unkie" thought about my having no money, I felt nothing. I would take my chances with Saint Cloud and the Ambers. Let the wealthy Caldwells keep their no-doubt ill-gotten gold.

By coincidence, Michael looked over at me in that moment and smiled. I was very much lifted by this sign.

39

How much more reliable than the effervescent Brett! I must concentrate on that.

"We are entering the fern forests now," he said. "You will see how much greener, more tropical it is."

I looked out and saw that though the landscape had changed subtly from the barren leeward slopes to the mountain country, we now quickly, and with startling effect, descended into the thick, shadowy world of giant ferns. They overhung the road on both sides in such profusion that we drove under a tunnel of greenery which dripped down on the car from time to time, as the fronds and spears and leaves grew too heavy with the showers from intermittent rainclouds. The sunlight, when it did come through, sifted down from the wet and lacy roof of this living tunnel, casting a peculiar green light over our faces. The heat was still with us, muggy this time, and thick with moisture, making it difficult to breathe. Until I became used to the curious sensation, I felt stifled.

Suddenly, between Michael and me, Miss Nell stirred and sat up. She pointed excitedly ahead. "This is where my Ellen's property begins. Just at that boundary on the left." She turned to me. "Ellen owns all of that ground, as far as you may see to the east, to the Atlantic, very nearly."

Laughing, to show that, of course, I did not mean it, I asked, "You are quite sure the volcano is harmless?"

I had expected the others to laugh at me. Instead, "How curious!" remarked Cousin Isobel in a reminiscent voice which gave me a shiver in spite of my resolve not to let her sly darts affect me. "Ellen always says— said the same thing. Because, of course, the creature still lives, beneath the surface of the land. Ellen said that at night she could hear it breathing. . . ."

"And Ellen is right. I have heard it! and felt it! The rumble, the shaking like a giant child, wanting to make itself noticed," murmured Miss Nell, closing her eyes again.

"Good God!" said Michael in a low, angry voice, and I was surprised to see David Earle look back at him from the front seat and shake his head in an unmistakable warning. I had not suspected that David Earle carried so much influence with Michael.

Overhead, the atmosphere grew darker and thicker,

so that some minutes later, when we turned off the main highway onto a twisting, serpentine secondary road, full of long-imbedded stones and occasional lava blocks, the whole scene resembled a twilight seen through a veritable cloudburst.

I had been expecting that the ferns and other crowded jungle vegetation would clear out suddenly and I would behold my sumptuous residence, the Amber House, which I pictured in my mind's eye. When we reached this residence, I was a good deal surprised to find that there was only space between the giant, dripping ferns and the long, narrow plantation house for a single badly rutted road that passed the length of the house and wound its way into what seemed impenetrable jungle beyond. The house itself was a one-story affair, with a veranda running the length of the house, heavily screened by netting, and a great, empty-looking interior beyond. From the car it looked dusty, dirty, and exceedingly dark, but that may have been the effect of the shutters, which gave every appearance of dating back to the French rule, a hundred or so years ago. The shutters were open. Otherwise, I really think I should have turned and run madly for the nearest point of civilization. As it was, I was half afraid to enter the black, hollow interior.

"Now, there!" said Isobel, in the manner of someone having proved a point. "You cannot possibly say we have led you under false pretenses, Cathy dear. You were afraid we intended to bribe you, for some sinister reason. But as you may see, Amber certainly needs your touch."

It needs something. A good bonfire to destroy it, I thought, but I did not say so. What creatures must be stirring inside that wretched old plantation house, lurking there in closets and under rugs? Leggy, hairy insects, or—good heavens!—snakes!

"Are there any poisonous snakes on Saint Cloud?" I asked, not thinking how it sounded.

David Earle looked astonished at this *non sequitur*, but Michael laughed openly, and I was cheered by the sound.

"No. None that we have found here at Amber."

"How can you say that?" Isobel demanded reproachfully. "You know perfectly well, Michael, nothing could be more poisonous than the fer-de-lance. You must not lie to the poor child. Think how she will feel when she first walks into one."

Whatever a fer-de-lance might be, I was so entertained by Michael's efforts to keep from exploding his hot temper that I lost all fear of snakes. He just barely succeeded in remaining calm under this extreme provocation.

"David, will you drive Isobel home? I'll walk. I am going to show Cathy around the house and, incidentally, scotch all vipers . . . poisonous or otherwise!"

I said demurely, "Thank you. One never knows quite how to go about killing poisonous snakes in the house. So little practice where I come from." I would not, for worlds, let Isobel know that she had succeeded in making a jelly of all my courage.

Michael helped Miss Nell out of the car and would have given her his hand up the step to the wooden floor of the roofed veranda, but she shook him off, announcing regally, "I am no stranger to Ellen's house, Mr. Amber."

It was pouring down rain when I got out, gratefully accepting Michael's assistance to avoid the rapidly filling pools in the muddy road, but no one seemed to think this downpour in the least unusual, so I braved it to the veranda, where David had set down my bags, and there I felt gingerly of my new white straw hat with its tiny green veil. It would never be the same again, poor thing. Nor would my open shoes, which had taken the full impact of a false step into a puddle of water. While I was wriggling one foot experimentally in the soggy shoe, David Earle drove off through the tunnel of ferns, and I could hear the car in the distance bouncing over stones, fallen tree limbs, and any other obstruction that vainly threatened the skillful overseer.

Michael opened the door for us, and Miss Nell strode through into a short, cool, moist-feeling passage, which cut the house into two long halves that appeared to be only one room wide. The short passage opened at its further end into a gorgeous profusion of color which I took to be the garden, although I had never seen anything remotely as rich, as overpowering, in an American garden. Even at this end of the passage, I could see dozens of varieties of tropical blooms, each more beautiful than the other, and they appeared to go back an enormous distance into the jungle behind the house.

"You will excuse me if I go and lie down," said Miss Nell, with her hand pressed to her forehead.

I said guiltily, "Of course, I'm so sorry. Let me help you."

Michael set my suitcases down in the passage and took her arm, but she released herself carefully, and he made no effort to do more.

"She will be better after she's had her tea," he explained. "She probably hasn't eaten since last night."

Miss Nell, who had started alone into the door Michael opened for her on the left of the passage, turned and gave us a tired smile. "I shall be the better for my tea," she said. "But don't trouble Soochi. Ellen will bring it."

Michael must have guessed my uneasiness at this; for he took my hand. "Come along. You will like the garden. Where the deuce is Soochi?"

After a moment I asked, "Has she lost her mind? Miss Nell, I mean?"

"Just tired. The poor creature has had nothing to care for during most of her lifetime except your half-sister, and I'm afraid she can't quite cope."

"How awful!"

He did not say anything but led me out to the garden before I could change my shoes or remind him of the rain. It had been puzzling me how the various rooms in either wing of the house were reached, but I saw that each room opened on a stone-floored walkway bordering the garden at its long west side and roofed over so that the rain poured in heavy gushes along the runnels of the roof and down the sides at either end. where a great stone wall completed the two sides of the garden.

I looked around at everything, more impressed with the plantation, now that I saw the huge garden, whose eastern end I could not even guess at for the growth of bougainvillea and hibiscus that masked the end of the vegetation. But after I had asked a question or two about how far east the garden did extend, and whether, as I suspected, I might get lost in my own garden, I realized that Michael Amber was not listening to me. He was staring at the north wing of the house.

"I wonder which room she has taken," he murmured, without actually addressing me. "She often did her sewing in Ellen's room and would not leave it when we brought Ellen back from the pool."

"How odd! Because she complained to me in the cafe this morning that she had been imprisoned there against her will. . . . By the way, how did you find us at the cafe?"

"One of the Amber boys from the tender saw you." He looked at me and said in the calmest way, "I don't intend anything shall happen to you, Cathy." While I was wondering what dangers he had in mind—romantic or bloodcurdling—he went on, the man of business again. "Besides, there is little I can't find out that goes on in Saint Cloud. It is, after all, a very small world. She didn't annoy you, I hope."

"Boxed my ears," I admitted. "I can feel it yet. No doubt I deserved it, taking Ellen's property this way."

"If she gets no better, she will have to be taken away where she can be looked after. I don't want her putting you into a panic."

I started to protest, but he took my hands between his palms. "You see? You are trembling already. Are you frightened of us all? You mustn't be. I'm not quite the ogre your friend Mr. Caldwell thinks I am."

I could have called his attention to the fact that I always trembled when I stood in a downpour of rain, but I abandoned this unromantic truth as the rain itself slackened. I was hunting for some suitable way to continue this interesting discussion where it was more dry, if less romantic, when the great, flowering blooms beside Michael began to sway and were presently parted by a human hand; something bright and blue, as large as a hydrangea, seemed to peer out at us from the garden jungle.

For one horrified instant I had the illusion that a flower itself was staring at us. Among the foliage at about my own height I made out the outlines of an exquisite oriental face beneath a blue, carefully tied madras turban. When the young woman pushed her way through the flower bushes, I saw that she was dressed, in the fashion of so many decorative West Indians of the French islands, in a frilled blouse and full skirt of bright blue pattern. On anyone else I felt sure

44

it would have looked too theatrical, but this stunning creature appeared entirely at home in it.

Michael heard her almost as quickly as I saw her, but when I pulled my hands out of his, he gave me an amused look before releasing me. Then he said in what I felt were remarkably cool tones for a man to use to such a little beauty, "Soochi, this is Miss Cathy. You will take your orders from her. You understand?"

Soochi's smile gleamed on her wide, full lips. She had large, stunning white teeth, and I caught myself thinking of a gorgeous Pekingese I once saw with just such white, flashing teeth. However, the smile on the Pekingese had heralded the attack to come from those useful teeth.

"I understand, Mister Michael. Believe me, it's my pleasure to welcome you, Miss Cathy." She made a graceful little gesture, almost a curtsey, and when I thanked her and said I was sure I could rely upon her, she gave me her big smile again, lowering her head to agree with me, yet never lowering the stare of her almond-shaped eyes. An idea came to me that she was mocking me for some reason.

"Mister Michael," she said, as we turned back to the house, "here is a small difficulty. It is Miss Nell, if you please."

"You must go to Miss Cathy with your problems now, Soochi. I told you that."

"As you say, Mister Michael. But she has taken the room I prepared for Miss Cathy. It is the Master's room."

"We'll settle that!" Michael began to walk very fast across the garden, trampling the delicate little flowers at his feet and making me almost run to keep up with him.

"No, please, Michael. It doesn't in the least matter to me. Soochi may put me anywhere. I don't care."

"Don't be foolish. You must assert your authority now, or you never will. That tiresome woman must either conform or leave. We've been patient too long."

Soochi seemed to float along beside us in her full skirts, her sandals moving rapidly yet never showing the exertion it took me to keep up.

"It is not my place to say, Mister Michael, but Miss Nell tells such stories! They make my blood run cold.

If I were to believe, I should go quick and buy a *ouanga* from Doctor Torri to guard me from the evil things she sees."

Michael waved this aside. "Doctor Torri has enough sick patients to attend to, without delving into that Haitian talk. If I ever catch him at voodoo, he leaves this island, sick patients or no!"

"You speak so, Mister Michael?" asked Soochi. "That would be bad. Most bad!" Yet through her voice ran the most curious little ripple of something light but evil—something like amusement, yet not harmless. Not at all harmless. I felt this as I would have felt a rich perfume that nauseated me.

When we reached the portico and walked along toward the last door on the north wing of the building, I took this chance to plead with Michael not to disturb Miss Nell, but although he had plainly told me Amber was now my affair, he had no intention of letting me handle it. The portico door was locked, and when Michael tried the door we could see Miss Nell peering out at us through the long bamboo curtains. After what seemed to me an endless time, she unlocked the door and said pleasantly, "How nice! Have you brought my tea?"

Before Michael could say anything I cut in quickly, "Miss Nell, wouldn't you rather have a—a sunnier room, or a larger . . ."

"This is the largest, ma'am," said Soochi, obviously anxious to be as little help as possible.

By this time Michael had calmed enough to suggest that Miss Nell move into a room which had, as he put it, "a more cheerful look. You will not want to occupy the room in which Miss Ellen's father died will you, Miss Nell?"

Under this, and Soochi's grinning presence, the woman became confused, and it was not long before Michael and Soochi had her in tow and she retreated meekly down the portico to another room, nearer the main passage.

By now I shared Jessica Nell's headache and was anxious only to be alone, to get my bearings. Michael sensed this. After commending me to the care of the smiling Soochi and saying he would bring over papers for me to sign tomorrow, he left us and walked down the wet jungle road. I went out to the veranda, and when he looked back I waved to him like a good hostess, but for the moment I was almost as tired of him as of everything else about Amber.

I returned to Soochi, ordered lunch for Miss Nell and myself, and while she was preparing whatever she had in her kitchen, into which I did not venture, I walked through the house alone. All the rooms that opened on the portico on the east end of the house had an extraordinary conformity. I felt that any room might be mistaken for any other large, square, unimaginative box, some with windows as well as the screened and curtained windows in the doors. There were several rooms which faced on the road and veranda, large, shadowy rooms for the most part, obviously used, in the past, for the stately reception of company.

There were two small rooms, near the servants' quarters at the south end, that were separated from the rest of the house by another east-west hall. These had obviously been children's apartments, for the furniture was still there—just such heavy ornamental pieces as were popular about forty years ago, not old enough to be antique nor modern enough to be useful. But each piece was extraordinarily clean and free from dust. I was impressed by Soochi's care of them. She did not look like the housekeeping sort to me. One heavy cradle with the single word ELLEN carved into its head was touching. It was my first contact with my half-sister, and I rocked the cradle a moment, thinking of that little girl, her lonely life, and its terrible end. I began to wonder what Ellen's mother had been like. In my imagination I saw a pale woman with a delicate face and ash-blonde hair, rocking Ellen's cradle forty years ago. Now they were both dead, the pale, quiet mother and her pitiful little daughter. I began to suspect that these things, so carefully dusted, were not Soochi's province at all. Probably Miss Nell, in her devotion, was the person who came here and dusted these remnants of a time that could never be repeated.

When I came out of these quarters Soochi met me with a double Manhattan glass, in which she said was a "banana daiquiri." I drank the sweet concoction, suggesting that perhaps Miss Nell would like one. Soochi shrugged.

"Miss Nell falls to sleep now. When she wakes, she will be herself. You will see. She is not crazy, that one. Not she!"

While I waited for lunch, I went to the large north room that was apparently to be mine and in which my father had died. I unpacked one or two items from my makeup case and then sat down on the great bed and looked around me. The truth is, I disliked the room intensely. It was larger than the others, as Soochi had said, and overpowering, the worst offender being this monstrous bed. It had been carved out of some black wood, probably mahogany. The bedposts and headboard were decorated with demon heads. As I lay down for a moment to calm an uneasy feeling in my chest, I turned in bed and saw, staring into my face from the bedpost, a hideous human monster. The sight of this wooden fright made me sit up abruptly, my heart beating faster than ever.

The door opened quietly from the portico, and Miss Nell stood there. She was fully dressed, with her greying hair neatly coiled in place.

"Are you all right?"

It was a curious question, for I had not made a sound. I wondered whether she had been watching me through the window, and that idea gave me an unexpected chill.

"It is these carvings. They are frightful. So is the room."

She came into the room and ran her fingers delicately over the horrid faces on the bedpost nearest her.

"They are very well done, you know. Ellen says—" She hesitated and corrected herself, a small matter but one which encouraged me to think her former aberration must have disappeared. "Ellen used to say this bed is worth a fortune to someone with a taste for Primitives."

It would take a primitive to appreciate it, I thought, and got up. Seeing my lack of interest in the mahogany, Miss Nell offered to show me around the enormous garden grounds, and I accepted. She seemed completely normal after her brief rest. Unless, of course, Soochi was right in her hint that Miss Nell had never really been abnormal.

The gardens were still dripping from the rain, but a

48

lovely shaft of sunlight illuminated certain previously dark and rain-soaked areas, so I was more impressed than ever with the beauty of this flower jungle that extended further back than I could see, into the fern forest, where, as Miss Nell explained calmly, "the path through the garden simply narrows without one's awareness, and presently one is in the jungle. The Tangerine Pool is just off this path."

We did not walk quite to the end of the garden. I was terrified of going too close to the Tangerine Pool, and I had decided some time before that when I saw this place of death and horror, I ought to be in the company of someone more muscular than one old woman whose mind was slipping. As we returned to the house, I could see that I had been right. It would be easy to get lost in my own garden if I did not take great care.

Meanwhile, I found Miss Nell calm and quite herself. When I told her I did not want to go near the pool just yet, she said, like the old nurse that she was, "You are quite right. I told Ellen, times without end, not to pass the pool alone and at that time of day." She sighed. "But she would do so! And now— They say she might have been saved. If only there had been someone with her! It was my fault. I should have known. I should have *felt!*"

"What do you make of Soochi?" I asked.

"Quite a capable young woman. She has been here since her earliest childhood. Mr. Amber—Mr. Richard Amber, Ellen's father—found her clever, and I think he hoped Ellen would adopt some of her elegance and her saucy ways with the men. But my poor Ellen was . . ."

"Of course. Ellen was too fastidious for Soochi's ways," I finished quickly.

Miss Nell nodded her head, and it was only by the purest accident that I happened to glance her way and see a peculiar little smile curving her thin, dry lips. I was as surprised as though I had caught one of the mahogany gargoyles smiling. More surprised, I think. I would not have put it past the gargoyles!

Miss Nell was right about Soochi's capability. The lunch was excellent, and later in the day, after I had explored more thoroughly the dull, square rooms of the

49

house with Miss Nell, we were treated to a dinner which was even more inviting, with odd West Indian dishes that tantalized me; but though I wanted to know what went into them, Miss Nell shook her head, and after Soochi had gone, she warned me, "You will enjoy it more if you do not know the ingredients."

As I was just then eating a spoonful of some delicious dessert, both sweet and sour, with bilious green trails of color through it, I took a deep breath and decided Miss Nell was right. I did not ask.

We were dining on the portico, for I had taken an immediate dislike to the dining room. Like the master bedroom it was full of huge, ornamental mahogany furniture, all heavily carved, the perfect haven for an African witch doctor. Darkness came while we ate, and the sounds of the jungle were very near—occasional bird sounds, hoarse and cawing, with now and then the chattering sound of other creatures. I looked out into the garden, whose profusion of light flowers resembled many pale but luminous moons in the tropic darkness. I could have sat there dreamily all night, but Miss Nell had been yawning, and I knew she must be miserably tired. She looked over at my room several times, and the last time she did so, I saw a wistful look in her eyes.

"Why don't you use that room?" I suggested, and added honestly, "I dislike it anyway. I'll take another room."

"No. Soochi would tell Mr. Amber, and there would be trouble."

"Well, why not try it for tonight? Then I may tell him I prefer the other room."

"But you won't tell Soochi?"

"Of course not."

When Soochi had gone to her quarters, I moved a few of my things into a smaller room whose window faced on the portico next to the central hall. The furniture here was cheap and ordinary, with no decoration, no gargoyles; it was rather like a commercial hotel room. It suited me admirably, for nothing could be less terrifying to my mind.

I lay awake for a long time. Though I was tired, I was curious about the house, the Ambers, and that huge garden which I could see outside my window, groping eastward until it was swallowed in the jungle of ferns and wild, secretive things. I began to wonder what creatures were out there in the night making those odd, subdued scurrying sounds that occasionally burst forth into a shrill climax. The idea did not lull me to sleep. I turned my head and saw the opposite wall, and I pictured what lay beyond it—the bathroom next door and the veranda. Then the narrow road and the enormous expanse of jungle again. I could not get over the feeling that the jungle of ferns on either side of the plantation house had somehow crept much closer under the cover of darkness.

I wished the bamboo curtains were not so thin. If I could not see that wild barrier everywhere from the window and door, and in my mind's unpleasant thoughts, I might not feel this curious sense of being closed in, imprisoned, and watched by many eyes. I was half determined to get up and do something about it when the muggy air of the night was cut by a shrill and horrifying shriek. I sat straight up in bed, clutching the single coverlet and wondering what kind of jungle creature had made that sound, and what hideous thing was being done to it.

It was several seconds before I realized the sound was not that of a jungle creature surprised by its enemy, but a human sound, torn from a human throat. In this house!

FIVE

I FUMBLED FRANTICALLY for my peignoir which had
fallen off the foot of the bed, and I rushed out onto the
portico, still in my bare feet. Under the starlight, a
thousand luminous eyes stared at me from the garden.
Each flower seemed, if not my enemy, at least a hostile
witness. As I peered into this multitude of heads,
trying to discover the source of the ghastly sound I
had heard, a breeze swept through the garden from the
jungle beyond and set me shivering. I knew I should be
looking along the portico, to see if either Miss Nell or
Soochi, at the opposite end of the garden, were in
trouble. But I had a morbid dread of turning my back
on those malevolent flowers.

"Evening, Miss Cathy." The voice came from the
shadow of the south portico, an unctuous, sly voice I
was fast learning to dislike. "Was that you screamed
just now?"

Soochi stood there in the half-dark with her arms
folded against that gaudy, beautiful dress of hers, the
points of her madras turban swaying like little feelers
in the night breeze.

"No, it was not," I said shortly, and I started along
the portico toward Miss Nell's room. I did not have to
go far. The nurse lay in her dishevelled clothes, half in
and half out of the doorway of her room, the whole
pitiful heap faintly outlined by the starlight. I ran to
her and knelt on the cool floor, raising her head as
gently as I could. I was relieved to see that she still
breathed; for that awful shriek had sounded like a

death cry. Her face was ash grey, terribly lined, ugly and defenseless. But her mouth was the shocking thing; for it was still open, pulled apart like a tragedy mask into a hideous, silent shriek, as though, even in her unconscious state, she still relived some monstrous experience.

"Get me some water," I told Soochi, "or some brandy."

"I will get rum," Soochi contradicted, and she moved away with her silent, floating step.

She returned while I was unbuttoning the high neck of Miss Nell's old-fashioned nightgown, and although it seemed to me that the nurse breathed more easily, she had not yet recovered consciousness. I tried to pour a few drops of the liquor into her mouth, but when she did not react, I was afraid of choking her and could not venture further.

"I wonder if she is in shock. I know nothing about things like this," I told Soochi, hoping she would have some suggestion. "We must get a doctor here at once."

"Try the pulse," said Soochi calmly. "You find it rapid. Not slow as when one is suffering from shock. You see, this has happened before."

I had tried Miss Nell's pulse and, finding the beat, had assumed merely that she was alive, without asking myself why it raced when the woman was sick and unconscious.

"What do you think happened to her?" I asked.

"But, of course. She saw something. You will notice she had fallen toward the door. See her arm extended so. She was trying to . . . touch something. Something that she found she could not touch. And so . . ." she shrugged. "The lady cried out and fell as you see."

"Yes. But what was she trying to touch? And why couldn't she touch it?"

Soochi's lips gleamed wetly in the starlight, and I saw her big, flashing teeth.

"So simple. She saw Miss Ellen at the window. She got out of the big bed and opened the door to Miss Ellen. But when she reached out to touch her, she could not. Then she knew . . . and she screamed."

The flesh of my arms had grown cold and damp in the night air as I clasped them with my fingers, and I rubbed them to restore warmth. Soochi watched me.

"Are you cold, Miss Cathy? You should not be. It is very warm tonight."

"Never mind that," I said briskly. "I do not believe in ghosts, and if I saw your late mistress at that window now I wouldn't believe it. So you may as well save these stories for the natives."

Soochi's smile grew broader. "Of course, Miss Cathy. The dead do not come back to haunt us. It is only the Others that come back."

"What others?" I demanded, and then I could have bitten my tongue for yielding to her suggestiveness.

"The Shades of the Dead, ma'am. The Wandering Ones, who died unshriven, come back to find their murderers."

Suddenly, this began to make sense.

"Do you think my half-sister was murdered?"

Soochi shrugged gracefully. "I do not think anything, Miss Cathy. I only see a sheeted thing that Mister Michael and Mister David bring through the garden and say to me 'prepare a room for Miss Ellen's body. She has drowned.' And I do this. I do not ask questions. But I have lived at Amber all my life, and I have never fallen in the Tangerine Pool. Nor have others."

"Then you don't think Miss Nell saw anything?"

"That is for others to say, ma'am. I say she did not see flesh and blood. She saw the Ombre—the shade of Miss Ellen, who will not sleep in her grave until she is avenged."

"But you did examine Miss Ellen's body. It was actually Miss Ellen?"

"There is no doubt. I have known Miss Ellen all her life. Her body was dead. I say nothing of that. But her Shade was not there. One can tell these things when one makes a body ready for burial. Her Shade is still here. . . ." She made a gesture toward the garden and then, vaguely, beyond, covering the fern forest and the path to the Tangerine Pool. "Is it Miss Ellen's Shade that made Miss Nell scream? I wonder."

"Go and call a doctor!" I said with as much firmness as I could muster. But she read in my voice an unsteady quality that I could not hide.

"I cannot call. This is a night when Doctor Torri is not at home."

I had never heard of such nonsense. "Well, call him wherever he is then."

"It is not possible, ma'am. He is . . . outside. There are no telephones where he is tonight."

"Then call Mr. Amber and ask him what to do."

"Mister Michael lives near Eastbourne on the coast. It would be more than an hour for him to come."

"Yet he walked there today."

"Oh, no, ma'am. He said he would walk, but everyone knows Mister Michael. He would be picked up and given a ride. It is important to please Mister Michael."

"Call him!"

"And then—he is often away from home in the early night."

If I had known how, I would have gnashed my teeth. I restrained myself from violence with great difficulty. Her deliberate stupidity was the most annoying thing in the world, in the face of poor Miss Nell's crisis.

"Are there no other doctors?"

"Only in Port Anne or at Eastbourne, ma'am."

I looked up at her, remembering something Michael had said about the doctor's outside activities. "You know where Doctor Torri is tonight; don't you?"

She nodded, more slowly than was her usual habit. It struck me that she had begun to look uneasy herself.

"Then go to him and bring him to Amber. You understand me?"

"Perfectly, ma'am." She turned away, but stopped long enough to add, "I am gone some time. Maybe an hour. But . . . if you say, I will go. If you do not object."

"Object to what?" I asked, putting the glass to Miss Nell's lips again; for I thought I detected some signs of a return to consciousness.

"But . . . to Miss Ellen, of course, ma'am."

"Miss Ellen is dead!" I was very firm on that point.

"As you say. Miss Ellen is dead. . . . But I ask myself, if her Shade was seen a few minutes ago . . . where is it now? Do you think of that?"

She left me. It was just as well. I was tempted to throw something at her. With Miss Nell across my lap I could not move, and with my back to the garden I had the most horrid sensation that my dead half-sister's Shade floated out there among those many-headed flow-

55

ers, perhaps creeping up on me at that instant. I tried not to shiver, for the involuntary movement disturbed Miss Nell.

Whether or not I believed in Shades, ghosts and other haunts, and I had always been firmly convinced that I did not, I still found no explanation for Miss Nell's dreadful scream. Aware of the garden at my back, and all the implications of that lush growth, I tried to concentrate on pure fact, uninfluenced by Soochi's superstitions. Perhaps Miss Nell was subject to some sort of physical illness which would explain the shriek. If not, what, precisely, had frightened her?

When I looked down at her face again, it was a shock to see her eyes wide open, staring up at me. I called her name, but she gave no indication of hearing me. I tried the rum again, and this time she swallowed mechanically and made efforts to get on her feet. I helped her. Though she did not appear to recognize my existance, she let me guide her in to the big, carved bed, where she lay down with her feet dangling over the side of the bed, and one arm shielding her eyes from the glare of the lamp I turned on. I tried to make her comfortable, lifting her legs onto the bed and pulling up the sheet to cover her.

Her manner of ignoring me had lulled me into a false calm; for as I finished covering her, her hand reached out suddenly and seized my wrist in a tight, pinching grasp that made me wince. Her other arm came away from her eyes. She stared at me unblinking, and with a quick, secretive motion of her head, she indicated the garden, as though she were under surveillance from someone or something that I could not see.

"Out there," she whispered. "Be careful. It's out there. . . ."

Then she covered her eyes again and lay there as though she slept, with the carved mahogany demons glaring down at her from the two bedposts. I moved away from her slowly, trying to nerve myself for another and more careful look at the garden.

As I stepped out on the portico and made my first tentative venture onto the springy turf of the garden, the grass under my bare feet cooled off my fears considerably. I looked around with a boldness that surprised me.

56

The pale faces of the flowers swayed before me in the night air, turning occasionally, like the heads of a silent throng watching something my own eyes could not see. I fancied once or twice that a luminous and unearthly Thing floated just beyond my vision, but when I swung around quickly, there were only the great blooms, taller than I, and behind them, acres of jungle growth. It occurred to me that if I, in a reasonably normal frame of mind, could imagine that Shades were floating among those giant flowers, it shouldn't be difficult for Miss Nell to "see" the dead girl.

Meanwhile, I was not going to prove my courage, if any, in bare feet. Not only had I sneezed once or twice, but I suddenly stepped on something wet and slimy that I hoped was only a damp, crushed flower head.

After glancing in at Miss Nell I returned to my room, got one of my own personal towels and fumbled around for light switches until I reached the only bathroom in the north half of the house. I had rubbed my feet dry and was stepping into my handiest pumps when a door closed somewhere in the house. It must be Soochi returning sooner than I had expected her. It would be a relief to have the doctor here. I listened, hoping to catch an unfamiliar male voice which would be his, but heard no further sounds.

From the bathroom I went into the dank and shabby hall which separated the two wings of the house, realizing a little late that in my thin, low-cut gown and robe I was not dressed for strangers; but I wanted to see this Dr. Torri before he examined Miss Nell. There was no telling what Soochi would make him believe about the unfortunate nurse.

I found no one in the hall, nor in the large, musty-smelling parlour which had a kind of wicker-and-Maugham look. I had half-expected to find Soochi, Amber's answer to Sadie Thompson, spying on me from some doorway, perhaps tastefully hidden behind a length of swaying bamboo curtain. I was beginning to be puzzled by that slamming door, and I tried to remember whether the night breeze had been strong enough to blow it shut. Snatching my plastic raincoat out of the closet in my room, I put it on and stepped onto the portico. The garden looked silent and serene. The moon was coming up, and in the added illumination, the flowers appeared less sinister to me. Then I glanced over at Miss Nell's room and saw that her door, which I had left closed, was now swinging gently back and forth. It had been slammed too hard and slipped the latch. I hurried over, but even before I reached the room, I could see through the window that Miss Nell no longer lay stretched out on the bed where I had left her. She was nowhere to be seen.

I called to her, not knowing what to think, but my voice made an annoying echo through the empty, desolate house, and I soon stopped that. There was still the possibility that she was sick and in the bathroom. I retraced my steps but found the room as I had left it, the door still open.

When I returned to the garden I made out under the brightening moonlight the bare footprints of Miss Nell's long, thin feet in the wet earth, headed toward the eastern end of the garden, on the path she had warned me about, which led past the Tangerine Pool.

Of one thing I was convinced: I, who had refused to pass the Tangerine Pool in broad daylight, accompanied by a seemingly normal Miss Nell, was not going to wander past the pool at midnight, in pursuit of a woman who was either sleepwalking or demented or on some sinister errand. I felt, however, that I might safely venture to the end of the Amber garden, in the hope that, somewhere along the way, Miss Nell would find her strength gone, and I might get her back to bed. I followed her footsteps quickly through the garden, several times catching my raincoat and the longer gown underneath on wet fern fronds and flower stems, which were still laden with the weight of the day's rains. Even with the rising moonlight, however, I could not make out Miss Nell's tall, lean form through the jungle growth ahead. I stopped to listen, hoping I might hear her thrash her way somewhere ahead of me, but although her footprints were still readable, in mud and in rotting dead leaves, I could not make out her form. She must be several minutes ahead of me.

It was only by luck that, when I walked out of one of my pumps in a particularly muddy place and stopped to recover it, I saw the boundary of the Amber gardens, a broken wall only a foot or two high near the path, masked by heavy growths of great red flowers. I stood there scraping mud off my shoe while I balanced precariously on one foot, wondering what on earth I should do about that crazy woman. It could not be much further to the pool. It would be in keeping with her mental state if she tried to destroy herself there, blaming herself for Ellen's death. But why, then, had she whispered a warning to me against whatever had startled her? If she fancied she saw Ellen, surely she would not consider it necessary to warn me. Or was Ellen evil after all?

I had never considered that before. An evil woman in life would presumably make an evil Shade. I remembered that queer smile on Miss Nell's face when I spoke of Ellen's fastidiousness, her shyness.

It was a tangle. I did not know whether to go on through this dangerous, unknown jungle or to turn back and afterward blame myself if anything happened to the nurse. But it was growing darker and darker as I moved deep into the jungle, and very shortly I should be unable to see my way at all. A stiff breeze came circling through the heavy growth as though it had swept off an open glade. If there were a glade ahead, there would be moonlight, and I might see Miss Nell after all. Before turning back I gave myself another minute or two for the pursuit, slipped my foot back into my shoe, and set out again, pushing aside the grasping ferns that tried to hold me back. This time I called to her repeatedly. I had been right. Ahead of me, perhaps a hundred yards, was an open space; for I could make out a dappled light that must be the moonlight slanting through the southerly jungle into an open space. But between me and that glade was a stubborn barrier of ferns and flowers so interwoven that I wondered how Miss Nell had made her way through them. I stopped to reach up and break off a vine between my fingers, and as I did so, I was paralyzed by the sudden tearing away of the vine; in its place, not two feet from me, was the face of a dark giant, the whites of its eyes glistening in the faint moonlight. Before I could recover enough to scream, the dark face spoke, in that soft, peculiar, half-British, half-French patois that I had noticed already among the people native to Saint Cloud. "Miss Cathy, what you doing out here?"

I stammered out Miss Nell's name and tried to explain that I was following her, but he said before I could finish,

"Were you not told it is unsafe? You might fall or lose your way. Let me help you."

In spite of the dark giant's nearly naked body—for he wore only torn and grass-stained dungarees and sandals—I recognized him now as David Earle. But seen like this, at midnight, only half-dressed, he did not look nearly so safe nor so civilized as he had appeared today in the Amber launch.

Nevertheless, I started to tell him about Miss Nell. He interrupted me with an authority I had seen him use toward Michael Amber.

"I know, Miss Cathy. We found her near the pool. She is quite safe. But you shouldn't be out here like this at night. Anything might happen. Someone might . . ."

I had already turned back toward Amber. Nothing would make me happier than to be safely locked in my room, but his words gave me a little jar.

"What do we mean—*we?* Are there more of you out here tonight?"

"No. No. But there are always strays here at night. One does not know. You understand."

He put his hand under my elbow to hurry me along, but I had noticed a curious phenomenon in the glade behind us. The moonlight was, in fact, much too bright and too lurid to be moonlight.

"What are those lights?" I asked, as he rushed me along the jungle path.

"Nothing. Probably men from the fields. A labor meeting, I expect."

I tried to look back. It was difficult, with David Earle's hand so insistently leading me back to Amber. There were moving figures now crossing the glade, stark, half-naked human forms which I could make out dimly between what I took to be covered lanterns. As the overseer had said, a labor meeting, no doubt. But the silence of that strange company was unnatural. I had seen labor meetings. I had never seen one that broke up in such extraordinary silence. It was almost as though a pall of fear hung over the glade.

60

"You're quite sure Miss Nell is safe? Why did she run away?"

The overseer said calmly, "The lady often goes to the pool where Miss Ellen died. Michael—Mr. Amber —thinks it is insanity. And maybe it is. But . . ."

"But you don't."

"Well, Miss Cathy, it is this: If the lady is mad, why hasn't she jumped into the pool? Why does she stand there and look . . . and look? What is she looking for? A soft place to jump? I do not think so."

I could not make out heads or tails of this. "What on earth is she looking for then?" I asked.

He paused, his keen eyes searching and finding the stone boundary of Amber before he replied, as we reentered the garden, "For evidence, do you think?"

"You mean evidence that someone murdered Ellen?"

"Someone. Yes."

I thought I began to understand. "Then Miss Nell is not crazy at all. She is trying to solve the mystery of Ellen's death. But that is very brave. And she may be in great danger. Don't you think so?"

He snapped on the portico lights, and when I looked at his face, I did not see the reassurance there that I had hoped to see.

"It is true she may be in danger, Miss Cathy. But what if she is looking for evidence which she herself left . . . by accident?"

He smiled as my eyes opened wide in fresh alarm.

"Now, Miss Cathy, it is only a thought. Mr. Amber does not agree with me. Only—watch yourself. And perhaps, if anything strange occurs at night again, you will leave the jungle to us. It is better so. A stranger to the island may see odd things which puzzle and confuse him. Things that are simple to those of us who have spent our lives here."

"What shall I do if Miss Nell isn't back?" I asked as he started to cross the garden on his way back along the jungle path.

"She is in her room. See for yourself, Miss Cathy. Good night."

I went past the window and looked in. He was right; the woman was stretched out on her bed exactly as I had left her earlier in the evening, before I had gone to bed.

I might almost have imagined the whole miserable walk through the jungle if I hadn't looked down and seen the grass stains and jagged little tears in my clothing.

I opened the door, which still swung gently back and forth, and went in and stood looking down at her. The bed clothes were tucked around her. She breathed with the even, slightly stertorous sound of a sleeping person. My first intention was to leave her. But I must know for sure that she had been out tonight. Her footprints and David Earle's report that she had been found—and by whom?—were only circumstantial evidence.

I raised the covers, slipping them out from her tightly closed fingers, and saw one of her feet, that long, bony foot with the blue veins prominent across the instep. It was quite clean and free from the mud of the jungle path; so she could not have been walking in her sleep, unless she bathed in her sleep as well. The natural explanation was that she had known what she was doing all along.

But . . . I did not know what to think.

The gargoyles on the bedposts knew though. They had witnessed everything that had happened in this room tonight. I could read it in their nasty, grinning faces. How glad I was that I had given up this room!

It was only after I had closed the door again and walked down the portico that I dwelt on this last thought of mine. No one but Miss Nell had known that I did not sleep in this room. Whatever Miss Nell saw that frightened out of her that unearthly scream had been meant for me!

SIX

AFTER MY baptism of terror that first night, I should have been a good deal surprised to be told I would sleep soundly, not only through the midnight arrival of Soochi with Dr. Torri, but even through a torrential rain in the early hours of the morning. When I did wake up it was with the annoying if not downright sinister awareness that someone stood at the foot of my bed watching me, and worse, pulling at the sheets. I distinctly remembering having locked my door the night before. This seemed to have had no effect on my visitor.

While I pretended to be asleep, I managed to study the intruder from beneath my lowered eyelashes. It was Isobel Amber, looking fashionable to the point of idiocy. The state of my mind after the previous night may be judged by my delight at beholding this fugitive from a *Vogue* cover. She might be acid beneath the sugar coating, but at least I knew what to expect of her. After the happenings of the night before, I was uneasy at the prospect of dealing with David Earle and, by implication, his employer, Michael Amber, and I was downright afraid of Soochi and Miss Nell. How refreshing to deal with Cousin Isobel, whose malice was clear and whose every word was suspect! You knew where you stood with Cousin Isobel, I told myself.

"There, my dear, awake at last!" she said cheerfully. Evidently I hadn't fooled her. "I've been tugging at your sheets this hour at least." She raised one exquisitely gloved hand, examining the forefinger for a fleck of dust, with a half audible "tsk-tsk!" and a shake of the head, as though she blamed me, but forgave me for ruining her pristine smartness.

I sat up trying to put my hair, at least, in some kind of order. I was still so unused to the house that I glanced around at the plain neatness of this bedroom, wondering who had slept here before me and why it lacked the exotic flashiness of some of the other rooms.

"How is Miss Nell?" I asked presently, seeing that Isobel was simply perishing to talk.

"Quite comfortable, my dear. I am given to understand she is sleeping. Doctor Torri returned this morning with Michael and me. He says the woman is overwrought. The Ellen matter still troubles her. That is all."

It was enough, I thought. Then I remembered. "Good heavens! How did you get in here? The door was locked."

Isobel laughed and, after daintily patting the edge of the bed into a convenient hollow, sat down. Her bright, malicious blue eyes seemed to take in every misplaced hair on my head, and then to make a self-satisfied excursion over my unpowdered nose and unpainted lips.

"But my dear Cathy, every key at Amber works in every other door. I assure you the only purpose of locked doors here is to keep them from banging in a high wind."

These were uncomfortable tidings. Perhaps a chair under the doorknob would do tonight. I was beginning to miss Brett Caldwell's presence; for he would at least have protested loudly.

Isobel reluctantly moved aside while I got up and reached for my peignoir.

"How very odd!" she resumed, as I got things together for my bath. "Now, why would you want to lock the door? Surely, you can't be afraid of a feeble-minded old lady and that harmless little Soochi? . . . Or is it because this was poor Ellen's room?" Her hand went to her mouth in a distinctly stagey fashion. "Oh, have I said something I shouldn't? But, of course, I thought Soochi would have told you."

I turned around and looked at her full and long without speaking. I think, for the first time in our acquaintance, she was disconcerted. She blinked and, after a pause, smiled maliciously and murmured as if she had made a great discovery, "Well, well, well! It should prove interesting to know what drove you to lock the door."

On my way to the bathroom I said to her, "It would prove interesting to know why you are paying such an early call, Isobel."

She arose from the bed with a sigh and followed me. "Dear me! I hope that does not mean I am unwelcome. I so look forward to visiting Amber. How happy I shall be when Michael gains possession and restores it to all its former beauty and luster!"

Knowing Isobel, I could not believe this was another slip of the tongue. It was said for a purpose, as was everything she said. While I bathed in the ancient tub and Cousin Isobel chattered to me outside the door, I tried to figure out how Michael could gain possession of Amber if I refused to sign over the estate. I had, of course, understood all along that the main reason for the Ambers' pursuit of the rightful heiress was to restore the plantation, and that for them to do that, the heiress must give her consent. But how did they intend to make me give consent if I did not wish to?

From something Miss Nell had said, I gathered that my half-sister had refused her permission; yet they hadn't been able to coerce her.

Or had they? Ellen Amber had been removed from consideration in the most permanent way. And by some sleight of hand I was now established in Ellen's bedroom—the place, as Miss Nell said, where Ellen's shrouded body had been laid out after it was returned from the Tangerine Pool. Wasn't this also the room in which Miss Nell had been imprisoned? Or was that part of her delusion?

What horrid thoughts I was entertaining! A desire to escape loneliness was not enough to make me put my life in jeopardy. If I could be absolutely sure I was in danger, I would sign over the entire property and hurry back home. I wasn't anxious to be a heroine. Particularly a dead heroine like my sister, Ellen. On the other hand, it seemed a pity to let a nasty-nice creature like Isobel scare me out of an estate that was legally my own. After all, I had no concrete proof that Ellen hadn't fallen into the pool through her own carelessness, and there was even less evidence of danger to me. I must remember to ask cousin Michael what would become of the estate if I were dead. No! Why give anyone ideas? Better to ask what would have become of Amber if they had not found me.

When I had finished my bath, made up and dressed, I found Amber full of guests, all standing around the dreary dining room, waiting for me. Isobel fanned herself with a stiff paper fan advertising a well-known Free Port shop, but paused long enough to roll her eyes at Michael when I came in. This, I take it, was to call my tardiness to his attention. Michael, I was happy to note, turned his back on her deliberately and gave me that warm and personal look which always lifted my spirits immensely. I saw David Earle in his white suit, looming massively in a dark corner. He had been talking to a lean, well-dressed Negro of middle age, whose eyes seemed to burn in an extraordinary way as they focused on me. It wasn't possible that everyone on Saint Cloud disliked me, I reminded myself. Maybe, in this case, it was merely the effect of the unusual whiteness of his eyes around the dark pupils.

Michael said briskly, indicating the stranger, "Cathy, this is Doctor Torri. I believed he arrived after you had retired last night. He has just been making another call on the nurse. She is taking breakfast in her room but insists on getting up."

I thought it might be interesting to discuss the recent events with this doctor, particularly what David Earle had been up to last night, wandering around the jungle only half-dressed, with his silent, zombie friends —"The Labor Meeting" as he had called them. I asked the doctor if he knew what had frightened Miss Nell.

Michael said abruptly, "It seems to have been a bad case of nerves, nothing more."

"And was it nerves that made her scream?"

"The lady remembers nothing whatever about a scream," Dr. Torri said with bland innocence.

I thought of getting Soochi's testimony to back me up, but I had no very high opinion of her honesty, either.

"Nevertheless," I said, determined to have the last word here at least, "I want to see Miss Nell immediately after breakfast."

No one made any objections. They treated me like a willful child they were humoring, and when Michael pulled out my chair at the head of the table, there was nothing to do but obey him and sit down. I had some thought of requesting Dr. Torri to sit at my left, so that I could talk to him while Michael and the others were busy at the foot of the table, but everything seemed to have been worked out ahead, and Dr. Torri wound up at the foot of the table beside Michael, while I was flanked by Isobel and David Earle. No one seemed to have thought of gaining my consent to all these extra breakfast guests, and I did not quite feel up to mentioning it to Michael in public. I was impressed, though, by the relationship of the overseer to Michael, as I had supposed David Earle would dine with Soochi. But the two men seemed to be more than employer and employee; they seemed more like old and valued companions. As the breakfast conversation progressed, and I got to know David Earle better, I was not surprised at their relationship. Closer acquaintance with him showed me that part of Michael Amber's success was due to the help of this keen and talented aide.

Discussing the acreage that lay fallow beyond the sweep of the old volcanic path across the north and east of Amber, David said to me, "In school Michael and I always hoped there would be another major eruption. We were crushed, Miss Cathy, each time old Soufriere blew off harmlessly. No thrill in that. Michael suggested dropping grenades into the cone, and for a while the idea was very promising. We intended to steal the grenades from our Vichy neighbor Martinique. During the war, you understand. This was after Michael was refused the R.A.F. And for such a reason! He was all of fourteen; weren't you?"

"I was as fully competent as anyone twice my age," Michael said sharply, as though the disgrace still rankled. I'm sure he believed every word of his boast.

I looked eagerly from one to the other of the two men. "Well? What happened about bombing the volcano?" I asked.

"I'm afraid," David admitted, "I had an attack of conscience. I became a coward and threatened to tell Mister Richard."

"I very nearly killed you for that treachery, you dog!" Michael called from the other end of the table. "But coward you were not. What a fight that was!"

David Earle smiled and added gently, "If I'm not mistaken, I won the fight."

"Can't recall you winning at all."

"You couldn't recall much of anything," Isobel interrupted. "My cousin Richard was all but threatening poor David with the authorities. If it hadn't been for Ellen, I really think . . ."

While I was making a silent bet that David Earle would not be able to beat Michael today, Michael contradicted his cousin quickly, brusquely.

"My cousin Ellen had nothing to do with it. I would never have allowed them to blame old David. He and I had been sailing across the Channel when the Great Battle commenced. Ellen wanted the schooner that night, and it was all over blood. My blood! That's why she asked her father not to interfere. It inconvenienced her."

"Now, why do you suppose Ellen wanted the schooner?" Isobel murmured with a side glance at me. "I suppose her journal would tell. She was always scribbling in those wretched little books. What secrets they could reveal if one knew where to look for them!"

For once I agreed with Isobel.

"Soochi says Ellen had been burning pages from them for some time before she died," said Michael, and I was severely let down. I did not want to pry into Ellen's secrets, but there might be many revelations in those pages that would help me to know what to do; for since my arrival I had been in an almost permanent state of alarm. I felt helpless to take the right steps.

Dr. Torri coughed and remarked, "I do not know how Soochi does it, but the food at Amber is always superb. Do you find it so, Miss Amber?"

"Why did my sister want the schooner that night?" I asked, into a huge and gaping silence.

If I had not been so curious, I might have laughed at what followed. Michael, David and Dr. Torri began to speak, and I could have sworn each of them had a different tale to tell. In deference to Michael's position, the two West Indians abruptly broke off, leaving Michael to carry on.

"Ellen often shopped for artwork on Haiti. It's a stiff sail from Saint Cloud and beastly hot by day, so the crew usually started in the afternoon. Ellen then spent what remained of the night on shipboard in the harbor of Port au Prince."

This sounded so plausible I wondered why I kept remembering that one of Haiti's more interesting products was voodoo. I felt a strong desire to throw a lighted firecracker into the midst of these clever strangers, so I asked, abruptly, "Doctor Torri, do you know Haiti at all?"

He looked up from his plate, his manner no more surprised than might be expected at this unlooked-for attention. "Quite well, Miss Cathy. I was born on a plantation outside Cap' Haitien."

"I understand there is still considerable voodoo that goes on in the back-country there." As I spoke, I crumbled up the remains of my toast, and I found that my fingers were trembling. I wondered just how dangerous was this ground I had ventured on. But although the doctor's eyes began to study me with some intensity, I think he was as much astonished as the rest of us when we heard a peal of light laughter, and there was Soochi, removing plates.

Standing behind Michael, Soochi said, "How like a tourist Miss Cathy is! But if the people of the islands were as interested in voodoo as the tourist, we should all wear charms to fend off the evil; isn't it so, doctor?"

"That will do, Soochi," said Isobel, with her charming condescension. "You really must not enter so freely into the conversation. You have been warned before. Did not Miss Ellen tell you so?"

Soochi smiled disdainfully. "I wonder what Miss Ellen could have told you all about voodoo. . . . Will there be anything else, Mister Michael?"

"You must ask Miss Cathy that," he told her as I secretly bristled. It would appear that I was neither fish nor fowl at Amber. Neither guest nor mistress. Under orders, Soochi glanced at me, her eloquent eyebrows raised. I wished with all my heart that I could think of something to upset Michael's composure, but nothing occurred to me, and I agreed stupidly that there was nothing else. She might go.

I was more positive with Michael, however, and when the breakfast broke up, I told him I would like to speak with him in private about my situation at Amber.

"Of course," he said pleasantly. "I have been intending to speak to you about it. Did you wish to talk to me before or after you see Miss Nell?"

I was so annoyed with myself for forgetting that I almost bit my tongue. And I had made such a commotion over seeing Miss Nell, too! It was frustrating to have Michael Amber always in the right and myself always corrected.

"I have left a mild sedative with Soochi," the doctor explained, hearing this polite little riposte between Michael and me. "She has my instructions to give a capsule to Miss Nell upon the lady's retiring, or at any sign that the lady is about to wander off the estate. I think you will not be troubled tonight. It has been a pleasure to meet you, Miss Amber."

We shook hands and he left, closely followed by Soochi, who saw him off in his small British Ford while Michael and I went to Miss Nell's room at my suggestion.

"Or more precisely—your room," Michael corrected me as we walked along the portico, which was now crisscrossed with the slanting sunlight; for a piercing blue sky hung over the garden and the jungle beyond. "Why did you change rooms?"

"If I hadn't," I said suddenly, "I would be the one Doctor Torri came to visit last night. Miss Nell really saw something, you know."

"Ridiculous."

I said nothing.

After a moment he went on in quite a different tone: "What do you think she saw?"

"I think she saw my sister, Ellen."

I had braced myself for his burst of laughter, even for disgust at my naïveté. Instead, he appeared to accept this, which did not ease my own superstitious feelings.

"How do you know that it was Ellen?"

"Because of something Miss Nell said to me when I got her back into bed the first time. She said I must take care. That 'she' was out there in the garden, watching."

"And you are quite sure it was Miss Nell who told you that?"

Absurd question. I hadn't talked to anyone else about Ellen's Shade. Or had I? And then it came to me. "Of course! It wasn't Miss Nell. It was Soochi. She kept talking about my sister's Shade floating about the garden, and how Miss Nell had seen it."

"I thought as much," said Michael. His satisfaction only made me more aware of my own gullibility. I had been taken in by that treacherous housekeeper.

"I ought to let her go," I said, half to myself. But as I might have expected, Michael overruled me.

"I doubt if that sort of talk will annoy you as much as losing her services. And then, too, she has been here all her life. She is mentioned in your father's will with a small legacy. Removing her might prove difficult. However, if she persists . . ."

I hadn't understood. This power of Soochi's was only one more proof of my own lack of power, and before we went into Miss Nell's room, I mentioned it to him.

"I must know what I can and can't do at Amber. At every point I am held back. I am not a guest, and yet I have no power as owner of the plantation. Last night I was ready to leave the island and return home."

He paused with his hand over my head, on the door of Miss Nell's room, and looked down at me gently.

"Cathy, I am counting on you. If, after certain matters are settled, you find you still dislike it so much, then I shall take you back to New York or wherever you like. With the income from Amber you need never have another problem . . . of that sort." He smiled. It was difficult to be angry when he smiled at me in such a way. "But I hope it won't come to that. I hope, in the end, you may feel that Saint Cloud will be your home to the end of your days. As it was your father's and Ellen's."

I tried to smile back at him, but the chill of that final comparison was too much, and I failed. He noted the quick revulsion that made me shiver at the memory of those two who had both died so suddenly, and he lowered his hand to my hair. For a moment I thought he was going to kiss me, but he merely traced my hairline

71

with a feathery touch and then abruptly moved away and opened the door behind me.

In the room, darkened by the bamboo curtains, Miss Nell's fully dressed, lean figure towered over me, and I realized that she had been standing there at the bamboo curtains, watching my little scene with Michael.

"I was about to go into the garden, if you will excuse me." She behaved as though last night had never happened. She was about to walk around me and out the door without any more explanation than that, but I took hold of her forearm. I remember being surprised at its sinewy strength, but at the same time, I felt the quick beat of her pulse and knew that however calm she appeared, she was greatly unnerved by something, which may have been our presence.

"Not yet, Miss Nell. I want to talk to you."

Michael stood where he was and leaned against the door frame, crossing his arms as though he expected this to take some time. I had a distinct impression he was making fun of me.

"This is my cousin's hour for interviews, Miss Nell. You must not mind. I am promised an interview later."

I felt like kicking him, but he pretended not to notice this tart humor. Besides, the nurse was trying to edge by me, in spite of my grip.

"Miss Nell, what did you see last night that made you scream? Was it my sister?"

"If I did scream, it must have been in my sleep. My Ellen is dead, you know. I saw her body when they brought it back. There was no mistake. I sometimes tell myself she isn't dead. It eases my conscience. But I know better."

"Then you could not have seen Ellen—or her Shade —last night in the garden?"

She swallowed and flicked her tongue over her thin, dry lips. Her gaze seemed to dart from me to Michael as though she could not settle on one of us for long. "Naturally not," she said. "How absurd! I do not believe in ghosts."

"But a Shade isn't quite a ghost, Miss Nell. Soochi tells me that a Shade is what remains of the soul of someone who was . . ." I paused just long enough to give myself courage. " . . . who was murdered."

This time there was a definite stir, not from Miss

Nell, whose ruddy, mottled face seemed frozen out of all expression, but from Michael, who had changed his easy stance. I could imagine him growing tense.

"And this is Soochi's idea?" he asked, in a voice that sounded ominously threatening toward the absent Soochi.

"What do you think, Miss Nell?" I said, as though he hadn't spoken.

She made a hurried movement and escaped me. Michael put his arm across the doorway, and she paused at this barrier.

"I don't know. I should have been with Ellen. It was my fault. I let her wander about alone too much."

"Where are you going?" I glanced down at her feet and saw that over her stout, arch-support shoes she was wearing galoshes. I was absolutely sure where she was going. It was as though her mind were transparent to me at that moment. She had a fixed idea, to find some clue at the Tangerine Pool. Whether it was a clue that bound her to the murder, or one that gave her proof of someone else's guilt, I didn't know. She had gone there last night and been turned back by David Earle or some of the Amber plantation hands. Having failed then, she was on her way there this morning.

"Never mind," I told her quickly, afraid that Michael would spoil everything by keeping her in the house. "I'll go for a walk with you in the garden, after you've had breakfast."

"I had my tea long ago, thank you. But if you care to go with me . . ."

Michael said slowly, "Are you sure you want to do this, Cathy? I have some papers for your signature—estate business."

"Later," I said. "Miss Nell was showing me around the garden yesterday. I want to learn more about some of those plants. I never saw any like them."

Frowning, Miss Nell looked at me and read in my face something that made her trust me. She sighed, and her nervousness seemed to melt away in that sigh. "I should be happy to, Miss Amber. You have some of your sister's ways. I think you will do well here."

This time, Michael lowered his arm and let us go, but when we were both out in the garden and Miss Nell had begun to give me some Latin names for a series of outlandish blooms, I saw that Michael still watched us from the portico, with a puzzled look. It was plain that he didn't trust one of us, or both together. What was he afraid of?

When he could no longer hear us, I spoke plainly to the woman who seemed, every minute, to grow more calm and easy in my presence. She might prove to be my only ally in this eery place. "Miss Nell, I think I know where you want to go, and why. You are looking for some tangible proof, some evidence. You believe my sister may have been murdered. That is why you keep returning to the pool, even at night. And you were on your way there last night, when one of the men brought you back."

She lowered her head, pretending to examine the stamens of a large red hibiscus, but I heard her hoarse, whispered reply.

"I never quite got there. I am always followed. Even last night, when it was so dark I could scarcely see the walls of the pool. Even then, they were watching me, and one of that accursed David Earle's clan forced me to return. They think of everything. They even humiliated me by insisting that they, and not I, must wash the mud off my feet. As though I should go back to bed knee-deep in jungle mud! Treating me as if I were mad!"

"Did you find anything at the pool?"

"Not yet. But I will. I will!"

"Whom do you suspect?"

She smiled in a sad way that made her uglier than ever, and yet gave her ugliness a firm dignity.

"The Good Book says 'What shall it profit . . . ?' For that, read 'Whom shall it profit?' Is there another heir to come after you? If you did not cause my poor Ellen to be murdered, then it is your heir we must find. Who is your heir?"

I saw that Michael had moved away from the portico and was inside the house. I wondered if he were still watching. Miss Nell noticed my glance and whispered, "Now! Before they mark which path we take."

As we made our way between the high, masking growths toward the broken wall which marked the boundary of the garden, I told her I had no idea who my heir was, as my only relations were here on Saint Cloud.

"Your situation is more and more like Ellen's," she muttered savagely, to my discomfort.

"Do you suppose my sister could have told us anything in the journal she kept?"

"Ah!" she said. "You know about that. But those journals are gone."

"Burned up, Soochi says."

Miss Nell smiled grimly. "That may be, but there is not a day since Ellen died that I haven't torn apart a pillow, or ripped up a mattress, or pried the head off a bedpost, to be quite sure Ellen hadn't hidden a few pages there. I still am not done. She never went anywhere without one of those tiny notebooks, hardly two inches long. She used to sit by the pool and write in them. Yet, when they brought her body back from the pool, her notebook for that month was not on her body." She turned to me as we passed under a ticklish, acrid-smelling fern frond. "D'you think it could have fallen off her body into the pool somewhere?"

It was possible. I hardly saw how it could be recovered from a pool of mud and water large enough to drown a human being, and I told her so. She shrugged. She knew this path very well. On several occasions I might have taken a wrong turning, but she was ready to choose among paths that were impenetrable to me. We reached the clearing where, last night, I had seen those strange, silent men passing in the moonlight. It was a pleasant, green glade by daylight, dappled with sun, but cool enough under the twisted tropic growths that bordered it. Shining in the sunlight was a crushed beer can which certainly went far to put down any of my extravagant ideas about 'voodoo ceremonies' out here last night. If it had been voodoo, it was a singularly modern form.

When we had left the glade and were making our way through the jungle beyond my discovery of last night, the path widened, and presently we came, with a suddenness that jarred me, upon the very rim of a huge, scooped-out place in the midst of black mud and decaying fern. It was twenty-five feet or more across, and looked a long way down when we stood on the muddy bank, our feet sinking into the ooze. The water of the pool was speckled with fallen leaves and other unidentifiable debris, but even at our distance, at least ten feet from the surface of the pool, we could see the reflection of the sky and of overhanging greenery, and when I studied the sloping lava walls with their coat of mud and moulding vegetation, I could see what a terrible thing it would be to lose one's footing here.

Miss Nell apparently shared my thoughts; for she said shakily, "I think I'll—I'll rest a moment, if you will excuse me." She shuffled to a tangled clump of tree trunks that seemed to proceed from the same parent trunk, much further away from the pool. She leaned back, shielding her eyes with one hand, which shook noticeably.

I took advantage of this moment alone and walked around the pool's edge, being careful not to step too close to the treacherous mud that rimmed the pool. I could understand why Miss Nell had never seen anything here which could help her to solve the mystery of Ellen's death. Indeed, from the look of the pool, there was no mystery about it. One careless step and Ellen would have *had* it! I was fascinated by the occasional outcroppings of rock that proved to be hardened lava, and I stopped to examine this lava, which was the closest I had ever come to a volcano. There was one place that had been carved out, by the natural act of the lava's tremendous flow, into an arm chair, as though by special order from the Fire Gods. Gathering up my skirt, I sat down in it with gingerly care. As I did so, I leaned further over the pool, and from this vantage point I saw what appeared to be a white leaf, or even a piece of paper, washed flat against the muddy side of the pool. It was temptingly close, and I leaped to the conclusion that it must be a piece of Ellen's missing journal. How lucky if I could find it and solve the whole mystery in one day! It was too far to reach without getting up from my lava chair, and that movement would be noticed by Miss Nell. I decided not to tell her about my discovery.

She shifted her position across the pool and took her arm away from her eyes. I saw that she was staring at me, but her sight was confused by the late morning sunlight overhead.

"What is it, Miss Amber? Why have you stopped?"

"This chair," I called to her. "We ought to have it at the house. It's more comfortable than any of the man-made ones." I got up and finished my walk around the pool. As I came back to Miss Nell's side, where the path wound close to the pool's edge, I looked across and could still see that little bit of white clinging to the bank about three feet under the lava chair. But if one had not seen it from close to, it would seem like a sun-faded leaf or an effect of the light on an outcropping of rock.

"I do think we had better return later, Miss Nell," I said, "when you are more yourself. You need your strength for this."

"Yes," she agreed, and she moved away from the tree with an effort. She leaned heavily on my shoulder. "Perhaps tomorrow. Tomorrow I'll feel more the thing."

I hated to cheat her like this, as I dabbed at her perspiring forehead with my handkerchief and then dropped the handkerchief in the path behind us, but I was not absolutely sure that I could trust her. We made our way slowly along the path back to the glade where I stopped in a quick flurry of impatience.

"What a stupid thing to do! I must have dropped my handkerchief. Where did I last have it?"

After a confused moment of what appeared to be thought, she answered, "At the pool, I imagine. Or—a few minutes ago . . . I—I'm not quite sure." She looked exhausted, poor thing! "I see I've overestimated my strength. Perhaps when I return to the house . . . I may lie down."

"Yes, of course, and with some hot tea," I encouraged her. "Can you make it alone while I go back and get my handkerchief? You see, it is rather special to me. It belonged to my mother." That, at least, was true enough.

She scarcely heard me but moved across the glade, dragging her feet and giving a heavy sigh now and then.

I hurried back to the pool, not wanting to leave her alone more than a minute or two. In the path was my handkerchief where I had left it, and I picked it up and went on to the pool, stepping carefully around its edge

77

to the lava chair. Holding onto the "arm" of the chair with one hand, and tucking my skirt between my knees, I leaned far over the pool's side and caught the white piece between two fingers. I could tell at once that it was not paper, as I had hoped, but a piece of cloth, heavily fringed. A triangle torn from an old-fashioned knitted white shawl.

It probably meant nothing at all. Certainly it was hardly worth all this effort, and I had left poor Miss Nell alone for this. I took it into my palm and examined it closely. A good material—the fringe was silk, and the shawl must have been cashmere. It was not the sort of thing a young person would wear. More like a woman Miss Nell's age, or even one of the servants on the way to market. On the other hand, it might have belonged to a long-dead Amber woman—Ellen's mother, for instance.

But in that case, would the cloth stay this white, in such muddy surroundings? It would have worn out and washed away long ago. I was hypnotized by my discovery and heard no sound until a well-known voice called to me courteously from across the pool.

"May I trouble you for that, Cathy?"

It was Michael Amber.

SEVEN

I JUMPED as if I'd been caught doing something sinister, and I very nearly dropped the scrap of cloth into the pool. Fortunately, by reflex action, my fingers curled it up along with the handkerchief in my perspiring palm. It took me at least two minutes to make my way around the pool's edge, during which time all embarrassment at my own behavior was submerged in indignation at Michael Amber. How dare he spy on me? And on my own property, too! If I were to have no privacy at all, anyone would think I was a prisoner.

Two minutes were more than enough time needed to palm the scrap of cloth and approach Michael with my grimy hand outstretched. I was so obedient it must have been sickening to behold, if he suspected the truth.

"Heavens! You startled me," I said as I dropped into his palm the little ball of lawn that was my handkerchief, while I retained the important scrap of "evidence." "I can't imagine what you want it for. I'm always picking up things. But, of course, if you want it. . . ."

He pocketed the handkerchief without even glancing at it.

"Thank you, Cathy. This sort of thing can be very dangerous."

He looked concerned but not angry. I could almost imagine that he was concerned for my safety. I looked at him innocently.

"Dangerous to give it to you? I didn't realize."

"I meant . . . !" He restrained himself nicely after

that first start. He took my arm in a more amiable mood. "I wish you would not treat me as though you suspected me of trying to do away with you."

I said quickly, "I'm convinced you would never dream of doing away with me."

"That is something, at any rate."

I considered myself to be in excellent form after the way I had fooled him with the handkerchief, and I teased him without any sense of fear.

"But that's because I didn't know how important you are in Saint Cloud. Now, I see it would be much more proper for your—er—gang to do away with people."

I expected to arouse him again, but he was learning. It had taken considerable effort, but he finally entered into the spirit of things.

"There is a certain crudeness about a 'gang,'" he objected. "I prefer to rely upon my 'trusty henchmen' for the ordinary run of crime."

I had to laugh as I looked up at him. "I'm sure only the extraordinary run of crime can tempt you. Such as following people and spying on them."

I caught a slight reddening over his broad cheekbones, and I was very pleased with myself. Such a serious, dominating man was a natural target for teasing.

"There are certain matters better handled by me," he said in a voice that left no room for discussion. I wanted to mimic him but did not dare. It would be the one thing he could not forgive.

When we finally caught up with Miss Nell it was necessary for me to cut her off quickly as she was about to mention my handkerchief. I made a great fuss over her and managed to get her onto the subject of her own ills, while Michael helped her back to the garden of Amber. There we found Isobel busy ordering around two of David Earle's men who had been loaned to us to clean up the debris of the garden after the recent rains. It seemed like a futile job to me. Thunderclouds were gathering, and every object at Amber, even our faces, began to take on the mysterious, shadowy blue look of things seen under heavy tropic skies.

After I had sent Soochi to prepare tea for Miss Nell in that horrid room full of gargoyles that she chose for herself, I could not wait to get to my own room and hide my small scrap of cashmere and fringe. I could not tell whether it was gallantry or suspicion that made Michael ask me, as he escorted me to my room,

"Will you be busy this afternoon?"

"I don't know. Why?"

"I thought I might drive you around the island before tea. It's rather scenic."

This was promising.

"How close can we drive to the volcano?"

This time he was ready for me before I even thought of teasing him. "Not close enough for me to tumble you in. We merely skirt the mountain. Are you disappointed?"

"Infinitely. I'm a fiend for danger."

"Perhaps I can promise you some. Not, I'm afraid, the melodramatic kind."

Whatever that meant!

"I'll read my horoscope and see if it warns me against long journeys with strange men," I promised him as he opened the door to my room.

He motioned me in. "I hope we shall not always be strangers, Cathy."

When he had gone I repeated his parting words to myself several times in different tones, trying to discover whether I could really bank on them personally or whether—dull thought!—it was Amber he was after. But wasn't it slightly possible that he would rather have me included in the package deal? I sat down on the bed, hugging my bare arms in the mouldy dampness of the room, and reconstructed in my mind all the facial features of Michael Amber. How strange and exciting his deep-set eyes were! There had been moments, like the one I had experienced when he said we shouldn't be strangers, that had almost made me blush like a stupid teen-ager of my grandmother's day. And, of course, from his eyes, my mind leaped to his mouth, that cruel, beautifully sculptured stubborn flesh. I had seen sensual mouths and been kissed by sensual men, and I hadn't liked it. But Michael Amber's sensuousness was quite different. He was far more exciting to me by his reticence and bad temper. And even during times when I feared him, a part of me couldn't help speculating at the same time on what it would be like to have him make love to me.

So different from Brett Caldwell! From the day I met Brett I never doubted how he would conduct himself in any of a thousand situations, and he didn't disappoint me by a single move. He was so nicely, typically, all-American-football-hero Brett Caldwell! With a girl in every sorority and twice as many on Sunday! He would never be sincere and genuine, as Michael Amber was.

While I enjoyed these thrills provided vicariously and without his knowledge by my cousin Michael, my prosaic mind was darting about for a place in which to hide the triangle of cloth that Michael's actions had convinced me would be evidence in Ellen's death. My first project, when I could concentrate on it without arousing suspicion, would be to find out what had happened to the rest of the shawl. By that time I might trust Michael Amber enough to show him what I had found. On the other hand, I might not. A great deal depended upon what my horoscope said that day.

What a marvelous idea! I took my paperbacked horoscope for the Leo-born out from under my pillow and carefully placed the triangle of cloth between the pages for July. Then I flipped back the pages and read my horoscope for this April day:

> You are not as clever as you imagine yourself.
> Seek rather to encourage your natural sweetness
> and sunlight!

What a disappointment! It was much more fun to be clever!

I wrinkled my nose at the advice and put the book back under my pillow. No one at Amber was likely to read the astrological advice for Leos. I had made up my own bed this morning, out of habit, and Soochi or someone had already dusted in here. Not a soul at Amber had any legitimate business in my room except myself.

I found Isobel in the darkened Sadie-Thompsonish living room, instructing Soochi on the finer points of running a household. I immediately decided to put my keen detective sense into play while both women were together, thus pitting one against the other. It should not be difficult. I had a large backlog of crime literature to fall back on for ideas, if only I didn't scramble up Mary Roberts Rinehart's methods into those of, say, Mickey Spillane, with whose methods I felt I couldn't quite cope. Not for nothing had I read about heroines who puttered around in murder-infested attics, with their plaintive cry of "Had I but known . . ." The difference was, I *but knew*. I must not trust anyone.

"Brr . . ." I said, slapping my bare arms ostentatiously, thus calling the attention of both women to me. "Is it always this cold? I should have brought more sweaters."

"It's not the cold, dear," explained helpful Isobel. "It's the dampness. Amber is set so very oddly in the center of all this jungle decay and vegetation. But that's the way great-grandfather Amber was. Lascivious scoundrel, carrying on his nasty affairs with all the natives and half the dreadful East Indian imports as well." I should not have thought anything about this speech if Isobel herself hadn't broken off in great confusion. "Oh, Soochi. I forgot you were one of . . . that is . . . East Indian people are . . . But my dear Soochi, they were quite different from you, you know. They were such yellow little things with their quaint bowing and scraping manners! One would as soon take up with . . ."

I cut in hurriedly, afraid she would now antagonize David Earle's people who happened to be in the vicinity, and besides, she was getting me off the track.

"Well, I certainly could have used another sweater . . . or a stole. What I really need is a good, old-fashioned shawl. But nobody wears those any more, I guess." I paused, feeling particularly proud of myself when Isobel fell into the trap.

"Why don't you borrow one of Miss Nell's shawls? She set quite a store by them when she first came to Amber. I daresay she still has some. I seem to recall seeing her wear them, off and on. Or am I wrong, Soochi?"

"I have not noticed, Miss Isobel."

The housekeeper's voice sounded more than usually flat and expressionless to me, and through the dim half-light of the room I studied her dainty yet sturdy figure, crowned by its double-pointed headdress, so like a pair of antennae bobbing gently in the stir of air. I noticed that although her face was motionless, her fingers, half hidden in the voluminous skirts of her costume, clawed slowly, like the pointed headdress, expressing the direction of her thoughts, which were so carefully concealed in other ways.

"I wonder what my sister did about the dampness," I ventured, dropping the question between the two women.

Soochi disdained to answer and with a slight inclination of her head, left the room, while Cousin Isobel stared after her.

"Dear me," she remarked in her sweetest and most understanding voice, "I do hope I haven't offended her. Such an odd girl! All of them are like that. One never feels . . . quite safe with them."

"What did my sister do about the dampness?" I asked, giving the question more immediacy than I had intended; for now it made Isobel stare at me in her hard-blue marble gaze.

"Does it matter so much? I had no notion. But then, this place does put all our tempers on edge, doesn't it? When I think of the quarrels Ellen and Michael had, and the bitterness between Ellen and Soochi sometimes! Well, really, it's small wonder that dear Ellen had to be got rid of. Now, dear . . ." She began to massage imaginary creases out of her gloves. "I must be running along. My houseman has promised faithfully to be waiting with the car at the crossroads. And I do want to get home to my little hovel before the usual afternoon storm breaks."

While I was interrupting with remarks about "What did they quarrel over?" and "Why was Ellen angry with everyone?" she simply ignored them and while still buttoning her glove, she leaned forward and brushed my cheek with her cheek in the conventional kiss among female relatives who know each other too well or not well enough.

I thought, "She is saving up some ammunition for a parting word. Something that will startle me and make me worry after she is gone." As I walked to the front veranda with her I tried to imagine what it would be. It was almost a game to her. Sure enough, on the broad top step she paused and turned around to me.

It was coming. What would her evil, vicious little brain conceive this time? Something bloodthirsty, of course. And I made up my mind that whatever she said would not in the least worry me. It might even put me onto the mystery of this place.

"Goodbye, dear," she said with her sweet smile. "How I wish it were possible for Michael to love you!" And she went away, with a gay wave of the hand.

I had never hated anyone so much in my life.

Naturally, her words haunted me during the entire hour before lunch. I spent that hour in my room, which had once been Ellen's, launching a thorough search for any of the little journals that my sister had kept so faithfully. The room had a monastic severity, and there were very few places to look, although I got up on a chair and ran my hands along the dusty moulding and all along the shelves in the closet, collecting, for my efforts, an enormous amount of what I thought of as "wet-dust," a dampish form of mould that made my flesh creep. The bed was modern, with no bedposts hollowed out to receive valuable documents that would name her killer, if there was one.

Why was it so impossible for Michael Amber to marry me? Was there some dark, dreadful secret about him? Was he, perhaps, the illegitimate son of my father? I had run across that plot in a novel not too long before and had been keenly disappointed. It seemed a shabby surprise to come upon after three hundred pages of dull reading. No. She was probably insinuating that he had murdered or stolen or done something even more reprehensible, though not necessarily so in my eyes.

There was a knock on the door, and I heard Soochi's voice say, "Luncheon, Miss Cathy."

I looked around the room once more, shook out the throw rugs again, and satisfied myself that either Ellen was cleverer than I, or she hadn't hidden anything here. I was beginning to suspect, though, that she hadn't been quite the dull spinster that she was painted. I liked her better for it.

Miss Nell and I had lunch on the portico again, and she appeared to be rested, in much better spirits than I had ever seen her.

"I suppose you and Ellen used to do this often," I said, breaking the ice and hoping she would plunge in after me.

"Yes. Very often. When she was not away."

"Where did she go? Did she have many friends?"

Miss Nell broke off a piece of bread and considered it thoughtfully. "No. I should say she had few friends. But she often visited on the inner islands."

"I had the impression she was a student of voodoo." I dropped that into the conversation half expecting her to break off and scurry away, but instead she agreed at once.

"Yes. My Ellen was a student of voodoo and of mankind. She was curious about everything. She might have been a brilliant scientist, under other circumstances. It is odd. Her mother was so nondescript."

"How did her mother die?"

She appeared surprised at the question, but then smiled a dry, humorless smile. "I see. You imagine Mrs. Amber was murdered? Oh, no. She died prosaically in bed. Pneumonia. She had been caught in a rainstorm, just as Ellen was on the day she—fell into the Tangerine Pool. Only Mrs. Amber knew how dangerous it was to take that path during slippery weather, and she took the longer way. She caught cold. It went into pneumonia."

"In the long run the pool killed her too," I remarked, beginning to feel a distinct aversion to that lovely, treacherous place in the fern jungle.

"Perhaps. I never got on well with Mrs. Amber. In her ineffectual way she resented me from the day Mr. Richard sent for me to take care of Ellen. But you are on the wrong trail, Miss Amber, if you think Ellen's mother was murdered. You would do better to think about Mister Richard and Ellen. Both of them behaved in ways very unlike them, during the last hours of their lives."

"How is that?"

"But consider. No one knew better than Ellen how dangerous the path was during a downpour, especially when, as often happened, the sun came through the west and set the Tangerine Pool into a blaze at sunset. We often have sunset in one direction and a thunderstorm from another, you know. The combination can be blinding for an instant."

"Yes, but I understood my father was running when he strained his heart."

The conversation had begun to prey upon Miss Nell. I could see that her hands were not as steady as they had been and her thin mouth quivered uncontrollably.

"Don't let's talk about it. It is upsetting."

A phone rang in the house, disturbing me, but I don't think Miss Nell noticed it.

"But—it must be talked about," she contradicted herself with a sharp urgency. "No one else does. No one mentions how odd it was that your father was racing through the fern forest when he had his final attack. Here was a man with a fatal heart condition, who knew his own weakness. Why has no one asked what frightened him into risking almost certain death? What was he running *from?*"

Something moved faintly in the doorway of the dark hall, and I wondered how long Soochi had been listening.

"Yes?" I asked coldly, seeing her effect upon Miss Nell's already frayed nerves. "What do you want, Soochi?"

"Mister Michael's house just called, Miss Cathy. He's on his way to take you for a drive."

"Very well. Ask him to come in when he arrives, and tell him I will be ready presently." That ought to be cool enough so that he would not guess his importance in my life.

Miss Nell watched Soochi leave us and then leaned over the table and took my hand in her shaking fingers. "Catherine, I don't know what they plan, or who is party to it. I do know that from Mister Richard's death until this business with you, there has been a plan. If . . . if anything should happen to me, you may be very sure I was right."

"Very sure of what?" I whispered, hypnotized by her terrible intensity. But it was this very intensity which defeated her purpose with me.

"Very sure it was part of the plan. Don't trust them. Any of them."

Poor thing! I could see in her pale, tired eyes that

she was on the verge of that state in which I had first met her. Not insane, perhaps, but hopelessly confused. There was a fancy psychiatric name for people who imagined everyone was their enemy.

"In that case," I told her, as gently as I could, "you must preserve your health, Miss Nell, so you and I can get to the bottom of this. You do want to avenge my sister's death; don't you?"

"And your father's. Yes. Don't forget. Your father's too."

"Then you must get a great deal of rest and be very calm. I'll talk to you when I come back."

When I left the portico she was looking after me with a pitiful hope that made me want to cry. It depressed me so that when Michael drove up a few minutes later, he was much concerned at my expression.

"What on earth's the matter? Cathy dear, are you all right?"

How nice that sounded! "Cathy dear." Much nicer than when Isobel said it. I told him I was fine, but that Miss Nell's depression was contagious. He looked impatient at her name but did not let this rub off on our relationship. He helped me into the front seat of the small English car with more care than our brief acquaintance made necessary. As he tucked my full skirt in beside me, I watched his hands and thought how capable they were. Very strong. Very capable. Almost frighteningly capable.

EIGHT

WE HAD BEEN driving for ten minutes or so, through the fern forests that reached out greedily upon the narrow road, before I could think of anything to reply to his comments on the eery scene with its green shadow over the landscape. I kept saying "Yes, I see" and "How interesting!"

"Don't you find it oppressive?" I asked finally.

"I never regard it that way. I suppose because my earliest memories are of wandering through the jungle, pretending to be lost," he said, as though he had given the question some thought, which was clearly impossible; for he was busy swerving the car to avoid a tourist taxi that hurtled toward us on our right.

When we were alone on the road again, Michael put out one hand and dragged me up from my temporary haven, which had been as close under the dashboard as I could get. He was laughing at my predicament, and for a few seconds I scowled. But his good humor was contagious, and I confessed, "I just can't get used to cars tearing along toward me on the wrong side of the road!"

"Precisely my sentiments in the States."

How odd! I thought. Englishmen were so strange, not recognizing that our way was obviously the sensible one. But this quaint Britishness of his made him more masterful, and I liked it. Besides, I was afraid if I argued with him about it, he might remove his arm, which stretched across my lap to the door handle, acting as my safety belt.

We were headed north now, and presently the fern forest died away, and I began to see the white rollers of the Atlantic in the distance on the east, while between ourselves and the ocean was a curious, hard, lumpy dark stretch of land running as far as I could see across the landscape, like a frozen stream of darkness.

"This was the path of La Soufriere's last excursion," Michael explained, and I looked up nervously at the great green mountain with its horrid burnt side, looming over the whole northern half of the island.

"When did it erupt last?"

"Three years ago. Small outbreaks may come at any time. As to the big ones, I'm sorry to disappoint you, but they're pretty well a thing of the past. My great-grandmother saw the last disastrous one. She had just been brought to Amber at the time, and the legend is that every worker on the plantation was so busy removing villagers, children and furniture from this path, no one had time to be frightened until it was over and old Soufriere died out." He raised his hand and pointed in the direction taken by the lava. "It cuts entirely across the borders of Amber to the old harbor of Eastbourne. The harbor used to be the main careenage for pirate ships in these waters, but an eruption in the late seventeenth century destroyed it, and there is nothing left now but the barren cliffs and a couple of small artists' colonies built on the old lava flow."

Our highway turned eastward now, across the hardened lava flow, which did not look any more inviting at close quarters.

"Charming," I lied. "Simply charming." I was determined not to trust that bubbling, belching volcano for one minute. "Your great-grandmother must have been shocked to have such a horrid thing happen so soon after her arrival. Was she on her honeymoon? What a shock it must have been, after England!"

The remark had been automatic, an effort to make conversation, so that I might enjoy his voice. But, without knowing why, I knew that the minute I asked the question, he withdrew from me emotionally. What had I said that was wrong? When he replied, I wondered if I was being hypersensitive, or if it actually took him some time to answer me.

"No. She had never seen England. . . . As we come up over the rise here, you can catch a glimpse of Isobel's cottage. It is on the headland near the Beach Club. That huge pink monstrosity is the Beach Club."

I could barely see the tile-roofed cottage he pointed out, but the Beach Club was everything he claimed for it. The last word in Cigarbox Modern, it went up in flat, unimaginative layers of pink stone or stucco until it seemed the only object on the whole windward coast. This was a pity, because as we approached, I saw among the comfortable older villas of the residents the bright, careless profusion of hibiscus and bougainvillea cheerfully doing their best to make one forget the triumph of Man over Nature. It made me almost prefer my own fern forest at Amber, where nature still had its way with us.

It was surprising how easily I had become adjusted to thinking of myself as an heiress. I had no hesitation at all in calling Amber mine and standing very much on my dignity when Michael or someone else gave orders about the running of the household. Was it possible that only a week ago I had thought the summit of happiness would be a boat trip for some mysterious girl called Cathy Amber?

What a fortunate coincidence all around that Brett's family had demanded proofs of my background and that by my advertisement I had come to the attention of Michael and Cousin Isobel! I had a lot to thank Brett's aunt and uncle for. Suppose they had never questioned mother's lineage!

"What would have happened to the estate if you had never found me?" I asked Michael suddenly. "Who was to have been the next heir?"

"In default of anyone closer, I imagine your Cousin Isobel."

"Good heavens! No wonder she hates me."

He smiled. "You flatter yourself. She dislikes everyone, but she is too malicious, too self-satisfied, to hate. It would ruin her entire life if she had to stop being malicious long enough to carry a good, lusty hatred to its logical conclusion."

"You mean she isn't liable to murder me in my bed?"

"Nor elsewhere. You realize . . ." he paused and

smiled, not entirely at ease. "If and when you sell out to me, you will have no problems, no threats, no fears. You will be quite free—and modestly wealthy."

The road dipped down toward the sea, and I noticed a low-roofed white building on a finger of beach that pointed out into the Atlantic. As we descended steeply, many giant ferns and other green tropical growths poked their heads up from the center of the building, and I mentioned this to Michael.

"Yes. It is my house. Built in the Pompeiian style, around a pool and garden, a kind of combination atrium and peristyle. My grandfather designed it. Like his father, Jonathan, he was a sea captain in the China trade. How he ever found an affinity for the Romans I'll never know. Rather pleasant to return to, though, after a day in Port Anne."

He appeared to be a man who was instantly obeyed, for we were met at the gates to the property by a good-looking young Negro workman who took the car while we walked up the sandy path to the villa. I looked back and saw that the car had already disappeared, and I remarked on it with amusement.

"You are like a magician who can produce a genie at will."

"They know me," he said.

I wondered how I was meant to take that.

Although the path and the approaches to the villa had been hot and dusty, the moment we entered we seemed to be in an entirely different climate—cool, dark, wonderfully Oriental in flavor. The furnishings were simple and spare, so that an artist more knowledgeable than I could have traced the background of every ornament, the panelling on the walls, the exquisite bric-a-brac. Even in my ignorance, I knew that this house had a special beauty.

A boy in white, who appeared to be still in his teens, waited unobtrusively in the shadows beside an open archway. Beyond the arch I could see the lush, beautiful garden and the pool in its center. Michael turned to me.

"What do you drink? Billy Tamby will see to it while I find the blasted papers."

"Papers?"

"All the infernal red tape about Amber. You will

92

want to have them in your possession so you can boast how rich you are." He put his hand under my chin and raised it. "You cannot be murdered for your valuables until you have them, you know."

I was meant to smile at this, and did so, but only from my lips. Within, I was aware of a nervous fluttering that was not in the least romantic. When Billy Tamby came and stood in front of me with polite if silent persistence, I said that I would have whatever was good for a hot day and walked over to the archway to look at the garden. I had thought the pool would be like those great status symbols in the States, but I was amused and oddly pleased to find that, in spite of its length, it was only a couple of feet deep. It was covered with floating flowers, some of which grew there naturally, and others, petals of endless variety, had blown there from the surrounding bushes.

I hoped this sight would change the direction of my thoughts, for I was trying not to reflect that the charming drive and Michael's attention to me had been motivated by business and that the moment I received all the deeds and other papers pertaining to Amber, I should be a target for anyone who was jealous or malicious or coveted Amber. It had been much safer being poor with mother. I wondered if that was why mother had left Saint Cloud.

Michael came back with a sheaf of papers and brought me to the problems at hand. "There you are," he said. "Everything you will need if any mysterious, last-moment heirs pop up to make trouble."

"I wouldn't put it past those Ambers to have some unacknowledged heirs," I admitted ruefully, before I realized how this sounded.

Michael looked surprised, probably at my ability to shock him, but he recovered enough to ask me if I would care to make an inspection of the papers immediately. I said no, and he then suggested that he show me over the house.

Hugging my sheaf of papers as though I actually cared about them, I went along obediently and found that my first opinion of the artistry here was borne out by the increasing beauty of each room. Much as I admired Michael, I could hardly credit him with this exquisite taste. Perhaps the Amber sea captain in the mid-nineteenth century had brought home these simple, beautiful carvings from the Orient, the elegant furnishings, the occasional rug so well kept and unfaded though obviously old. I missed the cluttered, overfurnished look of the houses and apartments I had known all my life. At the same time, I found the absence of clutter restful to the nerves, and by the time we reached what I thought of as the salon, but Michael called the "lounge," I had nearly forgotten my uneasiness over the possession of my papers and my disappointment at Michael's motives. On the far wall, well placed above a beautifully carved little teakwood table, was the portrait of the most beautiful woman I had ever seen. It was not until I was much closer that I realized that the flawless golden flesh, the oblique curve of the eyes, and the small nose were marks of the Orient. Although the nose was different, and those lovely fathomless eyes in the portrait were not deep-set, nor were they hazel, yet there was a familiar look about the broad cheekbones, the stubborn yet sensuous mouth and the generally exotic contour of the face.

"Who is it?" I asked, glancing at Michael.

He was not looking at me, but at the painting. "I mentioned her at La Soufriere today," he said. "She is my great-grandmother. You see, she did not come to Amber from England, but from Hangchow. As a slave in an Amber ship. They used to import workers—as they called them—clear up until the American Civil War."

I had a premonition that my whole future hung on that moment. I was afraid to say any of the sweet clichés such a disclosure warranted, and I blurted out honestly, "I hope they paid a pretty penny for her. How lovely she was! It's humiliating to think they could probably have bought two of a modern woman like me for one of her."

"That would depend upon the purchaser." This time he did look at me.

"When I used to read history in school," I hurried on, "I wondered just how much I'd be worth at a quick sale."

"I wouldn't like that."

"Why not?" I was back on the clichés.

"I might not have been there to bid you in."

Suiting action to words, he gently but firmly framed my face between his two capable hands and bent his head to kiss me.

I could have murdered the caller who jangled the telephone somewhere in the house at that precise and, for me, critical time. Michael raised his head and said something in annoyance that I echoed to myself.

"What the devil is it?" he called out to no one in particular. "Will someone answer the confounded thing?"

I glimpsed Billy Tamby crossing the astrium at the opposite end of the pool as he went around to the interior of the villa. It seemed very strange that there were not phones all over the house, as would have been the custom in the States. But I was beginning to see that such indifference to mechanical conveniences might be welcome on occasion.

Self-consciously aware that Michael was turning his attention to me, I became intent upon the portrait of his great-grandmother.

"Was she ever freed?" What a question! I wished I had not asked it, but he did not seem to take offense.

"Oh, yes. And married my great-grandfather Jonathan Amber. You are a descendant of his elder brother, the stable Amber. Jonathan was the wastrel. Nevertheless, I think this was one of the great Amber decisions. . . . But I may be prejudiced."

I thought I had the explanation for Isobel's parting words to me, in this slave who had become Michael's great-grandmother, and I said thoughtfully, "So that's what Isobel meant."

He must have felt there was more to this than met the ear, because he sounded amused, as he said, "Perhaps you had better tell me and let me decide what she meant."

Remembering the full remark that it was "impossible for Michael to love me," I flushed at the mere idea that he might read my mind, and I finished lamely, "I—I forget." I looked over my shoulder at him in soulful candour, hoping he would let Isobel's nasty words go at that. I must have succeeded.

"Han Liu could have taken lessons from you, Cathy. From all I gather, she lacked your sweetness, that lovely innocence in your eyes."

I felt pleasantly guilty. And then I stiffened with anticipation as I thought I heard him move behind me,

95

but realized I had probably heard Billy Tamby, when that polite voice broke in: "The call is for Miss Amber, sir."

Michael gave me a little proprietary shove, and I followed Billy Tamby. I could not resist looking back. As I had hoped, Michael was watching me. I gave him a big smile, hoping this would keep him occupied with thoughts of me until that stupid, ill-timed phone call was over.

The instant I heard Miss Nell's nervous voice punctuated by her uneven breathing, I knew my brief, lovely time of enjoyment had come to an end. Even over the telephone the damp, mouldy fingers of Amber House seemed to reach out and fasten in my flesh.

"Yes, Miss Nell. What is it?"

Tiresome old woman with her eternal complaints and suspicions! Couldn't she leave me alone just one day?

I was ashamed of my own ill humor, but I couldn't censor my thoughts or my tone as I dealt with her.

"Miss Amber, I know I have found it! Let me meet you and we will examine them together."

"It? Them? What have you found?"

She coughed and cleared her throat before trying again to arouse me to her pitch of excitement. Poor thing! She was so proud of her detective work.

"Ellen's journals," she went on, "or at least some pages from them. I don't know why I didn't think of it before. She often used that place to change before going to another island or before returning to Amber."

Michael's footfall sounded on the bare, gleaming floor.

"Who is it, Cathy?" he asked. "Can't you get rid of him?"

I hoped it was a desire for my company that provoked his irritable question, and not merely an excuse to spy on me.

"I heard that," came Miss Nell's voice, lower this time, and more careful. "Don't tell him, for God's sake! Can you get him to drive you over the cutoff into Port Anne on your way home?"

"I don't know," I said, uneasily conscious that Michael might be able to hear in spite of her care.

"I want to meet you at the cafe where we—where you found me yesterday. You remember?"

I distinctly remembered the slap in the face.

"Well then, meet me there in two hours. And do get rid of him. Make some excuse so that we may talk alone for a few minutes. Send him off to a shop or—or something."

What a project! Besides, I had a sneaking suspicion that Michael Amber was seldom hoodwinked by women with no more experience than Miss Nell and me. But mindful of him behind me, I merely said "Very well" to her and hoped she would understand.

"Good. I'll ring off. Remember. Two hours. At the Cafe Carrefour."

I set the telephone back in its little unobtrusive niche. Michael did not ask who had called. That was a bad sign. Did it indicate that he knew? I realized I must not move too quickly, but now I was impatient to have the whole lie done with. The prospect of trying to fool him made me fear him again, even while I was fascinated by him. When Billy Tamby brought in a tray of drinks, mine being a colorful planter's punch that was not nearly so satisfying as a plain gin-and-tonic, I drank with one eye on some figurative clock in my brain. I kept wondering how long it would take to drive to Port Anne, and what would be in those pages of Ellen's—assuming, of course, that Miss Nell had hit upon their hiding place.

I had sat down in a gingerly way on the edge of a chair and was startled when Michael said suddenly, "You are bored; aren't you?"

"No. Of course not. I love it here. That is . . ."

"This is the fourth time you've looked at your wristwatch since you began on that drink."

I apologized and reached for my first lie, in order to get us into Port Anne, at least.

"I was only thinking that I have some shopping to do, and if I go back to Amber I might still have time to borrow a car and get one of the men to drive me into town before sunset."

"There is no car at Amber at present. Ellen did not know how to drive. She had Miss Nell or one of the servants drive her, or she took a taxi." He set his drink down almost untasted. "Why don't I drive you home by way of the town? That will save time."

"If you could, I'd be ever so grateful." How easily

he had fallen into the trap! He was not so difficult to fool, after all.

"You see, I wasn't prepared for this kind of climate," I explained as we left the cool serenity of the villa for the villainous afternoon heat of the road. "I mean, when I left San Francisco, I brought spring things for New York. How was I to know I'd wind up in a muggy tropic island like this?"

"Is it so very bad?" he asked with rueful sympathy, as if he honestly cared. It was dear of him to fall in with everything I said.

I admitted that I was getting used to it. "But I simply must get a few sundresses, and perhaps look in the shops. Isobel's perfume place looked exciting."

"Of course." He reached over and took my hand when he started to drive, and I sat there, pretending I did not notice, but occasionally returning his interest by a strategic exploration of his palm with my fingertips. I felt like a treacherous Mata Hari, playing him along this way, lying about Port Anne and the perfume and the rest of it. But I did not feel noble enough to forego the pleasure of his hand. Besides, from the faint little smile around his stubborn mouth, I was fairly sure he enjoyed my answering touch. Either that, or—heavens!—he knew what I was up to and was amused at my efforts to deceive him.

I had expected him to return over the road across the foot of La Soufriere, but instead we drove on around toward the south, passing the old pirate port of Eastbourne, which still looked like a New-World Pompeii from the top of the cliff over which the highway wandered. Michael pointed out, however, that artist colonies and a museum did a flourishing trade among the ruins of the ancient harbor, and I stopped being awed by the desolation I fancied I saw there.

The view beyond the old town was fabulous. It seemed as though the whole Atlantic Ocean rolled away before us, clear off to its further shores. It was choppy today, with many whitecaps and a look of enormous depth. Gradually, as I stared at the view, I became aware of a drumming sound, muffled and far away, and I wondered if it could come from that dead town at the foot of the cliffs. Eery, a little offbeat, the drumming annoyed me and made me remember all the people who must have died below us, long ago.

"What is that sound?" I asked.

Michael looked around to the right of us, where the vanguard of the fern forest approached the road. The forest was shabby here, with dusty leaves, and no imposing overhead archways. The fern forest was no force to withstand the sweeping gales off the Atlantic. Yet I realized now that the drumming sound came from somewhere within the fern forest, and as I stared in that direction I suddenly remembered that somewhere in the heart of that green monster lay my own home, my Amber. Did the drumming come from there?

"Some sort of native ceremony," said Michael, but he glanced again at the edge of the forest.

"What kind of ceremony?"

"For the dead."

"For someone dead? Is it a funeral?"

"For someone about to die. It is a warning."

I shuddered. "Do let's drive on."

It seemed to me that for an instant he still looked puzzled, as though the silly superstitions of Saint Cloud's people meant more to him than to an outsider. Then he did as I asked. But I, who yielded to no one in my dependence on superstition, felt a distinct malaise at the idea that this level-headed man should be disturbed.

Presently, the highway branched off, one road turning to the south, skirting the island, passing most of the other well-known plantations; but the road Michael took cut directly across over the main mountain range of Saint Cloud and dropped down into Port Anne much sooner than I expected. We had exchanged very little conversation along the way, but there was a sensation between us that made talking unnecessary. It had taken us just over an hour and forty minutes, but, of course, we had started some half an hour after Miss Nell's call, so she would probably be awaiting me.

The dusty, bougainvillea-lined streets of the hilly outskirts gave me an idea. They suggested heat and headaches, both of which I determined to use. I sighed, making a big thing out of this, and of rubbing my forehead wearily.

"Tired?" he asked, brushing a wisp of hair out of my eyes. Like most of the drivers on the island, he managed to maintain his fast speed, glance over at his passenger, attend to my hair in this charming fashion, and still use the car's little insolent horn to warn the dark-skinned pedestrians out of his way.

"A little tired," I confessed. "Must be the heat. It's given me a nasty headache. The worst of it is, the shops will be closed soon."

"I imagine some of them will remain open for a little while. Not Alain's, though. They close at seven. Would you like to stop for an aperitif, or tea, perhaps?"

I debated aloud about how I could get to Alain's before it closed and whether I should have a cup of tea first. By juggling these two terrible dilemmas back and forth, I finally got him to make the suggestion I was working on.

"If you will give me the names, I can drop you at the Carrefour and stop by Alain's for you."

"Oh, if you would! How sweet of you!"

He looked at me, but without smiling. I almost fancied he was cross, and I couldn't imagine what I had said to change his mood, unless—had I overdone the enthusiasm? But I was nervous at his gaze, perhaps because of my guilty conscience, and began to point out a tea shop across the corner from the Cafe Carrefour.

"There. That would do nicely. I'm sure my headache will disappear in no time."

"I have no doubt it will," he said drily and let me out in front of the shop. "When you've done with your shopping, *and* your tea, perhaps you'll be so kind as to let me tell you what I have in mind for Amber—if we come to an agreement."

I did not like the sound of that. His motives were beginning to show again. Had he stopped thinking of me as the hand-holding girl? Was he back to thinking of me once more as that tiresome heiress who had something he wanted other than her feminine charms?

"You haven't asked me what perfume brands I want," I said, changing the subject. He listened with an abstracted air while I told him. I then made a great to-do over my headache and waved him away feebly.

In spite of the inadequacy of his rear-view mirror in the little English car, I waited until the car had turned the corner toward the Careenage before I crossed the street and went into the Cafe Carrefour. At this time of day it was crowded with idlers, most of whom appeared to be French types with a fascinating mixture of West Indian blood. There were few women in the open-air cafe, and almost every man in the place looked at me curiously. I went up to the middle-aged female in black who stood behind the espresso machine and asked where Miss Jessica Nell was.

"Not here, miss," said the woman, not mincing words.

I explained that the lady was to meet me here and that she was probably waiting upstairs in one of the rooms.

"Not here."

I did not know what to say in rebuttal except that I would wait until she showed up.

"Not here," repeated the woman firmly. "We are busy here. There by the street is one vacant chair. While you wait, you will have an aperitif, of course."

"Of course." I felt that I could hardly get out with my scalp if I said less. I went and sat down at the table, surrounded by three stout, middle-aged men with enormous black eyes, each pair of which turned with one accord and glowed at me. At first I was embarrassed in case they should find me attractive, and then, upon reflection, I was embarrassed in case they should not. I sat there counting the minutes and wishing myself anywhere else.

The woman behind the espresso machine brought me a Cinzano, and I was so nervous I drank the warm, thick, sweet drink in about two gulps, trying all the while to look as though I expected to be met momentarily.

When the Cinzano was gone, one of the men at my table leaned forward and inquired courteously,

"May I buy the lady her next Cinzano?"

The other two men listened avidly, no doubt playing off this gentleman's technique against their own and wondering if they would succeed in event this one failed. He failed, but only just. I was so nervous I could hardly stammer out that I thanked him but expected to meet someone "any minute."

He nodded understandingly and gave his friends a

significant look. He obviously didn't understand at all.

Michael must have been gone twenty minutes, and still there was no sign of Miss Nell. I did not know what to do. But as the embarrassing wait dragged on, I decided I would have to go across the street to the tea shop and make the whole thing look legitimate to Michael. As I arose, the man who had offered to buy me the Cinzano got up with alacrity to help me; he was followed on the other side by one of his silent friends.

I protested lamely, "No, really. I'm quite all right. I don't think my friend is coming. . . ."

They kept right on assisting me. I felt that any second they would accompany me across the street when another, and this time authoritative, hand clapped down upon my shoulder from behind me, and Michael's voice at its chilliest said, "Come along, Cathy!"

The two men dropped away from me as though I were poison, and the heretofore silent one ventured apologetically, "Your pardon, Mister Amber. We did not know. . . . We had no notion the lady was waiting for you."

All the way across the street I was protesting to Michael, "I decided I didn't want tea, but an aperitif. I saw down there and they . . ."

Right in the middle of the street, with little cars sailing around and past us at perilous angles, Michael stopped and looked down at me and said, "She isn't coming, you know. So spare me the drama."

"What do you mean?" I managed to ask in a tone of outrage. "Who? What *she*? What are you talking about?"

He pulled me over to the narrow sidewalk in front of the tea shop. Several interested bystanders stopped to hear the outcome of this interesting melodrama starring one of their leading citizens and an unknown female.

"Miss Nell is not coming! Now, please. No more lies. I'll take you home."

"How do you know I was waiting for Miss Nell?"

"I am not deaf, and it is impossible to miss that voice of hers, even on the telephone."

Questions drifted around in my brain, some of them scaring me, and then the worst of them came out. Everything else I could explain by his overhearing Miss Nell's call. But one had a shocking answer.

"How do you know? Did you phone to Amber?"

"Certainly not. I told you. I recognized her voice on the telephone."

"No." The horrid suspicion rolled over me like one of those Atlantic rollers I had seen today. "How do you know she isn't coming?"

NINE

I THINK HE was too angry to reply. This very anger of his reassured me somewhat.

Gazing at his face—what a temper!—I went on calmly, "You needn't look at me that way. You can't possibly choke me out here on the sidewalk. Everyone is watching us." I felt that any man who could not control his natural feelings any better than he could not possibly be a subtle, murderous villain.

"Come inside," he said, and he made a very good effort to get me into the tea shop without any assistance from me. I surprised him by sitting down meekly at a funny, old-fashioned little English table in front of the curtained windows. It was comfortable and shadowy, with a smell of fresh lemon and delicious Banbury cakes in the air.

I looked at him sideways and remarked pleasantly, "This is much better. Now you may do anything you care to. The shop being English, like you, they'll probably offer to get rid of my body, just to help you out."

"I suppose you imagine you are being amusing," he said, trying to preserve his dignity and the general manner of infallibility that he had cultivated in the minds of these islanders during a lifetime of bad temper and arrogance. He did not think me a bit funny.

"If it isn't Mister Amber!" said the pleasant little English lady who came to wait on us. "We haven't seen you for ever so. What may we do for you? Just anything, my dear sir. You've but to name it."

"Thank you, madam. Tea!" said Michael, not giving in an inch.

"And cakes," I added.

Michael looked at me, trying with a great effort not to break out of his self-satisfying mood of high temper. At last, he smiled. "I daresay she *would* hide your body, if I asked her."

While the lady was bringing our tea, with the lovely, spicy Banbury cakes and other delights, I was trying to think up an alibi that would cover my expected visit with Miss Nell. I had got over thinking Michael had murdered her or somehow stopped her from coming to Port Anne, but I felt that it was necessary to wait as long as possible, giving her every chance, in case some other cause had delayed her.

Michael guessed something of this. "What fantastic story has she regaled you with this time, Cathy?"

"Who?"

"Now, you're being tiresome. Jessica Nell wanted to show you some discovery she has made. What was it? If it was something about the Ambers, then don't you think I am the one who should properly investigate it?"

"But you are one of them," I reminded him.

The muscles of his face seemed to contract a little as I watched him, and he said after a pause, as though I had somehow wounded him, "Then it was not a joke, what you said out there in the street. Just how, may I ask, do you think I could have driven you into town and still managed to murder that old harridan?"

I confided as engagingly as possible, "Oh, I don't think you did—now. I only meant that she might know something scandalous about the Ambers and it would embarrass you to discover it."

He must think I was singularly stupid. Of course, David Earle could stop Miss Nell (not necessarily by violence, merely by locking her in) if Michael wished it. They had done so before. But let him think me more stupid than I was.

Michael said sardonically, "It would be much less embarrassing to discover some scandal myself than to have it broadcast through the length and breadth of the Federation by a couple of tongue-clacking females."

I should have been enraged by this, but I was interested in something much deeper. It seemed to me that Michael was growing more puzzled over Miss Nell's discovery. If so, then he could know nothing about the reason for her nonappearance in town. On the other hand, David might have kept her at Amber but failed to find those documents she intended to show me about Ellen.

Michael finished his tea and turned and called to the little proprietor. "Miss Hamish, may I use your telephone?"

"With pleasure, my dear sir. With pleasure. Just behind the potted plant there to your left. Ah, just so!"

I was not surprised when he called Amber House and spoke to Soochi. "Soochi, dinner will be late. Miss Cathy is with me now, in town. Will you put Miss Nell on? David had to lock her in today. She was threatening to run away again, and God knows where we should have found her this time. Probably in the pit of Soufriere."

I could hear Soochi's soothing, unexcited voice replying, "Very good, Mister Michael. I'll get the key and fetch her."

"Can you handle her?" Michael asked.

I could almost fancy the little Eurasian grinning, with her big, perfect teeth flashing in the tangerine light of sunset as it fell across Amber.

"But, of course, Mister Michael. . . ."

There was a longer pause than seemed necessary at the other end of the line. I supposed this was due to the angry struggle Miss Nell would make when she was released. It gave me the chance to demand sharply, "Is that why Miss Nell hasn't met me? Because you are keeping her prisoner?"

He waved this aside as inconsequential. "The woman is half-demented. You saw her when she was let to run about unescorted yesterday. She will hurt herself one of these times. She is much safer at Amber!"

Is anyone? I felt like asking, but didn't. He might be perfectly right. I hadn't forgotten the poor governess-nurse's dishevelled appearance when I first met her across the street at the sidewalk cafe. Nor would I forget that resounding slap she gave me. But why must that be madness? Couldn't it be the result, rather than the cause, of mistreatment? What if she did know some ghastly secret about Ellen that would explain my half-sister's death? And then—what about those journals of Ellen's? It was unlikely that they were a figment of Miss Nell's crazed brain. Even Michael owned up to their former existence.

"I don't like it," I said. "I don't think anyone should be locked in a room like a convict."

"Would you rather she—hush!" He waved me to silence and listened as Soochi's voice was audible over the telephone. It was bad news. I saw the beginnings of that well-known frown on his forehead, and then the tightening of his mouth.

"How the devil could that happen?" he asked in a voice that carried in spite of its low pitch. "Is David about the place? Well, find him first, and call the police at Amber Point." He covered the mouth of the phone with his palm and looked across the table at me. "Soochi thinks she used a key—probably one she had made yesterday when she was in town. At any rate, she's gone."

"That doesn't sound very crazy to me."

He scowled at me and took his hand off the phone to speak with Soochi again. "Good. And send out as many of the hands as can be located. Ask Doctor Torri. He always knows how to find his little disciples. They were at their idiotic death chants today, and you know what that means. Meanwhile, I'll return by Soufriere and see if there is any sign of her."

He put back the phone without saying goodbye, and when I would have asked a question, he interrupted to assure me, "The police will be patrolling all roads into Port Anne. They can't miss her. Poor devil! She had nothing else but Ellen, you know, and it's my belief she's got some notion of searching for her, when she behaves like this."

"She escaped from your 'custody' so she could meet me," I reminded him. Nevertheless, I was pleased that he showed some feeling for Miss Nell. At the same time, the whole matter gave me a deep feeling of uneasiness. She need not have taken one of the roads. It would be like her, in her present fuzzy-minded condition, to try to reach town by a jungle path.

"At any rate, it is your fault if the evidence is gone," I said, without thinking.

In the flicker of silence that followed, I knew I had said the wrong thing. He stared at me and asked in an odd, flat voice, "Evidence of what?"

I recovered my senses and decided that, whatever happened, he must not know about those journals of Ellen's, at least until I could be sure he himself wasn't implicated.

"Well—whatever Miss Nell wanted to see me about, of course." I had to change the subject quickly; for I could tell by his manner that he was going to pursue it. "I suppose you think that, just by talking with her, I can't learn a great deal more about this whole strange affair. As it happens, her word is a good deal better than yours."

He had signalled the little proprietor for the check but stopped to ask me with what was almost a smile, though of contempt or amusement I could not tell, "Really! And in what way is her word better than mine?"

This gave me the chance to say with gusto, "You promised to get me those perfumes, and you didn't. You spied on me instead." *That* should change the subject!

This time I could not mistake his smile. And a nasty, triumphant smile it was, too; for he reached into the pocket of his jacket and produced a carefully wrapped package with the name "Alain" and the word "Parfums" running all over the stiff paper in green tape. It was one of the most annoying things about him, that he so often had the last word without uttering it!

I took the package without thanking him, and we went out to the street in absolute silence. When he tried to usher me into his car, though, I balked.

"I'll wait for Miss Nell."

It was growing dark. There were few street lights. And passersby were looking at me very oddly, especially the men.

"Don't be childish. She isn't coming. They will have picked her up before she can reach town, an old lady like that. Besides, if she does make it, it will have to be by the Soufriere Highway. Come! We will meet her on the way."

This was just a sop to me; I knew that. But I didn't want to wait in this strange, foreign town all by myself.

"How long do they think she has been gone?" I asked him.

"Soochi says she stopped rattling the door and screaming about three hours ago. It never occurred to Soochi that there might be a reason for that silence."

Strange, I thought; for Soochi struck me as a person who thought of every eventuality. "Three hours!" I said. "But what can have happened to her? It would take her only an hour to get to town. Where is she?"

"We'll know that better at Amber. If anything has happened to her, they will call Amber first, and then my house. They would never think to call me in town."

"Yes, but—someone ought to wait here, just in case she does make it."

He looked down at me as though he were trying to read my mind. If he did, he found a jumble that certainly put him off the track of Ellen's journals.

"Have you any idea what she was going to tell you?"

"I wish you wouldn't keep talking of her in the past tense. If I must go back to Amber, then couldn't we set the police to watching for her in town?"

"Certainly. I intend to."

I wondered if he had actually intended to, but he did so now, getting me into the car and driving by a small office at the further corner of the Carrefour where he left word that Miss Nell might possibly arrive in town looking for me. I felt very guilty about leaving Port Anne when I had promised faithfully to meet her. But I also had one of those frightening premonitions that something had prevented her from keeping our appointment, and if that were the case, then Michael was right. I should be back at Amber to receive any messages.

We drove silently back along the dark highway that we had taken yesterday morning when we first drove to Amber. It was amazing how, once night had fallen over the island, the primeval forest took hold everywhere, and civilization, with its electricity and its big, zooming autos, became an infinitesimal part of this frightening, vital nature that still ruled the jungle half of Saint Cloud. We passed a police car very shortly, and the two men in it, recognizing Michael's car, stopped and reported that they had seen nothing of the missing woman.

"Maybe she was in a car," I suggested to Michael, but he shook his head.

"They know all the cars on the island. It is unlikely."

After we passed the experimental cane and pineapple fields, there were no passing cars at all for several minutes, and the lowering bulk of the great volcano oppressed us from the left now, while the Amber fern forest crowded in on the right of the road. It was very dark. Only a sprinkling of stars overhead and the lights of Michael's car made anything intelligible out of that massive night which enclosed us.

Great fern fronds groped out across the road ahead of us, sparkling in the car lights, where the afternoon showers had left them swathed in raindrops. On the distant horizon of the road I thought one frond seemed to glitter with an especial light, but I said nothing. The car was shaking more than usual, and I supposed Michael was driving faster. My imaginaton was already playing its tricks on me, here in the wilderness. The intrusive fern that bothered me was gigantic, growing out over the road just where the highway turned sharply to avoid an ancient lava flow, and as the car lights began to pick it up, I realized that what I had suspected was the glitter of raindrops was actually a floating greyness, like a tiny cloud that had no business hanging there only five or six feet above the ground.

Michael had glanced out at La Soufriere just as I saw the peculiar little misty cloud of grey ahead, and he remarked in a puzzled way, "I think that was an earthquake. Did you feel it?"

I was surprised that I hadn't, for I had known too many in my native California not to guess when those hideous tell-tale little tremors began. But I was staring at the turn looming up in the road ahead of us. At last, I knew what the cloud of grey was, and I screamed.

I suppose it was my scream that made Michael swerve; for the misty grey cloud formed itself more clearly. It was a tall woman in some kind of grey garments, with her arms outstretched above her head, waving to us. By swerving so sharply, Michael had thought to avoid her, but suddenly, to my horror, she plunged straight into the car lights and seemed to dissolve under the wheels like a wraith of fog.

"Good God! What was that?"

Michael had stopped, but whatever we hit was behind us. I had not felt the wheels strike her; yet, when I got out of the car to follow Michael, I was not surprised when he looked up from the woman lying in the weird, twisted clump at his feet and said, "It is Miss Nell."

My hands were shaking so that I covered my face for a minute, trying to get my bearings. Michael's voice brought me out of this eery sense that I was in a dream. "Cathy! Are you all right? Cathy!"

"Of course. Is she dead?" I tried to be very matter-of-fact, to kneel beside Michael and examine her, but I only pretended to look. I focused my eyes just beyond her so I would not have to see the pitiful lumpy bones.

"I'm afraid so. It was straight on. She seemed to leap into my path."

"It's horrible! Horrible! The poor thing."

"Cathy, she deliberately sprang at the lights. . . ." He stopped speaking and looked up at the giant shadow of La Soufriere directly to the north of us. I felt the tremor of the next quake, as if someone had given the road beneath us a short, sharp jolt. I began to tremble, and my teeth chattered. I was behaving like an idiot, but it was difficult to stop. Though there were no more earthquakes, I kept expecting one. I was grateful to him when, in spite of that pitiful woman at our feet, he put his arm around me and I felt the strength and warmth of his body, which seemed to act as a barrier against the horrors of the dark around us.

"Well," he said after he could see that I was more myself. "We have several alternatives. I can stay with her, and you can drive to the police. You will probably intercept them somewhere on the road. . . ."

"I can't drive," I said. "My mother always drove."

"Then—shall we take her with us?"

"No, no! What if she isn't dead, and we do something to her? We mustn't touch her until a doctor examines her."

"She is dead. There is no mistake. Feel her hand. Like ice. And her pulse . . ."

"Don't tell me."

"At any rate, we must do something. And quickly. There may be more quakes, with this unsettled weather."

"Maybe we could both drive for the police, and leave Miss Nell here in a—a comfortable position until we come back."

He frowned.

"No. I don't like that. There is something more to this whole thing than meets the eye. Very likely, if we left her here, she'd be gone when we returned. These damned locals, with their infernal voodoo!"

Poor Miss Nell! How she would hate that! I looked at her dead white face, and saw the pale eyes staring at me, wide-open, almost unbearably lifelike. Even her pale lips were parted as though she had been trying to tell me something. What was Miss Nell's secret? What did she know about Ellen Amber that caused Ellen's death and her own death? But that was nonsense. Michael had killed her, accidentally. I saw him. If only he hadn't looked away from the wheel for an instant when he felt that first earth tremor, he might have been better prepared for Miss Nell when she leaped out at the car. Even so, he had avoided her. What made her fall directly into his path?

"I'm afraid we must take her with us," Michael said finally, as he began to lift her. "There is no question but that she is dead. She seems to have struck the back of her head on the pavement when she—fell. There is very little blood. Her body must have taken the rest of the shock." He felt over her body with one hand. "No purse. No money or papers. Nothing."

I was glad it was dark. When he carried Miss Nell into the car lights I did not look. I only remembered her dead eyes staring up at me in the starlight. If she could have spoken, I knew she would have pleaded for the truth about Ellen Amber's death—the truth Jessica Nell had sacrificed her own life to obtain.

Suddenly, the whole scene blazed with light as a car

112

rounded the corner of the highway headed toward Port Anne. Seeing Michael's car, and Michael with Miss Nell's body, clearly outlined in his own car lights, the new-comer pulled up along the left side of the highway and two men in uniform walked back to us.

"Oh, it's you, Mister Amber," said one of the police in that friendly, half-deferential way that most of Saint Cloud used with Michael. "You've found the poor creature? The Amber housekeeper called the Point to warn us the lady was loose. They thought at Amber that she might have tried to walk through the jungle. Well, an old lady like that—and not born to it—what can you expect? How did you find her?"

I came up to the little group and put in shakily, "She ran into the car. It was horrible! Right into the lights—like a moth."

"Terrible thing." The two men made a cursory ex-amination of Miss Nell while Michael held her in his arms. No one seemed to think it particularly odd that a crazy lady named Jessica Nell had run into the car like this. They were very calm, and they offered to take her back into town to the mortuary. "Then, Mister Amber, when it's convenient, if you'd come in and make a report. For the record, as it were."

"Certainly. Later. Meanwhile, I think I had better get Miss Catherine home. She looks quite done in."

The two police looked at me curiously, which did not make me feel any more calm, and agreed that Michael's first duty was to me. It was all very strange. At home, I thought, there would have been all sorts of questions, and Michael would be down at the police station the rest of the night. They might even accuse him of delib-erately running down Miss Nell. But, of course, they couldn't do that here. They had my evidence that it had been impossible to avoid her.

And it was impossible . . . except for that odd mo-ment during the first earthquake, when he looked away from the wheel to stare at La Soufriere's formidable shadow.

"Nasty little shake or two, a few minutes ago. Did you notice them?" asked one of the policemen as they packed off Miss Nell to their car.

113

"Makes one wonder about old Soufriere," Michael said, with a nod toward the mountain.

They laughed and drove off.

Michael helped me into the car, although all I really wanted now was to be left alone, to think out this hideous accident. I was still shaking as we drove home along the narrow, fern-crowded little road to Amber, and Michael put his arm around me and pulled me to him, so that I rested my head on his comfortable shoulder. But I kept thinking . . . wondering. . . .

What a remarkable coincidence that accident was! Now, we might never know what Miss Nell had been about to show me. It was curious that if she intended to meet me, she did not have Ellen's journals on her person. Nor any money.

Soochi, who had heard the car, was standing on the lower step of the veranda at Amber House, waiting for us, holding a china lamp in her hand. The pink glow was like an eery moon in that jungle dark.

"Will you be all right?" Michael asked me.

I nodded.

He reached over and kissed me, but I was too numb to respond. I wanted only to get away and be by myself.

"I'll see you tomorrow," he promised.

I went in with Soochi, who said, smiling in her cold malevolent way, "You will be hungry, Miss Cathy. Will you wait for Miss Nell or will you eat now?"

She had to repeat it twice before I really understood.

"Nothing, thank you. I had tea and cakes shortly ago. I think I'll take a bath and go to bed."

"Yes, ma'am." She said it as though this were a fresh mark against me, but I did not care what she thought. I'm sure my mother would have called her an "impudent little hussy" and perhaps shaken her in the bargain.

I had not been fond of this bedroom at Amber. It was as unromantic, as frigid and old-maidish, as Ellen Amber must have been, but it was the only room where I felt I might rest and blot out what I had just seen—the death of a woman who might have been my friend. And friends were scarce enough on Saint Cloud, at best.

114

It was not until I had undressed, bathed, and got into bed that I remembered the scrap of the shawl I had found early today at the Tangerine Pool and which Michael had been so anxious to take from me. I reached under my pillow and drew out my horoscope book. It opened naturally to the page where the scrap of cloth had been; but—*the scrap itself was no longer there!*

TEN

I SHOOK OUT the book vigorously before resigning my-self to the truth. Along with possible murderers, voo-doo followers, and ghostly Shades (if that was what had frightened Miss Nell last night), this charming old ruin also housed a sneak-thief. How low could people be! It was surprising that no one had tried to murder me yet. Or was that to be the Cherries Jubilee of this whole affair?

I went to the door and called for Soochi. It always seemed to my suspicious nature that she appeared too quickly when called. No doubt the real reason was be-cause she moved so silently, but it never failed to give me a chill.

"Did you clean my room lately?" I asked her, hardly recognizing the sharp authority in my own voice.

Her exquisite black eyebrows arched with curiosity, and the cloth "points" of her Madras turban, urged by the breeze behind her in the hall, began to exercise their hypnotic effect, pointing their way inevitably toward me, like little feelers.

"No, ma'am. Mister Michael said to fetch in some help, so I did. Your room was cleaned by a girl from the village. I'm sure if it was badly done . . ."

"No. Not badly done. Rather too thoroughly done, if anything. What was the girl's name?"

"Bouramie, I believe. David Earle would know. He is acquainted with the family. He set her to work in here. Showed her how. She's to help out, now there's

116

more to do." She paused, and it seemed to me that in the slanting depths of her eyes a little fire was lit and the eyelids widened as she thought of something. "Or maybe Miss Isobel could tell you more about it."

"Miss Isobel! When was she in here alone?"

"A little after you returned from your walk with Miss Nell this morning. Is there anything wrong? You were in the bathroom, and she said she left a handkerchief in here earlier, when she was talking to you."

"Really!" I said. "One would think she had a better excuse than that. Of all the ancient clichés!"

"Just as you say, ma'am. Only there was a handkerchief in her hand when she came out. May I ask—is something missing? Occasionally we have pilfering among the locals. But if it's anything valuable, I'll have it returned at once." She paused and then made a little gesture, spreading her arms to indicate abundance. She seemed serious. "You see, they imagine the Ambers are all very rich like Mister Michael, and they wouldn't miss a fountain pen or a hair comb with paste jewels. Things like that."

"No," I said, having been given time to think. "It was not something missing. Merely that everything seems misplaced. This chair . . . the . . ." I groped for excuses. "The—bed cover seems different. And that old-fashioned cabinet doesn't seem quite in the same place."

"The armoire?" she suggested.

"Yes. It just seemed to have been shifted slightly." I was making this up as I went along, fumbling for any excuse to hide the identity of the thing that was missing. But as I am not a very experienced conspirator, I overdid it. Especially since I noticed, upon close observation, that Soochi's turban tonight was wrapped in the usual way, but the material was actually similar to the shawl whose scrap I had found. The pattern and color were different, but it did indicate that the piece I had found might belong to Soochi.

Her eyes narrowed, and she stepped into the room, staring at the objects I had mentioned. "You are right, ma'am. It was not necessary to move the armoire this morning." She suddenly switched that dark, penetrating gaze to me in a most disconcerting way. "What were they looking for—whoever did it? What could you have hidden, ma'am, that sets on a search like this?"

"I'm not an international spy, and I don't have coded papers hidden in my room, if that's what you mean."

She persisted. "But why should anyone think you have?"

I said haughtily, "I'm not responsible for the odd ideas people get. Anyway, I have nothing that anyone would care to steal." She did not move; her eyes continued their search of the room, and I added, almost losing my temper, "That will be all, Soochi. You may go back to your work now."

She gave me a nasty, fiery look, as though she resented my proprietary tone, but she left. To prove that I had no more problems with that room, I left too, going into the kitchen, where I found a scared, dark, teen-aged girl washing dishes and looking very much in awe of me. I asked her to make some coffee, and when she had poured it into a glass coffee container for me to carry to my room hot, I tried to make friends with her, but she was too shy, and I gave up.

Carrying the coffee and a cup and saucer on a tray, I walked along the portico, whose outer rim was faintly illuminated by the rising moon, and I smelled the cool, moist odor of the garden beside me. Suddenly, the cup and saucer began to rattle slightly, and the coffee in the glass container sloshed back and forth briefly, in a tell-tale way. Under my feet the stone walk jarred twice, and I felt the horrid imbalance that earthquakes always give me. It was just a tremor, but it made me a little sick after Miss Nell's death and the events of the day. I glanced up apprehensively in the direction of the ominous Mount Soufriere.

I waited, as I always did, to be sure the "Big Shake" wasn't going to follow, and in the night silence I heard Soochi's voice in a room somewhere off the portico. ". . . just like the others. The cowardly pretenders, with their fancy commands, their bossy ways. And she'll end like them—running—running. . . ."

There was a little silence and then Soochi again. I wondered why I could not hear the voice of the one to whom she was speaking.

"Scared away. What else? Like the others. Like me,

118

sometimes, when I pass that pool. . . . Because I remember him. I remember how he ran and ran. And all the time—his heart . . ."

The sounds died away. I tried to peer through the bamboo curtain, but the room beside me was dark. I was not even sure Soochi had been speaking in that room. Perhaps she had been in the room beyond. And to whom had she spoken?

One thing I knew now: the man "running—running" was my father. And men with heart trouble do not run, except under great, perhaps dreadful compulsion. So my father, and perhaps my half-sister, had been "induced" to die. If only I knew to whom Soochi had been speaking!

I tiptoed back to the kitchen, where the shy little maid was wiping the sink and dish pan.

"Who is in the house tonight? Besides you and me."

In a shaky, bashful voice the girl said, "Only Miss Soochi, ma'am. That's all. Mister Earle's been and gone these three—four hours, and the field boys went with him. They are looking for the tall lady that stays here."

"I heard someone," I said. "Someone in the house tonight."

"Must've been Miss Soochi at the telephone," said the little maid. And out of a clear sky she added, "Did you get your mail, ma'am?"

"No. What mail?"

"It generally is left by the telephone in the lounge, ma'am. That's what made me think on it."

This gave me an ideal excuse to walk in upon Soochi at the telephone—I had only to say I was looking for my mail. I wondered who would be writing to me, and I confess to a hope that I should hear from Brett Caldwell, whose uncommon and often idiotic sense I missed already. It was typical of Soochi's attitude that she had not told me of the letter.

I went very quietly through the house, through the silent, musty-smelling dining room, whose use this morning by my guests did not seem, in any way, to relieve the general feeling of disuse that pervaded every room at Amber. I crossed the center hallway to the north half of the house but neither saw nor heard signs of any unwarranted visitor here. Only my bedroom was lighted. Far to the south, next to the servants' unused quarters, there was a light in Soochi's room and, of course, the kitchen. That was all. I returned to the matter at hand, going out of my way in order to listen a moment at Soochi's door. She was moving about the room, obviously preparing for bed, and humming a little tune. I waited long enough to overhear any company she might have, but heard no sound beyond her off-key humming. I gave up spying and groped my way back through the house to find the telephone.

It was annoying that in this entire house there appeared to be only one extension, but as I was always threatening Michael and myself with picking up and leaving at the slightest provocation, I decided not to object to the telephone situation for the present. When I reached the telephone by feeling my way through the darkened living room, carefully avoiding the old-fashioned Sadie Thompson-type furniture, I set down my tray and ran my fingers over the telephone. It seemed warm. But then, the evening was warm. I could not be sure that Soochi had been using it. I felt around the telephone, on the stand, and found one letter. I could not read the handwriting, so I put it on my tray and went back to my bedroom, the room that once had been the unhappy Ellen's place of refuge.

The letter was from Brett, and it was very typical of him!

Doll, have you fallen for that teddiby British blighter yet? Beware of strangers bearing gifts. Also watch out for assorted Trojan horses.

On the serious side, do you ever think of me? It seems like years. How many months has it been since you left New York that unhappy (for me) day? Don't tell me it's been less than a week. I deny it vociferously (did I spell that right?) Don't forget. You know who to count on if the going gets rough. But by that time, wouldn't surprise me if you were so rich you wouldn't even tip your hat to your old buddy-buddy. Love you like crazy. What's cooking in the spook department? I'll bet your British Romeo had two or three wives buried in the garden of your precious Amber!

If you do decide, at long last, to listen in on the

tinkling music of my voice, call my answering service in San Francisco and they'll get me pronto. I'm working hard (horrible thought!), selling Unk's cabin cruisers. Can I interest you in a few? They're cheaper by the dozen. All this just to impress good old Auntie, so she'll see what a good influence you are, and so you'll see what you missed.

P.S. Don't forget to call me "when a fellow needs a friend"—I'm your man! Now, if you could see that too!

I laughed to myself. If only I could believe in Brett's much protested love, be quite sure he didn't mimeograph such letters, just so all the girls would benefit equally . . . It was hard to figure out why I persisted in feeling that he was a playboy. He had come clear to New York to prove his sincerity with me. He had even gone to work. Greater love hath no playboy!

At any rate, I was profoundly grateful to him. At a time when the horror of Miss Nell's death made me almost physically ill, his letter cheered me immensely.

I turned down the bed covers, came across my horoscope book, and wondered again who had stolen that bit of shawl material. Surely, only a guilty person would have a motive. Soochi? I did not know. She had more knowledge of these affairs than she should, but did she know about the scrap of shawl? And if she were responsible for these evils, why did she say in the one-way conversation I had just overheard, that she was "scared—like the others"?

On the other hand, David Earle might have taken the scrap to turn over to Michael for some reason—the same reason Michael had asked me to give it to him when he caught me at the pool today.

But then, there was Cousin Isobel, that strangely imperturbable unknown quantity. One might almost fancy that her own position in this mystery was to wait it out and pounce on the Amber inheritance when the conspirators had murdered each other.

Well, I could not solve it tonight. Pouring the now lukewarm coffee and drinking it while I held the saucer in my other hand underneath it, I wandered out on the portico and looked at the garden. All seemed serene. I wished I could say the same for myself, but although I was dead tired and ached in half a dozen places, I was also keyed up over Miss Nell. Soochi's strange, one-sided conversation hadn't helped me either.

I determined to forget these things, to forget even the great heads of the flowers in the garden as they shone under the moonlight, like knowing faces in a mob, watching me, their victim.

I went back into the house, thinking of Miss Nell and her last words to me on the phone. How odd they had been! Until now, I had not thought all of them through to their logical conclusion. What did she mean, for instance, by saying that Ellen "changed there when she went to the other islands or returned"?

Changed where? And even more important—changed *why?* Presumably, Ellen wore sailing clothes for her trips. Why does a woman change, except to suit the purpose at hand? Then Ellen had some other purpose besides the prosaic art purchases when she went to the inner islands. The Haitian visits, as so many other details here at Amber, suggested an interest in voodoo. But everyone knew that voodoo was only a tourist trap —or was it? Surely, even if she required some special clothes for her voodoo prowling, she would not wear them on a full night's journey across the Caribbean.

I had just put down my empty cup in its saucer, when the answer to my first question leaped at me as I stared around Ellen's monastic room.

Perhaps there was a purpose in Miss Nell's preoccupation with the Cafe Carrefour in Port Anne. She had asked me to meet her there because it was there, no doubt in one of the upstairs rooms, that Ellen had changed before going to the other islands. Excited over my deduction, I stepped out to the portico and studied Soochi's room at the far end. Her shadow moved now and then across the thin bamboo curtains. She had removed her turban, and I could see her shadow brushing out what must have been lustrous black hair.

The little shy maid came to the kitchen door, shook out a cloth and returned to her work.

I was alone. I glanced at my watch. It was barely ten o'clock. I went in to the telephone, picked up the heavy receiver, and called for the Cafe Carrefour in Port Anne. There was a good deal of static and confusion on the line, and while I waited to be put through, I looked around furtively, feeling enclosed by the musky dark. The room was illuminated faintly by one or two pools of moonlight on the floor matting, where the front curtains were split. In hurrying to the phone I must have touched a rocking chair, for it teetered back and forth silently, and I stared at it several seconds before realizing it was empty.

A woman's voice, with a heavy, impatient French accent, came on the phone then.

"Cafe Carrefour. What is it you wish?"

"This is Catherine Amber," I said, as low as I could without whispering.

"Eh? Speak up, Madame."

I repeated a little louder, and added, "Did you know my sister, Ellen Amber?"

"And if I did, Madame? What then?"

"I believe she rented a room at your Cafe. Did she leave some clothes with you? Or a suitcase, perhaps?"

"Perhaps."

"And—and . . ." I had the key suddenly. "And perhaps she owed you money? I will be happy to pay it."

How warm and effusive the voice became suddenly! "Ah, well, that is a different matter entirely, Mademoiselle. The English lady, her friend, has promised me my money this age, but not a shilling, not a ha'pence have I seen. Will Mademoiselle come and make the arrangements herself?"

Now that I had achieved the triumph of guessing where Ellen's hideaway was, I did not know quite how to use it. I could not very well call a cab at ten o'clock at night. Nor was I absolutely sure I would not be followed if I went to town tomorrow. Uncertain, I ran my finger nervously along the fluted edge of the telephone-stand, and in doing so, I remembered Brett's letter, which had lain here.

And then I recalled Brett's acquaintance in Port Anne, Joel Bingham, whom we had called from New York for news of the Ambers. Mr. Bingham had nothing to do with the Amber clan, as far as I knew. He just might be the man to help me. Besides, he had sounded very charming and friendly on the phone.

"I'll come myself, or I'll send someone," I said, and added, in case someone else arrived to collect Ellen's

123

things, "Are you acquainted with Mr. Joel Bingham, of Cross and Bingham?"

"Perfectly, Mademoiselle. An old and valued patron."

"Good. Then kindly deliver my sister's things either to me or to Mr. Bingham."

"And how will I know you, Mademoiselle?"

The amusement of having outcautioned myself stopped me, and I thought a minute.

"My passport name and picture ought to help. . . . And thank you so much."

"Not at all, Mademoiselle. My pleasure, believe me." She rang off.

I stood with the phone buzzing in my hands, while I peered around the dark, silent house. Nothing stirred, not even a breath of air, but far off I thought I heard a car engine chugging along the road. I listened carefully, but the sound was not repeated. Setting down the phone, I went out on the front veranda. The road shone pale and spectral in the moonlight. Only the giant ferns moved faintly on either side, sentinels of the unknown beyond.

I went back into the house and called the operator for Joel Bingham's number. The operator's sleepy voice gave it to me and then rang, but there was no answer. Nobody home. So much for that. Then I remembered his offices in town and asked her to ring there. I could not mistake the pleasant, very British accent of the man Brett and I had talked to from New York.

"Cross and Bingham. Bingham here."

I told him my name and was flattered by his quick reaction.

"I say! This is jolly good of you to look me up so soon. I'd been rather hoping you would. Wanted to learn how you made out and all the et ceteras. Are you actually the heiress, Miss Amber?"

I said I thought I was.

"Jove, what luck! Any way I can help you? Any way at all?" He laughed. "Help you spend it, for example? My forte, I assure you."

"As a matter of fact, you can help me," I said. "Could you come to breakfast tomorrow morning?"

For an instant he seemed too surprised to answer. I

couldn't blame him. Probably he had never thought his fatal charm would carry him this far so fast.

"Rather!" he said hastily after that betraying pause. "Name the hour. I'll be there."

"I wonder if you would be so kind as to pick up a—a suitcase in town and bring it with you."

"No sooner said than done. You checked your suitcase. Where?"

"Not mine. It's my half-sister's. Ellen Amber. At the Cafe Carrefour. There will be a charge. If you would be so kind as to pay it, I'll reimburse you at once. If you will trust me . . ."

"Nothing easier. I always trust heiresses."

"You—you couldn't get it tonight, could you, and keep it locked up until you see me tomorrow?"

"Anything you say, Miss Amber. Tonight it shall be. Been on the books all evening. Good to get out. It's only a step from here."

"And you will guard it; won't you?"

"Oh, absolutely. Old G—Miss Amber. Suppose I give you a ring-down when it's under lock and key. I promise I'll run all the way."

I thanked him and hung up. The next few minutes would be a long wait. I walked back to the portico and saw that Soochi's light was still on. Her shadow crossed the window, and then, while I watched, the light went out.

I stood a few minutes, inhaling the scent of the garden, trying to calm myself. The first faint soughing of a night breeze came to my senses before I was aware of the telltale sway of the foliage, but I welcomed the cool dampness against my flushed face. In the far distance of the fern jungle, beyond the Tangerine Pool, a sound like muffled thunder began. But it was too even for thunder. A native drum, probably. I wondered if the field hands of Amber were treking through the green darkness to some mysterious midnight rites.

While I thought of this, thankful that I was here and not out there as I had been last night, I heard the unmistakable creak of a footstep on the front veranda steps.

The car engine I had heard a while ago was not imaginary, then. But who would be visiting Amber at this hour? Very quietly, I turned and went through the center hall, intending to spy on my visitor before unlocking the door.

Suddenly, cutting through the night, the telephone set up its jangling noise. I must have jumped a foot before I recovered enough to move toward the living room. As I was about to enter the doorway, a cultured but alarming voice spoke to me out of the darkness.

"The message was for you, Miss Amber. Mr. Bingham wishes you to know he has Miss Ellen's suitcases under lock and key. He will deliver them in time for breakfast."

Someone here in the dark with me knew this important secret!

Shaking so that I had to lean against the door frame, I asked weakly, "Who is it? Who are you?"

The tall, lean man stepped into the edge of a pool of moonlight. In his dark, reticent face only the whites of his eyes were visible. It was Dr. Torri.

"And now," he said, "I think we have something to talk over. Don't you agree?"

His almost hypnotic quietness, his strange, hooded look, everything about him, terrified me. I said not a word as he came toward me.

ELEVEN

"Never mind that," I said at last, rudely, when I couldn't avoid speaking any longer. "What are you doing here at this hour? How did you get in?"

He appeared literally "taken aback" at my attitude and retreated a step or two.

"Pardon, Miss Amber. I would not have intruded without your consent. I was given a key many months ago when Miss Nell's illness first required my services. It seemed simpler and did not disturb Soochi."

Everyone was mighty careful of our precious Soochi, and I resented that as well as the idea that this mysterious doctor, about whom I had heard hints of voodoo, might come and go here as he chose.

He added briskly, "In Miss Ellen's things you may find the clue to her death. I say only—be on your guard. It is possible to discover what she wished kept secret forever. I do not know. I only suppose it."

Almost immediately I was ashamed of my own reaction, for no one could have displayed more tact than he did now; but it was annoying to find myself so frightened and to show it before a comparative stranger.

"Don't go yet. I want to ask you something. I'm sure you understand, doctor, that, as we are women alone here, it is better if no one comes in without being let in."

He bowed his head in agreement and at the same time, with the familiarity of long habit, calmly switched on a lamp near his hand. He did so, I was sure, to make me feel that everything was aboveboard, but it had an opposite effect. I was at once aware that he knew this house better than I did.

"The truth is, Miss Amber, I had no notion you were home. David Earle told me, earlier this evening, that you and Mister Michael were in town. I certainly would never have intruded, nor answered your telephone, but for that. However . . . now that I do know about Mr. Bingham's errand for you, may I suggest that any further investigations on your part should be conducted with the greatest discretion?"

I almost laughed. "I couldn't agree with you more. Unfortunately, you are now party to my—investigations."

"Ah, but I am not a danger to you."

"I have your word for that."

His dignified, almost haughty features tightened a trifle, but then he forced a smile. "I understand. You are already obliging me by carrying out my instructions. Please be as cautious with others. For your own sake. That is what I wished, particularly, to say to you."

"What others?" I asked abruptly.

Before answering me he picked up a blue, imitation leather case with three zippered compartments. I supposed it must be his medical bag but my mind was on so many evil aspects of this night that I half imagined it might contain the tools of a Jack-the-Ripper, it appeared so big and crowded.

"May I suggest . . . everyone."

"Excepting Michael Amber, of course."

He merely looked at me, the dark pupils of his eyes piercing in the pure white that surrounded them. I had my answer.

"Now, may I see the governess?" he added.

"She is dead," I told him without beating around the bush.

"Ah, that now." He hesitated, appearing not to be too surprised. "Suicide? She had inclinations, a very strong guilt complex, entirely based on false premises. She could no more have prevented Miss Ellen's death than—than . . ."

"Her own?"

He was startled. "What do you mean?"

128

"Michael ran her down on the highway to Port Anne."

He almost dropped the blue leather case. "Good God! Has it come out in the open then?"

Now what did *that* mean?

"She ran out into Mr. Amber's path," I said. "He swerved to avoid her, but it just happened. The police have taken her body into Port Anne."

He seemed to find this easier to believe. It occurred to me at the same time that if he were so perturbed, he himself must be innocent of complicity in whatever diablerie was going on here at Amber. I seemed to be exonerating everyone on Saint Cloud tonight!

"I see. It certainly bears out the suicide motif. An unfortunate case entirely. The woman had never made friends with anyone except Miss Ellen. She was crazed by the tragedy; there is no doubt of it. Well, then, once again I apologize for intruding. Perhaps, if I am needed, you will be so kind as to call me. Soochi has my number."

I walked with him to the front door like any suburban housewife. When he stood on the steps, he stopped and looked back at me in the moonlight.

"Miss Amber, any inquiries into Miss Ellen's past may cause serious difficulties. May I repeat, as an outsider, that you must use extreme caution? It was what I meant to say when I heard Mr. Bingham's information tonight."

"I could go to the police, I suppose," I said doubtfully.

He paused. "I think not. You will find that Mister Michael's authority is overwhelming on Saint Cloud. Anything you tell the police may get back to him. However, I know of nothing against Mr. Joel Bingham. He is well-known hereabouts and perhaps cleverer than he appears on the surface. And, he has one great attribute: He is not an Amber!"

Almost my very thought, uttered aloud by a comparative stranger. I stared at him.

He walked down the steps and across the road to where he had parked his ancient English car under the swaying ferns that lapped thirstily at its roof.

After he had driven away I was angry with myself for having asked nothing about the talk of voodoo in the neighborhood, and particularly the hints between Michael and Soochi about its practice. Or was it, after all, only a form of social club, a labor union without the ordinary weapons of labor's power and possessing, instead, some more subtle weapons—the power over the human mind.

It was as well I hadn't asked Dr. Torri. If I had, I should have slept worse than I did when I returned to Ellen's room and tried to banish Miss Nell's death and all that had happened since from my mind. What a long time it seemed since this afternoon, when I had been so thrilled by Michael's attentions at his villa!

There was also the worrying thought that if Dr. Torri knew of Joel Bingham's errand to Amber tomorrow morning, others might know as well. I could scarcely believe Soochi had heard me on the telephone; she had been too far away in her own room. But what was to stop some local resident from listening in on the party line? The more I thought of it, the more I prepared myself for bad news in the morning. By the time I got to sleep, some time after one A.M., I had convinced myself that when I did see Mr. Bingham, he would either have been hit on the head and have lost Ellen's suitcases, or he would not show up at all, for the same reason.

I was in a fine state of nervous expectation, therefore, the next morning when I heard a heavy, masculine knocking on the front door and hurried to answer it, prepared for Joel Bingham's sad story.

To my surprise he stood there in the pink of health, a lean man in his early thirties, with blue eyes, a jaunty black mustache, and a manner at once charming and airy. Beside him was a worn canvas suitcase, heavily laced with cord to hold it together, and a smaller, square vanity case that American women call a "train case."

"Good heavens!" I exclaimed, letting him in. "You still have them!"

He seemed to find this odd greeting quite in character, and after shaking hands with me, he assured me, "Safe as the Bank of England, Miss Amber. Safer, if I may say so. I can't say that they struck me as worth stealing, but one never knows. Gold brick hidden in

130

them, by chance? Ah! Perhaps the Amber fortune. I should have looked into them. Muffed it, by George!"

I laughed and assured him that it was much more prosaic. They were my souvenirs of the half-sister I had never known. We arranged the payment of what I owed him for the ransom of the two suitcases, and he took the money after some polite protest. It amounted to slightly more than twelve pounds. Poor Miss Nell could not even raise twelve pounds, after a half a lifetime spent in the service of the Ambers.

"I will just put your things out of the way, Miss Cathy," said a well-known purring voice behind me. Dear Soochi! Always underfoot when you wanted her least.

"Never mind," I said. "I want to get my best napkins out of one of them. Mr. Bingham, would you be nice enough to bring the suitcases along?"

"But Miss Cathy, breakfast is ready," Soochi interrupted a trifle breathlessly, eyeing the suitcases with great interest.

Joel Bingham must have trained himself not to be surprised at anything, for he lifted the bags and calmly followed Soochi and me into the dining room, where he set the two bags down, more or less under the direction of my eyebrows, half out and half under the big table. This meant that all during breakfast I could keep the calf of my leg pressed close against the larger case, to be quite sure they did not vanish in a puff of smoke.

"Well, this is more like!" Joel announced enthusiastically, taking his place opposite me after playing the gentleman in getting me settled. "Breakfast with an heiress! Jove! One never knows. And I owe it all to the little baggage."

"The what?" I asked, thunderstruck.

He pointed to the bags beside me, and I began to laugh. Then, remembering Soochi, I put my finger to my lips, ever so lightly, and he caught my signal at once, steering away from the subject.

"Did you know my half-sister?" I asked when Soochi had gone to the kitchen for the second course, which was scrambled eggs and Soochi's delicious preparation of Barbados flying fish.

"Only just. Quiet, reserved sort . . . or so I thought!" He smiled and finished his glass of juice. "One never knows. That was before I saw her up in Petionville, of course."

"Good heavens! Where is Petionville?"

"Oh. Sorry. We're so insular down here, we fancy everyone knows every nook and cranny of these little islands. Petionville is a residential suburb of Port au Prince. That would be the Haitian capital, you know. Frightfully swank suburb for such a poverty-stricken island. I had the impression she was to meet someone there, but I heard later that she'd gone down into the Haitian quarter for the actual meeting."

"Meeting? With whom? I gathered that she was interested in voodoo."

"Really? Shouldn't have thought it myself. Still . . . that would explain the native quarter."

Soochi came in with a platter and began to serve. Joel said with his customary enthusiasm, "Jolly decent of you to have me in on such short acquaintance. Riotous luck my knowing the Caldwells. Lovely people, you know. Really—lovely."

"You don't say," I remarked with what must have been conspicuous lack of excitement.

"Oh, quite! The old gentleman's of the Southern Colonel school, if I may say so. Shocks of white hair, mint julep on the breath, pleasant word for the underlings."

"Snobbish," I agreed.

"Good Lord, no. Not a snobbish bone in his body. Just that manner one likes in the aristocracy. Perhaps a touch of condescension, but in the nicest way. Good manners, you know."

"Delightful. Especially the letters they send out. What's the aunt like?"

"Sweet. Met her once at a reception. Shy and birdlike. But no fool, I'd say. Very Southern. I remember she had no use for the pompous local bigwig who was guest of honor at her dinner, and let it be known to Old Lester—that's her husband. Excellent judge of character."

What an infuriatingly stupid thing to say! For a minute I wanted very much to kick him under the table. Then I realized that he could not know of Mrs. Caldwell's letter to me, with its lamentably bad reading of my character and that of my mother. If it had not been for that letter I should never have advertised for my identity and, in all probability, never have come down to Saint Cloud to be threatened with idiotic mysteries on all sides.

"She doesn't like me, and neither does your precious Old Lester," I said finally, "so I'm afraid I can't say much for her judgment of character."

He seemed very much surprised.

"Fancy! I should have said they'd have taken to you at once. Well, maybe the old dears are jealous. Sometimes happens, I'm told."

I had a sudden idea.

"Mr. Bingham, as you may have guessed, these suitcases are something of a secret. Would it be possible for you to keep my housekeeper, Soochi, occupied with something while I look through them? I have an idea she spies on me."

He played up delightfully. "Love to. Nothing easier. Always fancied playing the Eric Ambler to the very depths of the attache case. I'll . . . yes. I'll be a passionate flower fancier. You make me feel I'm taking part in a charade, Miss Amber. You aren't going to turn as mysterious as your sister, I hope?"

He was as good as his word. When we had finished breakfast, he immediately engaged Soochi in a vigorous and knowing conversation about the garden, and she had no sooner made her first flat statement about one species of flower in the garden than he contradicted her, playing to the hilt the last exemplar of the stiff, arrogant English-Raj. I could see that she was puzzled, but she was forced to accompany him around the garden, growing a little more heated than was her custom, while explaining that, though he might be right about English flowers, he was quite mistaken in calling some monstrosity a begonia. Once, when they made a turn, bringing him to face me while she was pointing out a huge leaf to back up her argument, he made the Churchill V-for-Victory sign with two fingers, and I could not help smiling. He was a born actor.

Meanwhile, I had not long to search before finding an astonishing array of items in the big suitcase.

Almost leaping to my eye was a black-sequinned cocktail suit of extreme cut. In spite of wild efforts to conjure up a picture of the Ellen Amber I had heard about in this cocktail suit, I could not. But the black satin shoes were there also, with hideous overdone little bows and some lingerie that even a modern woman like myself would have hesitated to wear because of their bad taste. I was almost ashamed to go further into this secret "Mr. Hyde" life of my half-sister; for I could imagine how she would have hated for me to know or to humiliate her memory in this fashion. But it was probable that these garments would help to focus on the cause of her death.

Rolled up in a red satin slip I found several peculiar items that looked like the fetishes of some primitive religion. Among the amulets were a dozen teeth on a string. They looked like human teeth, but were they? There were other amulets: a tiny black gourd shaped into a shrunken head and stuffed with something that rattled like dried corn and finally a small, cheap doll carved of wood. It was dressed like a white woman, without a turban. A few strands of mouse-brown hair were glued on the bare, wooden scalp. The doll wore a small petticoat and odd, badly done leather-thonged sandals such as a modern woman might wear around the house and garden. The dress itself was a plain, white shirtwaist type. Perhaps the lonely Ellen had kept the doll as company, the way some women keep stuffed animals to decorate beds and dressers. If this were the case, though, it was an anomaly to find in the same suitcase with the black-sequinned suit and a red chiffon dress in the very latest mode. In fact, as I studied the doll, I thought it looked almost the way I would have pictured Ellen Amber herself, as she appeared to her plantation neighbors. I had a vague recollection of having read somewhere about dolls resembling certain persons. Voodoo. Yes. Something to do with curses and witchcraft. But what?

Ellen had obviously used the Cafe Carrefour to dress for her meetings on Haiti—meetings which could not take place at Amber or anywhere on Saint Cloud. Why? What was so secret about them beyond the obvious fact that Ellen was living two lives? Perhaps she was a psychopath, a schizophrenic. I doubted it, though. It seemed logical to me that her affairs on Haiti could not be conducted on Saint Cloud, because Saint Cloud had known her from birth as one sort of girl, and she had wanted to be this other one—the black-sequined glamor girl. Poor Ellen.

At the bottom of the suitcase I found what I had originally been searching for—scraps of paper from a cheap French note pad, one of the kind that is squared off for figures and graphs. I scrambled together all the pieces of paper I could find, and after glancing at the garden to see that Joel Bingham, like a sorcerer, had got Soochi clear out of sight, I hurried to my bedroom with the suitcase and changed, in a flash, to a full blue skirt with large patch pockets. I put the pages of Ellen's diary into the pockets and stuck a handkerchief into the top of each pocket. The suitcase I put into the armoire after hanging up Ellen's gaudy clothes among my own, and I threw Ellen's odd little self-portrait doll into my lingerie drawer.

I found nothing exciting in the train case, which was locked but yielded to the second of the many suitcase keys I had on my own chain. Inside the case I found exactly what I would have found in my own train case —the usual collection of plastic and glass makeup containers; the darker foundation tube with a telltale rim around the cap, as though it had been screwed on hastily by an eager hand; the watery lotion with white grains of sediment at the bottom; and dozens of eery green and blue tubes for eye shadow, eye liners and all the necessities to turn a girl like Ellen into the woman of the black sequins. Except for Joel Bingham's hint, I had always supposed that Ellen was a dry, virginal creature headed for spinstery old age. But all this makeup showed signs of heavy use. I could not help picturing Ellen as perhaps too heavily made up. It would be a natural consequence of the revolt of such a woman against the restraints of her life at Amber.

The key to all this, of course, was the lover, if there had been one. If he had been respectable, why couldn't he have met her at Amber? What was so shadowy about him? And why had she first gone to Petionville on Haiti and then met her lover in the later meetings so far from Saint Cloud? It is true that her lover might well have been a Haitian of mixed blood, but such matters were commonplace in these islands. It was puzzling.

Her journals, those sad little scraps of paper with their frantic jottings of events and moods, would mention the lover. I felt that his identity would explain all that had happened.

Another thought occurred as I remembered the fetishes, which I put in a corner of the armoire. I might be wrong about the entire matter. It was openly acknowledged that Ellen believed in, perhaps even practiced, voodoo. Was it possible that she dressed in this fashion to attend voodoo ceremonies of some sort? That would explain the fetishes, and it was also more in keeping with what we knew of Ellen than all my guesses about a secret lover whom she could not acknowledge.

I locked the case again, placed it on top of the other in the armoire and took out a few pages of the journal. Many of them were pencilled and water-stained. They looked as though they had been written on uneven surfaces, perhaps as her little boat crossed the waters on these secret journeys. Many were incoherent, and, of course, they were not in order.

". . . died. I knew it then . . . I heard the drums all that day. . . . I knew he would die. How unbelievably horrible it must have been to make him run like that, knowing he ran to his death! But it was after him. I saw the signs. I know. He had offended the Thing at Amber, the Thing that haunts the fern forest at night, the Thing whose eyes burn so fiercely from the pool at dawn and at sunset. One of the maids has promised me a *ouanga* to ward it off. It would not dare to hurt me if I have the *ouanga*. I could walk to the very brink of the pool and laugh at it. Perhaps I shall. But first I must have the *ouanga*.

I took several scraps of paper out of my pocket, and all were as incoherent. Ellen must have been driven mad by this place. I could not wonder at it.

Even in the gaudy morning sunlight I peered out anxiously at the garden to see if "It" was lurking around—whatever "It" might be. I saw instead the two figures of Joel Bingham and Soochi. Soochi was adjusting her turban in a way that suggested, though of course I might have been wrong, that she had just been kissed. I will always say these Englishmen seem to know how to get the most entertainment out of any situation!

I saw Joel pause suddenly in the path and appear, for the first time, ill at ease. I wondered what upset him until a shadow crossed my window, and I recognized a man's back as he stood on the portico staring at Joel and Soochi. It was Michael Amber. He did not speak.

Joel coughed and said brightly, "Morning, sir. Devilish fine weather we're having—considering the season."

This produced no response, and, greatly interested, I leaned against the bamboo curtain, watching Joel's effort to promote a pleasant, cup-of-tea friendliness.

"Shocking earth tremors last night. Thought for a moment old Soufriere was going to blow its top. Awkward for you if it had; that is to say . . ."

"Soochi!" said Michael sharply. "Has Miss Amber nothing for you to do?"

Soochi showed her perfect teeth but said nothing as she went off to the south end of the house, leaving Joel to manage alone.

"You were visiting Soochi?" asked Michael finally.

"Good Lord, no! Matter of fact," Joel explained with bland innocence, "came to breakfast at Miss Catherine's invitation. We're old friends, you know."

"No. I did not know."

I wondered if Michael could be jealous. It was very amusing. I enjoyed it.

"Oh, Gad, yes. Old, *old* friends. From New York, you might say. You have no objection to my visiting her, I fancy."

Frigidly, Michael assured him, "Why should I have anything to say in the matter? Amber belongs to Cath . . . to Miss Amber."

"Exactly. My very words to Kit. Said so at breakfast."

The devil he did! Joel's sense of humor was more than I had bargained for; because Michael clenched his fist, which I could see plainly near the window, and asked, "Am I to understand you discussed me with Miss Amber this morning?"

I thought it was time to interfere before poor Joel got his nice mustache knocked sideways. Michael sounded quite capable of it. I called out the window,

"Hello, Michael. When did you arrive? Too bad you missed breakfast with us."

He turned, saw my face dimly behind the bamboo strips and, with some effort, managed to turn that forbidding frown into a smile. "I can see I missed a great deal at breakfast. I came to take you to the funeral."

"What? Already?"

"These things are done rapidly here. It will be brief, but, of course, everyone connected with the estates will be there. You mustn't mind the crowds."

"Rather!" put in Joel, trying to be helpful. "It's all sort of a show for the natives. They eat it up, you know. Kind of white man's voodoo."

Michael reminded him, "We do not call the people hereabouts—*natives*."

"Right-o! Well, I'll be trotting. Unless, that is, you need me."

I was amused to see Michael's eyebrows rise at what he must have thought sheer effrontery, but I assured Joel that he might go. I left the bedroom window, went out with him to the road and leaned over the front seat of his formidable little sports car to say goodbye. Michael must have thought that our goodbyes were tender, but what I really said was, "If I need you, I'll call. You've been a darling."

The fellow actually blushed, saluted and rumbled away, feeling very dashing, probably.

Michael was standing on the steps when I turned around. "Do you think you need to be so effusive with the—*natives*?"

I laughed at him, but I was not altogether amused. For all I knew, he might be involved in three deaths. He had behaved most mysteriously throughout this whole affair. And he needn't think that because he had a certain animal appeal for me, I would be as cowed as Ellen had been.

However, my discoveries this morning proved that Ellen had been far from cowed. My fingers itched to take out more of those scraps of her journal, to find out the real reason why she dressed so elaborately, made up in so sensual a fashion, to visit a neighboring island. Was it voodoo? Or was it to visit a man? What was wrong with the man? Why was she unable to see him at Amber?

Michael took my arm but his rebuke was embarrassing because it was true.

"You seem very cheerful this morning. I thought last night you were going to get hysterical."

There was no answer to that. I could not tell him of my discoveries, which might solve Ellen's mysterious death, nor that Miss Nell herself would be the first to thank me for following her own detective work. After all, I might be talking to the murderer of both women. Nevertheless, I was subdued by his reminder.

In spite of his attraction he had such an effect on me that I felt almost as uneasy with him as Ellen had with her eery "Thing" whose eyes burned from the depths of the Tangerine Pool.

TWELVE

I HATE FUNERALS and avoid them like the plague. For some reason, they always make me think of my ancient nightmare, the one where I am running through thick, heavy-scented underbrush, running to something, I don't know what, and from some horror. By now I know what that horror was, but the nightmare will probably never die completely, and funerals are still a hideous chore to me.

I sat in the little French chapel on the edge of the careenage at Port Ann and thought it strange that I hadn't dreamed my nightmare since my arrival on Saint Cloud. All around me in the chapel the thick, overwhelming odor of tropical flowers and foliage made me sick, and to get my mind off the coffin and its contents, I fumbled in my pocket, pulled out my handkerchief, and with it, one of Ellen Amber's little rambling pieces of writing. Cousin Isobel, sitting next to me on my left as Michael was on my right, peered over at me, her bright eyes malicious and eager, but she saw nothing. I put the handkerchief innocently to my nose, then lowered the muslin, reading what it contained in its snowy depths, the way mind readers operate on the stage when they read the written messages from the audience.

. . . burn for him. It is wrong and evil. But I burn for him. . . . Today at the Tangerine Pool I was just in time and saw what must be the devil's eyes burning up at me from the depths, and I knew how glad those eyes were that I should sin like this. But I must have him, even if I break every law of God and Church and decency.

I felt my cheeks flush hot in sympathy and embarrassment for Ellen. It was wrong of me to read such intimate things. I knew that. But surely, Miss Nell would have done so, if she thought it might help to avenge Ellen. Did Ellen need avenging, though? She sounded almost deranged. Or did some forms of love after long repression affect people like this? Who was the man, and what were the barriers set up by God, the Church and decency?

Perhaps this man had murdered her. She never mentioned his name, as though trying to blot out his identity; for it was obviously his identity that gave her conscience such suffering. He was not just any unattached, ordinary male. Such a liaison would not offend so greatly. Or would it seem so to a woman of Ellen's strict, repressed upbringing?

Michael saw me make the same gesture again, with the handkerchief pressed to my nose, and I was ashamed when he put his hand on my free hand for a moment in obvious sympathy. I reassured myself, however, by telling myself again that I was only carrying on Miss Nell's work. I looked up, saw her coffin blanketed by flowers, and looked down again, feeling stifled.

The piece of paper on which Ellen had poured her thoughts this time revealed no more than the last. Mere ramblings and arguments with herself, favoring her unorthodox love affair.

. . . returning from the night in Port au Prince. No one recognized us, thank God. What would Papa have said, or any of the others? After my strong feelings on the subject . . . But I cannot live without knowing that I shall experience this again. No power can keep me from it, so long as I am wanted. . . .

The service was nearly over when I read a line that gave me a start. It was scrawled under great emotion.

141

How I hate him! How I hate Michael! Yes, hate! In these notes I was to cleanse my soul. *He* will not be cleansed, though. Very well. I shall hate them all. . . . Yes. Even Him. For the pain He gives me. . . . It will end by killing me. But whose hand? The hand beckoning from the bottom of the Tangerine Pool . . . those terrible, burning eyes. . . .

I shivered and was aware of Michael's shoulder, very close to me. What if he could read this? Did it refer to Michael? I tried to imagine how I would write such a melodramatic line, but I couldn't quite be sure that the "him" referred to in the first sentence was the Michael of the second sentence. Why did she hate "them all"? I felt the mephitic atmosphere of the room again. Was it possible that Ellen had been in love (and hate) with Michael Amber?

No, no. The thought sickened me. I would not admit it. . . . Only it was there. She loved and hated Michael because Michael wanted Amber and made love to her to get Amber. And had killed our father for the land. Was this the answer?

But if this were not known—and certainly no one had accused him—what could be the objection to Michael as Ellen's suitor? Why was it so shameful to love him? Surely, such a man could be welcomed as a natural suitor in the eyes of all Saint Cloud. Ellen was hardly superior to him. The note must mean something else. Perhaps Michael had found out something about her affair. It that case, his warning would very likely cause her to hate him. Yes. That must be it.

Michael looked over at me and smiled. He had such a nice smile and used it so seldom. I thought it would be a charming weapon in any courtship he might indulge in. With Ellen? He would meet all the requirements. I was studying the broad, exotic planes of his face with great seriousness and forgot to smile back. His expression changed, so slowly that for a moment I did not note the change. Then I realized that his glance had gone to my hand and he seemed intent. I half expected him to take my handkerchief up and examine it. I smiled tremulously, hoping he would think I had been concerned for Miss Nell. Apparently, he did, for he smiled back, and I loved that warmth in his face and that special, tender

142

quality of his smile. I almost understood Ellen's ravings about the mysterious lover. I, too, could be attracted to Michael no matter what stood between us or what secrets those strange eyes of his withheld.

It was over at last. There was a stirring among the people present, and I could not help thinking that they enjoyed this ceremony as a kind of treat or special show put on for their benefit. They kept Michael occupied for several minutes complimenting him on the beauty of the "display" and asking if he knew when many of them would be back at work restoring Amber plantation to its original productive status. Hearing some of this, I felt quite guilty. But I wasn't ready to give in yet to what probably motivated Michael's interest in me.

Isobel Amber, however, was much too busy watching me to notice the noisy throng as they poured out of the chapel, all chattering at once about the hymns and the flowers and the excitement of the day.

"Dear Cathy, how nervous you look! One would imagine you fancied yourself next in the dreary procession."

I looked up quickly, serving the purpose I had intended, for she stopped staring at my handkerchief and pretended she was studying my face instead.

"What do you mean by that, Isobel? Are you going to help me into that 'dreary procession'?"

"Good heavens, child! Where do you get such ideas? Do I look like a woman who would toss you into a pool or run you down in my speeding car?"

"You look like an incurable gossip," said Michael with finality, taking my arm and leaving Isobel to make her own way out of the church. "Someone ought to cut her tongue out," he said as we went to the car parked across the street.

It was a horrid thing for him to say, and I did not like it, though I hoped his disgust was on my behalf and not for some deep-dyed reason of his own.

Isobel came toddling after us, and there in the front seat of his car we promised to be cozy as three cats, all the way to Amber.

"Dear me, dear me," Isobel said, when she had arranged herself exactly as she wished, leaving the space that was left for Michael and me. "How touchy we are

143

today! Michael, my pet, no one blames you just because you ran the woman down. Good heavens! Everyone knows how you drive. She shouldn't have taken a chance."

"We were driving very slowly," I put in, hoping to ward off another of Michael's outbursts.

"Really? I shouldn't have thought—that is, the police of this wretched little island are all blind as bats, anyway, when it comes to an Amber sin. Don't you worry, Michael. They will be most discreet. They know to whom they must answer if they make trouble for you."

"I suppose you mean something by that," Michael said in a bored voice. He seemed so disinterested I was surprised and a little uneasy to see how his fingers tightened on the wheel; his face looked exceedingly grim. Of course, Isobel annoyed him. But she annoyed everyone. I wondered why he should be so upset now. Surely, he must have known her long enough not to let her needle him like this—unless his conscience bothered him.

"Mean? Mean? What on earth? I only made a remark, dear. One of those nice, funny brown policemen said to me that it was odd you hit the poor creature when your lights were on, and it did seem you could have avoided her. That's all I meant. It isn't as though your own family were going to accuse you, after all."

"Accuse me of what?"

I felt frightfully ill at ease between them, feeling the animosity clear through my body.

"You know, Michael. Like poor, dear Ellen." Isobel preened herself as though she were a splendid tropic bird, which, indeed, she looked, in her fashionable new electric-blue silk suit and accessories. It was hardly a funereal outfit. She tried to squint into the rear-view mirror, but Michael abruptly twisted it out of her hands.

"Poor, dear Ellen," he said in a voice that seemed seething to my ears, "was mad as a hatter. Everything was going to ruin. You may see now what it had come to, humoring her. Shattered. All the work of a century, nearly gone. Seeing the land die is like seeing a person die. But you wouldn't understand that. Neither did Ellen."

"I know she thought you wanted her property, dear.

144

That's not what I meant. She hated you for the other thing . . . you know."

The heat of the day seemed to have gone. I felt chilly, as though I were home at Amber, surrounded by the dripping wet fern forest. Surely, Isobel must have read the scrap of Ellen's paper that I had been reading during the funeral. Else why would she bring up such a thing now? Ellen had hated Michael, and Isobel knew it. It must be because he had been her lover, the secret one. What else could Isobel mean by "the other thing"?

I said briskly, trying to laugh and clear the air, "I don't think Ellen hated anyone. You must be mistaken. She didn't understand why Michael wanted to handle the Amber property. As Michael says, she didn't feel for the land as some people do."

Michael glanced at me as I looked innocently away. What I said and what I believed were two different things, and I didn't want to be swayed by that look of his, as I always was.

Isobel laughed, her brittle, sarcastic little laugh. "Dear, dear Cathy! It all seems so pathetic. Next year, we shall probably be dismissing you in the same way we now dismiss that pitiful Ellen."

Michael pulled up at the outskirts of the Port Anne hill, reached over me, and opened the car door beside Isobel.

"Get out! Go and sell your foul lies to someone else."

Isobel brushed her skirt daintily. "Oh, I couldn't very well do that, now, could I? What a fool I should be, to place myself in a situation where I might be run down the way you killed Jessica Nell."

I ducked my head instinctively, wondering if Michael would actually hit this frightful woman, but he did not. He closed the door again and drove on, without a word. I could feel his body, tense and stiff and ominously strong, beside mine. Isobel, on the other hand, was easy, imperturbable, smiling. Deliberately, she reached up and adjusted the rear view mirror again, so that she could see herself. Michael did nothing. His face, when I shot a scared glance at it, was pale and frozen with anger, and he looked straight ahead.

When we reached the spot where Miss Nell had been killed last night, the car swerved momentarily, and he slowed down as we rounded the curve. I could hear Isobel very quietly make a sound like "Tsk! Tsk!" with her lips pursed. I pretended not to hear, and hoped Michael did not.

As we reached Amber and Michael let me out, Isobel surprisingly said she would stay on too, "in case I needed her." I assured her that nothing was further from the case, but she insisted.

"You will be so lonesome. Heaven knows how the natives will act after this. I think you should have company."

I said goodbye to Michael, putting my hand out to shake his hand, just as he leaned forward and appeared about to kiss me. I tried to make it seem that I had accidentally avoided him, but I think he understood that I could not trust myself to his lovemaking; for he got back into the car, looking straight ahead, and drove away. With a sudden feeling of revulsion, I wished I could do the whole thing over again, tell him I didn't care about the gossip, the lies of Isobel, even the hatred of Ellen. Whatever he did, I would tell him, was for our good, and I trusted him. I wanted to tell him that, even though it was untrue.

I felt now that he had always been an outsider, whether because of the exotic background of his great-grandmother and his renegade great-grandfather, or because he had made his way by his own efforts, rather than by strict inheritance, as was the case with the weaker Ambers. It was for this reason, and his own peculiarly masculine attraction to me, that I wanted to be on his side. It would not be the first time (as I excused my feelings) that a woman was drawn to strength and masculinity rather than justice.

And now there was Cousin Isobel on my hands.

As we walked into the house, which was darkened against the noonday heat, I saw and heard the rustle of bright cloth in the lounge, and Soochi seemed to gather dimensions out of the darkness.

"There was a telephone message, Miss Cathy. A trunk call. They didn't leave a number."

"Long distance, dear," said Isobel helpfully. "I wonder who it could be. How frightfully exciting if it were that old boyfriend of yours!"

She must have eyes in the back of her head. I ignored

146

her and told Soochi I would make the call later. I went to my room and left Isobel to her own devices. Later on, I saw her wandering out past the eastern boundary of the garden, toward the jungle path to the Tangerine Pool. I did not think she would get far. She was still wearing her fashionable high heels and sheer nylons.

In the meantime I had read every scrap of the little papers on which Ellen Amber had unburdened her soul, or her heart, as the case might be. It seemed to me an effort on her part to reveal herself psychiatrically to her own consciousness. There was no other purpose in this outpouring of emotion and troubled conscience. I suspected she wrote these things on the suggestion of Dr. Torri. It might fit in with his words to me last night, when he had warned me that what I might learn of Ellen from her writing would be dangerous. Certainly, if in this accumulation of half-sentences and fierce exhortations, the name of one individual predominated, that person might well be her killer, and therefore a menace to me. But no name predominated. Her lover was always "he," and the others were always vague enemies. All except Michael. He was mentioned.

I supposed a smart amateur detective, like those in movies and paperbacks, would guess the villain in all of this, just by the hints from the shreds of paper onto which Ellen had poured her feelings. But I couldn't. I knew a great deal more about Ellen than I had before, and I felt ashamed for knowing such intimate facts about her. I could even guess that the "lover" in her life—or the person who held her to that enchantment, like a figure in a voodoo rite, might well be the one who had maneuvered her death, as well as that of Richard Amber. But Jessica Nell had died under my very eyes, by Michael's doing.

One scrap of paper had fallen from my pocket, and I picked it up off the floor.

. . . please, please, tear me loose from this evil Thing. . . .

I thought this over, reading in its plea something else, the whisper of voodoo that had run through Ellen's life. Had it, after all, been such rites, and not a corporeal lover, that had disturbed her so?

147

Here in my hand I had all the evidence I was likely to find of Ellen Amber's real self, her past that was unknown to anyone on Saint Cloud except her companion in this evil, and I still was no nearer to finding out what was behind the horrors here.

In putting away the scraps of paper, I pushed aside a pile of Ellen's things and saw a little doll at my feet. After a confused moment, I remembered that I had found it among Ellen's possessions. Perhaps a cherished memory of her childhood. But something about it seemed evil. Surely not the face, which was almost nonexistent. Perhaps the style. The doll was not dressed in the Madras and full skirts of the local dolls. As I had noticed, it was dressed like a white woman; yet it did not look like the dolls one gives a child in my own country. I wondered about this as I put it back.

I glanced out the window and saw Isobel picking flowers and giving orders to Soochi about something or other, so I took my chance and went into the lounge and made my long-distance call to the number in San Francisco that I had for Brett Caldwell.

As I expected, his answering service reported that he must have made the call to me that morning from Calistoga, a town in northern California where he actually intended to sell a yacht or two. I had to laugh at his confidence.

Before hanging up, I asked, "Is he really on business? You know how Mr. Caldwell jokes about such things." Actually, it was a foolish question. Since when had Brett taken business seriously? When I wasn't around, he simply turned for his amusement to some other girl, or rather, girls. It was so like him, I didn't mind. It was part of his Brett-quality.

To my surprise and pleasure the woman on his answering service replied quickly, "Mr. Caldwell is doing very well lately. He tells us he lays it to the influence of a good woman. I rather suspect that's you, Miss Amber."

I was enormously pleased, for while I did not find him quite so thrilling and overpowering as Michael Amber, he was much more comfortable, and I wanted very much to have him succeed on his own, if only to show his stuffy relations.

I told the service to ask Brett to leave the number where I could reach him with Joel Bingham, for I didn't trust anyone at Amber.

I wondered what would happen if I called his relatives and left the same message, letting them discover at the same time that the little nobody was now an heiress. I put through the call to Charleston, South Carolina, and presently found myself asking the Caldwell butler if I might speak with Mrs. Caldwell. When he asked my identity in that terribly polite, terribly distant voice of all butlers, I gave my new name, adding that I was a friend of Brett's.

I had to wait a very long time, but presently an imperious voice piped into the phone with an accent as thick as candied yams. "I don't recollect the name. You say you are a friend of my nephew. But he has so many!"

That was no news. I explained that she had known me formerly as Catherine Blake, but that I was actually Catherine Amber, and I had inherited the Amber estate on Saint Cloud.

"You don't say," said the little molasses voice. "My word! Brett neglected to mention that small detail."

"He called me on the telephone," I went on. "And I wondered if you would give him a telephone number by which he might reach me."

"Heavens, no, child. Shortly ago he was in Ottawa on some sort of business. He is a man of business now, you know, and doing very well, I must say."

She might, at least, give me credit for straightening him out, but it was clear, from her next words, that this never entered her head.

"Yes. My boy always found it difficult to be aggressive in the business world. He'd rather make people happy. . . ."

She could say that again!

"And for a long time, a business career for him was quite out. He used to complain of a bad heart, but it was psychosomatic. You can't fool me on such matters."

I remembered Brett's many amusing excuses for dating me when he should have been working. One time he claimed to have caught a touch of gout. I recall that

I blamed it on the excessively rich dessert he had eaten the night before, and he called me "heartless" and "unsympathetic," but he grinned just the same.

"Well," I said, "if you should hear from him, please ask him to leave any message for me with Mr. Joel Bingham. I won't wish his calls to come through this phone."

"Indeed! A Caldwell unwelcome on one's family telephone. . . . How strange! Should he happen to mention you, Miss . . . er . . ."

"Amber."

" . . . I shall convey your message. But I doubt very much if *my* nephew . . . well, we'll see."

The old witch! After the briefest amenities, I hung up, only just in time; for I heard the tinkle of Isobel's voice on the portico.

I was soon made aware of why she favored me with her company that day. She went straight through tea and dinner chattering about the appalling difficulties suffered by previous "Ambers" who had claimed the estate during the past few months and finally fled in terror. When I laughed and told her she would have to be cleverer than that to scare me, she made a little moue with her mouth and finally smiled.

"Then, Cathy, you are braver than the others. It happens sometimes. But that isn't your best proof of birth. Your sister and your father were not brave. See how they both died, in fear, running from . . . Well," she shrugged. "Whatever it is they were running from."

"Murder, I imagine," I said, and I went on eating, pretending indifference.

"And whom do you suspect?" she asked. For the first time in our dinner conversation I felt that she was not wholly at ease. She played with her dessert, a luscious tropical-fruit salad, in a way that was not quite like the poised Isobel Amber.

Her uneasiness gave me renewed confidence. I laughed at her in my most cutting way. "Don't flatter yourself, Isobel. You are only one of the suspects on my list."

She looked up. There were two red spots in her flawless cheeks. "Let me tell you something, Catherine— whatever your name really is! I needn't bother killing you. All I need to do is wait. Wait until Richard was dead. Until Ellen was dead. Until . . ."

"I am dead? But then, suppose you are not the next heir. Suppose you have Michael to reckon with in the courts?"

"Not if Michael were—where he could not inherit."

"Behind bars, you mean?"

She had lost that tiny flash of truth-revealing temper. Now she was her cool self again. "You have said it, Cathy. I haven't."

We finished dinner in silence, and when she asked me to join her in the lounge during the evening, I refused. I walked around the cool, damp garden for a few minutes and went early to bed, propping a chair under the doorknob. My nerves were not quite what they had been before this "Amber" business, and I needed every hour of sleep I could get.

I heard Soochi calling a taxi from the nearest village for Isobel, and presently I heard the sound of an ancient motor chugging away.

I went to sleep almost immediately and during that first hour of deep unconsciousness was only aware that my dreams were full of house-moving, roller coasters and other phenomena that had nothing to do with the house in the fern forest. An hour or two later I was awakened by a sharp earthquake and understood vaguely then why my dreams had been so lively. Apparently this was not the first tremor of the night. I lay in my bed in the semidark, with the moonlight coming through the bamboo curtains in tiny stripes across the pillow. No matter how many times I felt earthquakes, I never became used to them, and my whole body tensed expectantly, waiting to see if the tremor was but the beginning of a major disaster. It stopped an interminable time later, and I glanced at the clock. It was ten minutes before midnight.

The doorknob of the door leading onto the portico began to shake.

I sat up, frowning. The bed and the room were perfectly still. From long experience, I knew that the surest test was the small chandelier in the center of the room. But it was perfectly still. I watched the door. It seemed to me that the moonlight outside was blocked by a shadowy form at the door. Did someone have the

151

nerve to try to get into my room, perhaps to murder me? I was not so much afraid at the moment as furious at such effrontery. Everyone knew that I suspected the entire island of conspiring against me. I stared harder at the door, trying to discover whether that shadow I saw was actually a corporeal body. It seemed to me that the moonlight shone right through it.

The doorknob rattled again.

I waited, very long seconds. I could fancy I heard my own heartbeat. My nerves were in such a state that I felt I could not stand this any longer. The first weapon that came to my hand was a night lamp. I removed the shade and globe, and after unplugging the base, which was brass and capable of putting a dent in any skull, I went cautiously to the door. By a miracle, I removed the chair without making a sound. Raising the lamp base I swung the door wide open.

Something very tall, very gaunt, filled the doorway, towering over me.

"Don't be afraid, Miss Cathy," said Miss Nell.

She was all in grey, wearing the hideous robe she had used to wear that looked like a shroud. In her shadowed face was the sallow, dried, wrinkled look I remembered, with only the eyes glittering and the wrinkled lips spread wide in a hideous smile. She put her hand out, that big, capable hand, grey as ashes in the moonlight.

I stammered, "Don't—don't touch me. . . ."

My head was going round and round. I moved backward, stumbled over something, probably the rug, and struck my head hard upon the floor as I went down. I felt a prickling, black wash of darkness over me, and I fainted.

THIRTEEN

MY HEAD ached abominably, but I was never so glad to see a crowd of people as when I awoke and found every light in the house ablaze, casting a harsh yellow glare over the faces around my bed. Closest was Dr. Torri, professional, competent and strangely gentle, and at the foot of my bed, Michael Amber, looking very concerned, and beside him, David Earle, his handsome face taciturn, but with an expression of curiosity about the eyes, I thought.

Soochi came gliding in, staring at me with eyes that seemed to dart around my face and body, as though passing me under inspection, piece by piece.

"More cold compresses, Doctor," she said, and I felt the cool cloth upon my forehead in place of one that had grown warm and soggy.

"Cathy, can you tell us what happened? Soochi says she heard you fall," Michael said, leaning over the foot of the bed and putting his hand on the bedcovers. I could feel the warmth of that hand clear through the covers, on my foot.

Gradually, I began to realize that someone was missing. I tried to sit up but felt giddy and sick, and under Dr. Torri's ministrations, decided the pillow was best after all.

"Where is Miss Nell?"

Michael and David looked at each other. Dr. Torri's hands, moving through his medicine bag, paused, but he did not raise his head for an instant. I knew at once that they all thought that the fall had knocked me out

153

of my sense. The doctor turned to me again and seemed about to speak. Before he could do so, however, Michael came through in his decisive way.

"Miss Nell is dead and buried, Cathy. I saw her. I swear to you it is so. I don't know what they've been telling you, but . . ."

"Soochi, you may go," said Dr. Torri, using very good sense.

With the faintest smirk on her moist red lips, she moved out of the room, noiseless as always, looking back once, expressing her supreme contempt for the three men and "that idiot in bed who fancied she saw dead people." Although she did not express this latter opinion aloud, she did not need to. Her manner and her features spoke it for her.

"You don't understand," I said. "She was at the door—right over there—at about midnight. That's why I fell and hit my head."

David Earle went to the door, which was open. I could see the garden crouching there beyond it, some of the big, luminous flowers nodding their heads at me gently. The overseer seemed to fancy he could pry an explanation out of the door frame and even the doorknob. He tried everything briskly, thoughtfully, making me more annoyed by the minute. He seemed to be trying to match my story against hard reality, and I knew as well as he did that in hard reality it didn't stand up.

Michael asked Dr. Torri, "What do you think?"

Dr. Torri studied me. He did not smile, but I felt that his dignity and reserve covered a great deal of understanding.

"I think Miss Amber saw the governess."

"Now, Doctor, this is absurd. The woman is dead. Exhume the body, if you like, but I assure you, the woman is . . ."

"Nevertheless, Miss Amber saw something that she took for Miss Nell. I would stake my case on it."

I nodded wisely, and we both looked at Michael to see how he would take this. He looked disgusted and disturbed.

"Is it some sort of preposterous joke? First Miss Nell is frightened into a heart attack, and now Cathy

154

in this state. Obviously, they could not both have been frightened by the same spectre."

"I believe Miss Nell saw my sister, Ellen," I said. "I've thought that almost since she had her heart attack."

"But you say you saw Miss Nell," Michael objected. "And nothing could be less like Ellen than the governess." He called Ellen so familiarly by her first name. Well, why not? Weren't they cousins? Still, I was troubled. Jealous, perhaps.

Dr. Torri said quietly, "I think we need not trouble ourselves about such supernatural matters at the moment. I may have some ideas of my own when I have examined the aspects of voodoo that appear in this."

"Voodoo! No. Please, no voodoo!" I protested and was cut off sharply by Michael's voice.

"Doctor, I forbid you! I will not have voodoo on this plantation—in any form. I warn you!"

Dr. Torri shrugged and changed the cloth on my forehead.

"Mister Michael, whether you like it or not, you have voodoo on your plantation. . . . Miss Amber's plantation, I should say. And among your own field hands. To tear it out by the roots would be to destroy a harmless sedative, a form of entertainment, and in some cases—a treatment for mental disorders."

"And this terrifying of Cathy, I suppose, comes under the heading of a treatment for mental disorders."

Dr. Torri looked at him directly, a piercing stare which had alarmed me two nights ago.

"This terrifying of Miss Amber and of Miss Nell is not the result of voodoo among the workers. You may look to your own race for this mischief."

As Michael and I were the only Caucasians in the room, we looked at each other. For a ridiculous instant I felt guilty and thought I read suspicion in his eyes. Then he gave up.

"Well, if you have some method of determining the truth about this affair, I've—we've no objection."

"No, no! If you do, I won't stay. It's exactly what destroyed my half-sister. Voodoo!" I cried, quite agitated. I fancied the same pattern that had killed her was working on me.

"Rubbish!" said Michael. "You are a strong, healthy girl, not a weak neurotic like Ellen. You aren't going to let a little thing like an imagined apparition scare you away."

"It wasn't an imagined anything!" I insisted. "It was real. It was Miss Nell . . . or—or something. . . ."

"She must have seen something," put in David Earle, to my surprise. But he spoiled it all. "A few hours ago the moon would have struck just here. When you consider the power of that light, with these endless shadows of the garden . . ."

"It was real!"

"Yes, yes. We believe you," said Dr. Torri soothingly. I wasn't at all sure that Michael and David agreed with him, but Michael, at least, had the decency to go on scowling, as though my apparition puzzled him. David Earle did not look the least bit worried or concerned. It was almost as if he were getting close to something, and therefore was no longer disturbed. If he knew something, I wished he would tell.

I said, "Maybe I saw someone in the house. Soochi, or someone."

Unnecessarily, David Earle reminded us, "Soochi is a head shorter than the governess. I think we'll have to look further."

"I wish Isobel hadn't left when she did. She is such a snoop, she'd have been sure to see something," I said, thinking aloud.

Michael raised his head sharply, "What time did she leave?"

"More than an hour before I saw this thing. And besides, she is smaller than Miss Nell, too."

"Are you sure she really left?" Michael wanted to know. He seemed worried, which was nonsense. Nothing could be less like the gawky giantess, Miss Nell, than our fashionable little relative.

"Well, I saw her—that is, I heard her leave," I finished lamely. I thought they were getting pretty far afield, suspecting Isobel had stayed behind and masqueraded as Miss Nell.

He and David considered the matter, and Michael went to the lounge and called Isobel on the telephone. I heard him call to David.

"No answer. She must have left four hours ago, at least."

"Maybe she went into town to spend the night," David suggested, walking out of my room and speaking to him from the hallway. "In Saint Cloud there's some old lady with blue hair that she is friendly with."

I smiled at the "blue hair."

Presently, Michael called Soochi, who insisted that Isobel had left shortly after eleven and that only the taxi driver knew her destination. It was curious about Isobel.

Dr. Torri put away his medical equipment, which reassured me somewhat; but the knowledge that he and the others would be leaving was not reassuring.

"You need some sleep, ma'am," he told me when I objected.

"Yes, but not in this house alone!"

"You have Soochi. She can call me if anything—if you feel unwell."

Soochi! What comfort!

"Please don't go. *She* might come back. You don't know how awful it was—all that grey stuff floating on the breeze, and Miss Nell beckoning to me in that old way she used to do . . . just as if she were alive."

"Nonsense. Miss Nell is dead. If you did see anything, it was a prank, and I am sure Mister Michael or David Earle will get to the bottom of it."

"Unless one of them is the prankster."

Dr. Torri zipped up his case quickly. The noise of the zipper grated on my nerves.

"Well, Miss Amber, what else do you know?"

I motioned him nearer to the bed.

"I read those notes Ellen made. Did you tell her to write all those torn bits of paper, so incoherent, so senseless?"

"Ah." His dignified face and manner were at war with the gleam of interest in his eyes. He finally gave in. "Yes. I thought it good therapy. Whatever ailed her was mental, and it seemed the natural thing—to purge herself of her thoughts."

I nodded and said no more, watching him, while I pretended to arrange my bedcovers. He was exceedingly interested in my story of Ellen, but he was trying to retain that medical indifference.

157

"Well?" he prompted me. "What did she write?"

"She was in love, Doctor. And with someone she considered ineligible. Someone she thought it a sin to love. Or else, it is possible it wasn't one man, but something else that held her in its power. Something she thought of as a kind of lover. And you know what that was." I was about to mention voodoo, when David Earle walked into the bedroom and Dr. Torri exhaled rapidly. He must have been very angry at this interruption, for his eyes darted from the big overseer to me, and when he saw I wasn't going to speak, he bit his lip, and I felt sure he barely refrained from asking me to explain my last hint. Let him think about it. I didn't trust any of these people. The only thing I asked was that they stay in clumps around me, so that none could harm me without witnesses.

I said rather saucily to David Earle, "Do all the residents of Amber House see ghosts? Or is this treat reserved for newcomers?"

He grinned, a big healthy grin, refreshing (or was it callous?) in the present grim circumstances. He did not seem afraid of anything, unlike Dr. Torri and Michael, who were both upset.

"Miss Cathy, anything you see—if you really see it —is no ghost. Just remember that."

"Maybe I ought to have a weapon, in that case," I said, to test him.

"What, ma'am? To shoot through a ghost?"

"You said it would be real."

"I said—if you really see it!"

I was so mad at him I wanted to fire something at him, but nothing was handy, and I tried to avenge myself by turning my back on him and talking to the doctor.

"Don't you think I ought to have a gun or something?"

He hesitated. David Earle surprised us by laughing.

"Get out of that one, man! That's all we need. A nervous young lady with a gun, loose at Amber. And the first thing she pot-shots is one of your crazy voodoo followers."

Dr. Torri said haughtily, "I've told Mister Michael this is not voodoo in the true sense. If you choose to make it seem so, you may have your reasons."

David Earle, speaking harshly for the first time in my memory of him, said, "Don't you know it would be better for everyone if it was voodoo? Every death so far has been due to terror. Why not leave it alone? Put a stop to the mental suggestions that voodoo always presents. You'll keep from killing other victims by suggestion if they know that's what it is. Let it be voodoo. If it's voodoo, you can defeat it by closing your mind to it. Isn't that so, Miss Cathy?"

I did not answer. He gave me more credit than I deserved. As a matter of fact, knowing so little about voodoo, I was half of a mind to suspect they could bring the dead back to life, and that in this way, each of the dead had frightened the next to die. It was silly, but this whole affair was unreal, based on something impossible in the light of day.

Dr. Torri patted me professionally on the shoulder, told me to get some sleep and finished his preparations to leave. When Michael came in, I protested that I didn't want to stay alone, and if I did stay alone, I wanted a gun or something.

Before answering me, he said in an aside to the overseer, "I don't like that business about Isobel. She isn't at the hotel in town. I suppose she stayed with some friend. But it seems odd."

"At least, she isn't here to stick pins in your image," David Earle remarked sardonically. "You are her favorite victim."

Michael ignored this and gave his attention to me in an embarrassingly public way; for he refused me the gun, politely, and then leaned over me in front of both men, and kissed my forehead and told me to go to sleep, "like a good girl."

Both the doctor and David Earle exchanged glances, and the overseer shrugged as if in answer to an unspoken question. Michael said gently to me, "I'll be staying here until breakfast. If any ghosts come, I'll shoot them for you."

He smiled at me and then went out on the portico, following the doctor and the overseer.

With the lights out, I could see that it was nearly dawn. The hour seemed gloomy and full of horrid spectres. I closed my eyes but snapped them open a short time later when something scratched ominously upon the window, and a shadow seemed to beckon to me through the bamboo curtains.

Miss Nell!

I screamed and jumped out of bed, my head pounding so hard and so painfully I could feel each thump. Before I could get to the door, it opened, and Michael came hurrying in.

"Out—out there!" I managed to stammer, as I clutched at him with an unpleasant death grip. He scooped me up in his arms in a very competent way and carried me out on the portico, where he showed me a tangled branch of hibiscus and ivy, scraping at the window. I felt stupid in his arms, half afraid I'd fall out of them, strong as he was. But then, I wasn't used to being carried.

"There. You see? Not Miss Nell, at all."

"Well . . ." I covered my embarrassment, "it was before!"

He laughed and remarked prosaically that my feet were cold, and carried me back to bed. It was very comfortable now in his arms, whatever his guilt or innocence, and I supposed that, with practice, I might get quite used to it.

When he left, I started to rearrange my bedcovers which no man ever gets right, and as I did so, I saw that one of those little scraps of Ellen's diary was lying here between my bed and the armoire. I got up and tore it into even tinier pieces and threw them into the darning basket I had been using as a wastebasket for my cleansing tissues. There was something in the darning basket which would be found in almost all baskets, except this one—a tiny pair of scissors. It was the natural place for the scissors, but I knew I had removed them when I turned out the contents of the basket and began to use it for my used tissues. I examined the scissors. They were not mine. Ellen's, probably. Caught in the rivet was a shred of cloth which looked familiar. The shred was large enough for me to recognize it as part of one of my dresses, a blue linen sheath. Holding my head, against the furious disturbance within, I stood up, opened the armoire and fingered my clothes until I came to the blue linen. There, down one panel of the skirt was a large, neat, square hole. A piece of material about four inches square had been cut out!

My anger at the phantom of Miss Nell was nothing compared to this vandalism. I wrenched off all my clothes from their hangers and examined them minutely. Nothing else had been mutilated. Then, as an afterthought, I opened the drawer on the side of the armoire, in which I had my lingerie. The top nylon slip and one stocking had also been cut up, neatly and carefully. The remainder of the slip and the stocking had been folded as before, with only a large, square hole in the material, ravelled around the edges and starting innumerable runs. Gradually, my fury diminished. The cold, damp hours of dawn crept around me. I could almost feel the drip-drip of the ferns in the forest beyond the garden, with each raindrop falling on my bare shoulders. I began to be terrified. My teeth chattered.

I knew that when I had gone to bed my clothes had been whole and the sewing basket had been empty. Otherwise, I would have seen the scissors when I threw in my tissues after removing my makeup. So this hacking at my clothes had been done some time after I saw Miss Nell's ghost, and before Michael and the doctor arrived.

But why? Why not after Michael arrived? Either David Earle, or the doctor, or Michael himself might have done it. Still . . . it seemed like a woman's trick. And the scissors were so small—one could not imagine David's great, shapely hands curled around those little scissors. Nor the other two men. They were all big men, husky or rangy, with hands to match.

But why this vandalism? It seemed peculiarly horrible to me that this cutting and haggling had been committed beside my unconscious body. What would have happened if I had come to consciousness unexpectedly? Would those scissors have been used on me?

Across the room where it had fallen out of the lingerie drawer in my hasty scramble, Ellen's little doll in its dowdy, Ellen-like dress winked its beady black eyes at me, catching the first light of morning. I stared at the doll, wondering why it seemed to bring me some message that I was too stupid and too frightened to comprehend. Gradually, my eyes closed, and although I shivered under the bedclothes, I slept.

I woke up just before the heat of morning, and I doubt if I'd have been roused then by anything less than the telephone clanging noisily. I could hear voices on the portico outside my door—Michael saying something sharp to Soochi, who mentioned my name. Then Michael said he would take the call, and he went inside. I was sure it was for me. Before I could pull myself together to go and challenge the dragon at my door, I saw Michael return to the portico. David Earle was just coming into the garden from the direction of the Tangerine Pool, and Michael met him in the garden. They discussed something for a few minutes, glancing occasionally at the house. In my hypersensitive mood I was sure they were discussing "my" phone call, which Michael had taken. Well, it was too late for me to rush to the telephone now.

After a few groans and the cursory examination of several black-and-blue marks from my fall last night, I managed to get dressed, though I still looked rather like a washed-out Miss Nell myself.

Since Soochi and Michael had quarreled over the phone call, I bypassed Michael by going through the house until I found Soochi cleaning the dining room table with her little dark-eyed helper, whom I had quizzed in the kitchen last night. The girl almost jumped out of her skin as I appeared in the doorway, and Soochi, who had her back to me, turned slowly, saw me, and dropped a nest of dirty dishes with an appalling crash.

I was delighted to have turned the tables and frightened her for once.

The little kitchen girl cried out at the calamity of the dishes, "Oh—oh—Ma'am Soochi!" And then, to me, "Oh—ma'am! They said you was sick—asleep." She seemed as much terrified by Soochi's reaction as by my appearance.

"You can see that I am not sick—nor asleep," I said in my chilliest tone. The coldness was as much for Soochi as for the little maid. "I do think you might pick up the scraps," I told Soochi, meaning to start out ahead of her for once.

Soochi's hands shook as she knelt to pick up the

162

crockery, and her meek "Yes'm" seemed to stagger the maid, who stared at her in astonishment.

"The phone rang a while ago," I said. "Was it for me?"

Soochi did not look at me. She was busy with her work and growing less nervous as she made herself useful.

"Yes, Miss Cathy. It was from town. Mr. Bingham, I think."

I certainly wasn't going to call him from here. I decided to order a taxi and go into town to see him. Then I could make a long-distance call to Brett, since Joel Bingham's message to me was sure to be from Brett.

I turned away from the mess on the floor, then thought of something. I really had my knife out for Soochi this morning, and everything conspired to help me.

"By the way, Soochi, what happened between you and Miss Isobel last night?"

I could have predicted her reaction—the insolent look, the shrug, the remark that after she had called the taxi and sent the lady on her way, she had nothing more to do with the affair. Instead, Soochi made a grab for a broken water glass, and to my surprise, and the horror of the little maid, we saw her wince, as a nasty little stream of blood spurted between her shaking fingers.

"I don't know. I just can't understand it, ma'am. I— I— It's not possible!"

"What isn't possible? Here. Let me help you wrap that." She was managing very badly. But she snatched her hand away from me.

"I mean—she must be home. Where else would she be?"

"An interesting question," I replied, feeling oracular, and left her to her own devices and the frantic help of the kitchen maid.

I would not have put it past Isobel to have staged this mysterious little disappearance of hers deliberately.

Still—I could not help feeling that Soochi had behaved about it in a way entirely untrue to her character. If, by some remote chance, she had something to do with Isobel's nonappearance at home, I felt she would

163

have brazened it out. But no. She seemed extraordinarily worried, either because of a guilty conscience or complete innocence.

But I just could not believe that cocksure Cousin Isobel was in trouble. She was much too fond of herself. It smelled rather like a trick of some kind to me.

I wondered why level-headed Soochi, with her Oriental calm, who took every horror in stride, should feel so upset about it.

FOURTEEN

HOPING MICHAEL would not hear me, I went to the telephone and called the local taxi company at the village adjoining the crossroads near the center of the island. I still had my headache which kept me from being hungry, but I was so anxious to contact a few sane "un-Amber" people for a change that I would gladly have suffered more than a hadache.

I considered myself clever when the cab pulled up a few minutes later and chugged away with me inside, while David Earle ran down the road, calling to me to come back. Perhaps he thought I was leaving forever. If I weren't so stubborn, I might have done so. But no one was going to scare me out of my inheritance. This was the inheritance I had once been so squeamish about accepting, but I felt I had now earned it on the soggy, fern-infested field of battle: Amber Plantation.

"Where to, missus?" the driver wanted to know.

"The first village where there is a public telephone," I told him.

I saw his dark eyes studying me in the cracked mirror above his head. I did not explain. He said after a moment or two of bouncing and jouncing over the impossible road, "Things happening very funny at Amber; don't you think so, missus?"

I thought, as Brett would have said to that: "you're not just beating your gums, boy!" However, I smiled and said briefly, "It's the ferns, I think. They soak into the blood and turn everyone into a homicidal maniac."

165

I could see by his expression and his quick looking away that he wasn't too sure of *me*, right now.

"There is a good deal of chanting and drumming and that sort of thing at night around here," I went on presently, watching his face in the mirror. "Do the people of Saint Cloud think it has anything to do with the deaths at Amber?" I was waiting for him to say the word "voodoo," but he steered all around the word instead.

"No, missus. It is no harm to sing. Mister Michael does not like it, but David Earle is with us sometimes. He says it does no harm. I think ye speaks to Mister Michael and makes him not to stop us . . . them."

"Do you people like Mister Michael?"

He raised his head. I thought he was going to speak, but he shrugged instead, and I had to pursue the matter myself.

"I mean—have you had any dealings with him? Is he popular? Or what is the attitude toward him on the island? He seems to have great power."

This time the driver smiled, one of those enigmatic smiles so impossible to read in a race that is not one's own. "Maybe it's the power that makes people wonder . . ." he said.

"Wonder about what?"

"I mean the things at Amber. He tells all the hands at Amber what to do, what not to do. Yet never has an owner of Amber given him the house, the power on paper to do these things. The power, you see, is inside Mister Michael. We do not like him. But without him, we would maybe all be nothing, have no job, no boats for trading. Not anything. We think he is a great man and—maybe—terrible. Do you know La Soufriere, our volcano?"

"Too well, I'm afraid. I don't like those earthquakes it's been sending out the last few days."

"That is because La Soufriere will blow one day soon. The doctors who sit up there and look into the Old Woman of Fire, they have said so. But what I mean is, Mister Michael is like La Soufriere. There is much boiling under the surface. There is much strength on the outside when he chooses. And he gets his power from no man but from himself, within. You see? He is La Soufriere. He is what is called 'made-by-the-self.' "

This told me very little that I hadn't known before. Privately, I had long been convinced of Michael's explosive and volcanic propensities. What I wanted to know was, did they cause devastation or not?

"Do you think he could have caused what has happened at Amber?"

He shrugged. "Maybe. Maybe not."

"And if not Mister Michael," I went on, probing, "then perhaps his friend David Earle, who does so much of the work for him."

"Ah!" said the driver expressively, the dark pupils of his eyes glittering in a strange way. "He was one of us. But has he sold his soul to the devil? That is the thought that we sometimes think; for he is not one of us now. And if not, then what does he belong to?"

I tried to get him to go on about the overseer, but he shut his mouth, and at the end of the ride I had all I could do to get him to tell me where I might find the public telephone in the village.

The little village seemed to grow out of the fern forest, almost as a part of it. The houses, many of them, were on stilts. Water ran under them, and ferns grew dark and cold and dank under there. There were children everywhere, darkly handsome, their ebony flesh gleaming like scrubbed and polished wood. The ancient French influence was strong in the faces of the people, and it showed in the fact that though there were scarcely two dozen houses fronting the main highway, there were five outdoor cafes, all of them crowded with men lazing at the tables over their morning *café au lait,* or whatever. The women of all ages that I saw passing back and forth, most of them carrying loads and bundles, were, almost without exception, beauties, dressed principally in full-skirted, bright, electric-blue cotton, with pointed red cotton Madras headdresses like Soochi's.

The heat, at about this time of morning, was beginning to lay in like blankets over the whole island, but especially in these open spaces where the sky, so piercingly blue a little earlier, was now brassy with sunlight. Prickles of heat seemed to rise all over my body, as I got out of the car and went to the nearest of the several cafes to make my telephone call. At first my skin seemed dry as bone under the density of that heat, but then, the humidity began to make itself felt, and soon my skin was as damp as that of the few other Caucasians I saw in the village. Everyone in the cafe paused in drinking to look at me. The men were very polite, and I heard no comments, but as I asked to use the telephone and arranged about paying for the toll charge into Port Anne, I saw the cafe-sitters exchange low-voiced remarks, through which the word "Amber" was audible. They knew who I was. Such things as the affairs at Amber got around fast on such a small island.

Joel Bingham had been out on the docks, but while I waited, someone from his office went to get him, and eventually I heard his comforting, musical British voice say, "I say! This is jolly decent of you. I daren't hope it's an invite to another breakfast. You have such a fierce dragon for a watch dog. I've a notion he was jealous. High compliment to me, I assure you."

I laughed at this description of Michael, but then I got down to cases. "No. I really wanted to ask you about Brett's long-distance call."

"Hard lines for me! Nothing but a blasted go-between. Well, that's the way she blows, as my pirate ancestor would say. Yes. Late last night I got a trunk call from Caldwell. Heaps of squawking noises and a chatty operator with a nasal twang, which I daresay is infallible sign of a trunk call from the States. He is flying down to rescue you. Thinks the dragon's going to devour you whole. Much more likely to devour Caldwell, as I told him. His suggestion was that he come immediately to Amber and "punch the bastard in the nose." I merely quote, you understand."

"Oh, no. He mustn't! Michael would kill him!" I cried out in panic. That idiot Brett knew how I felt about such amateur violence. Besides, I didn't want Brett hurt, or conversely, I didn't want Michael's dignity ruffled. Any man with so little sense of humor couldn't afford to look ridiculous, even to himself. Curiously enough, it was his lack of humor that gave Michael the one weak spot which made him even more attractive to me.

"Precisely my sentiments. So I took the liberty of suggesting some sort of meeting between you and Caldwell before you present him at Amber. Thought you might want to caution him and what-not, as they do on the flicks. Then you may decide the next go in battling the dragon."

Bless this Bingham! He thought of everything.

"You did just right. Where should we meet?"

I could see now, by his tone, that Joel Bingham was justifiably rather satisfied with himself.

"There's a little hole in the corner over on the south end of the island. Place I go to occasionally, with a particularly choice bit of a dish. . . ." He broke off so quickly I knew he must have been about to reveal his romantic secrets, and I tried not to smile as he changed his dialogue in a hurry. "That is—you know, guests from the States, or out from home."

"I understand perfectly," I said, and added, just to devil him, "You haven't any choice bits of—that is, guests out from home there at the moment, have you?"

He laughed and took my teasing goodnaturedly. "Might make it a bit awkward, what? No. No choice bits there now. Until you come, if I may say so."

"What time?"

"I'll drive Caldwell over from the interisland boat landing. He should be arriving about now at Charlotte Amalie. That allows him time to take one of our Cross and Bingham boats and reach Saint Cloud about three this afternoon."

"You are an admirable arranger," I told him. "I can't thank you enough. Where do I meet you?"

"I expect you might take a taxi to some meeting place, but . . ."

"No. I don't think they like me dashing off like that, trying to get rid of them. This morning Michael sent his overseer running after me. If I could just amble down some path, you know, as though I were looking at the scenery . . ."

"Exactly. And I know just the place. It's a back road cutting through the fern forest at the eastern end of Amber plantation. If you walk through the forest back of Amber House, you can't miss it. The lava flow from the last eruption crossed about where the road meanders through the forest."

"I understand."

"You might arrange to meet us there about three-thirty or a few minutes later. I'll wait."

We were about to hang up when Joel Bingham said

suddenly, "By the by, what's the to-do about Miss Isobel Amber? There's talk in Port Anne that the police are on the lookout. Don't tell me you've made her the fiend in the Amber plot. Hardly the type, I should think."

I said briefly, "I wouldn't put it past her."

He chuckled. "No. Indeed not. Quite a formidable little lady, if she's the one I'm thinking of. Credit not too good, though. Always being rescued financially by your dragon, Michael Amber."

"I couldn't care less, to tell the truth. She's a dreadful gossip and perfectly hateful."

"No doubt. Still . . . one doesn't like to think of her at the bottom of some lava pond, or running out into the way of a lorry some dark night, now does one?"

What a horrid thought! After I had hung up, I wished he hadn't left me with such a notion. I much preferred to believe that Isobel was hiding somewhere, just to devil Michael Amber.

I stepped out of the telephone alcove, which served also as the entrance to a communal restroom, whose facilities (there was no door) seemed rather inadequate, like a lean-to, attached to the outside of the cafe. As I started out through the cafe I saw David Earle's big form, easily noticeable in his white clothes, and he seemed to be questioning the men at an outside table. One of them pointed in my direction, but I had ducked behind the telephone alcove, and I went out through the communal restroom and up a path behind the cafe, which led into the fern forest.

This cat-and-mouse game was played for the sole reason that it annoyed me to be found out and dragged back to Amber by David Earle. But I couldn't think of anything else to do with my time, and besides, I was hungry for some of Soochi's good food; so I took another path down to the road to Amber and sauntered along toward "home," knowing perfectly well that it would not take the overseer long to find me. As I had expected, he soon drove along the road behind me. I wondered how long it would be before he felt it safe enough to beard the lion (me) and ask me to get in the car without my embarrassing him by my screams which would be heard in the village.

I took him out of his misery by glancing around and waving him on. He drove up, leaned out, and said, "Miss Cathy, you had us all worried. Mister Michael thought you tried to run away."

"Does he think so still?" I asked, wondering at the past tense he had used.

"Oh no. I called him at the village. He has so much to do today that I didn't want him to hold up on—on our account. He'll be back to take supper with you."

I made a face. It would have satisfied my selfish soul to think of Michael still at Amber, brooding over my whereabouts. Besides, I would probably be having dinner with Brett and Joel.

"I'm tired," I said. "For heaven's sake, give me a lift back home."

He grinned. "Sure, Miss Cathy. I told Michael you weren't the type to run out like the others." He appeared to think those last three words a mistake, for I heard him catch his breath for an instant, and then he began to change the subject to something about there being rain expected in the afternoon.

Determined to be difficult, I caught onto the three words he wished forgotten and said coldly, "I take it the others were frauds and I am genuine. Or am I a fraud in that choice nosegay too?"

"No, ma'am!" he exclaimed emphatically. "You're no fraud. You're Miss Catherine's daughter, right enough. She was brave like you. I always thought she left because she wouldn't share Amber with . . . with anyone."

"Anyone . . . who?" I asked curiously.

"Why with—with your father's first daughter, Miss Ellen, of course."

Was that what he had meant to say? I wondered. Had mother left Amber because she would not share the plantation with Michael Amber, perhaps? Even in my father's time, Michael had run his own business on the island, with the boats and the cargoes and all that he and David Earle had built up. And such power would be bound to interfere with father's property, just as Michael encroached on my rights now. Was that what David Earle had been about to say? Or was it something else that had driven mother away from Saint Cloud and the fortune and the estate? But it wasn't

171

like mother to run away from a fight with a man like Michael Amber, who must have been very young—a boy, in fact—when mother left Saint Cloud. It was pride that would make mother give up, not fear of a fight. How could mother's pride have been so injured at Amber that she would banish even the name from her life, giving her only child a false name and the smirch of illegitimacy? I could not imagine anything Richard Amber could have done for which he would deserve to be wiped out of my mind.

When we reached Amber, Michael had already gone over to Isobel's house to see if he could discover what she was up to; so I ate my late breakfast alone in the big dining room, under the slanting, watchful eyes of Soochi. At any rate, I felt much better since learning that I would be seeing Brett this afternoon. Then we could talk about what was best to do and whether I were safe here at Amber until something was settled about the estate. He might advise me to sell it to Michael and get out. That would be sensible. But if I did so, I should never see Michael again, of course.

I wished I felt as infatuated with Brett as I was with Michael, or, contrarily, that I liked Michael as much as I liked Brett. What a pity that one man could not embody the best features of both men! But that would be asking a little too much.

Anyway, either Brett or Joel Bingham would have an explanation for Miss Nell's ghost, and the holes cut in my clothes, and the other horrid things that had happened. I reflected that by this time tomorrow Brett and Joel would have helped me decide what was best to do, and all the horrid suspense would be over.

Just then the telephone rang, and as I started to the lounge I met Soochi, who said without expression, "A man to speak to you, Miss Cathy. He is a trunk call. Much noise on the line, and he speaks so funny it is hard to make him out."

Good heavens! Brett and his southern accent! And after all the messages I had left about not calling here. I hurried to the telephone. It was Brett. The line had cleared up now, and his warm, friendly voice made me think of the silly, clowning days in San Francisco, our dates, the joking about marriage, his constant glances

172

at other girls . . . all the safe things I had lost when I came to Amber.

"Well, sweetie! Guess who this is."

I could not play his game. I was too anxious to be assured that he was coming today, that there would be safety somewhere in the world.

"For goodness sake!" I cried. "I made a three-mile trip to avoid using this phone today! Please don't say anything on this line. There may be people listening somewhere."

He went right on, paying no attention to my warning. "All right, sweets. Don't play. I just got in to the Virgin Islands. I told you you'd never get on with that Bluebeard. Has he tried to make love to you yet?"

"None of your business. Have you been carrying on with any interesting beauties lately?" Woman-chasing Brett in the Virgin Islands! It struck me as singularly appropriate.

"None of *your* business, doll! Hey! See how well we get along? We're born for each other. The minute we meet, we quarrel. What married couple could ask for more?"

"Your aunt and uncle!" I said, a little more sharply than I had intended.

"Auntie? Uncle Caldwell? Forget them. Just their sense of humor. That letter—I've told you a hundred times, it didn't mean a thing."

"I suppose it didn't mean a thing when I called her —your aunt—long distance, and she was exactly the same."

There was a long silence. I wondered if he had left the phone, but then he said, "You—called my aunt? What—what did she say?"

"That assuming you ever mentioned me, she would be happy to tell you I had called."

He was obviously relieved, and I, in turn, was a little let down. It seemed to me that he cared more about her opinion and his uncle's than he pretended he did. Well, that was Brett Caldwell. One mustn't expect miracles overnight.

"Look, hon. I can't wait to see you. Are you all right? Will you be safe 'til I get there? Joel says there's all kind of hanky-panky going on down there with that Bluebeard cousin of yours."

That was better. He sounded genuinely worried. I reassured him, hating to have him go off the line, because his voice gave me a sense of security that was gone when I looked over the phone at the fern forest across the road. The frayed leaves trembled in the sudden breeze, as a rain cloud passed over the sun and threw everything into deep shadow.

"Well, sweets," he made a kissing sound over the phone. "See you in a few hours. Joel knows the place. If I had my way, I'd walk into that house of yours and knock old Bluebeard's ever-lovin' block off! Do you yearn for me?"

I was still laughing at his "ever-lovin' " description of Michael but agreed that I yearned for him, and he hung up. As I did so, I heard footsteps creak suddenly on the hall floor, and Bouramie, the kitchen maid, came in, her hands nervously clasped in her bright, full skirts, as she spoke.

"Missus, I worry. I said this to Ma'am Soochi, but she doesn't listen to me. So I worry."

"What about? You mustn't be afraid, Bouramie—is that your name? You must speak up. Soochi can't hurt you, and neither can I."

"No, missus. But—there's others. They hurt people. Maybe they hurt Ma'am Isobel. Out in the ferns."

My heart began to thump with those first painful signs I now recognized as the beginning of the Big Fear. "What do you mean?" I asked. "What do you know about Miss Isobel?"

She was frightened again. "No! No! Nothing, missus. Nothing, I swear! I only saw her walk out to the Pool, the one they call the Tangerine Pool, where the devil's red eye glares up at you. That was last night, before I finished the dishes. I say to Mister David when you are sick in the night, 'where is Miss Isobel?' and Mister David says not to gossip. I say to Ma'am Soochi, 'where is Miss Isobel?' and she is very frightened and shakes me and says 'what do you know?' But I know nothing. I only saw Miss Isobel go on the path last night, and then this morning the field people say Miss Isobel goes like Miss Nell."

The field people. They had guessed right about Miss Nell. And yet that lying Dr. Torri had said voodoo wasn't mixed up in this.

174

"And when you told Soochi, she was frightened?" I asked the girl, wondering at that, although it did bear out my own observation of the housekeeper this morning.

"But that is the thing I don't understand, missus. When I speak to Ma'am Soochi again this morning, she is not frightened, and she says, 'Hush, you are a fool!' I do not know what to think. So I think I will come to you, Miss Cathy. And I ask you— Did Miss Isobel go last night in the taxi, or did she never go from Amber at all?"

We were full of jolly thoughts today. Mine, immediately, was that Isobel's body might lie at the bottom of the Tangerine Pool.

I grabbed the poor girl by the shoulders, scaring her half to death.

"Bouramie, come with me, at once!"

"Yes'm." And then, as I started toward the portico and the garden—"Where, missus?"

"Don't call me missus. Call me Miss Amber. And don't ask questions. Just come along." My cross voice, which hid a frantic anxiety, served its purpose. The poor creature was apparently used to being ordered about, and she trotted along beside me across the garden, although I saw her eyes behaving nervously as we left the garden and took the path through the overgrown jungle to the Tangerine Pool. I couldn't blame her. Only my pride kept me from darting side glances at all the fern fronds which seemed, like beckoning fingers, about to entice us off the safety of the path.

The usual afternoon shower caught us halfway to our destination, and Bouramie threw her top skirt up over her head from behind, and I wished I might do the same. Aside from the discomfort of getting soaked, my headache had come back, and the lump on my skull, where I had hit myself last night, was throbbing unpleasantly. But I kept thinking of Isobel, floating like Ellen Amber in that filthy pool.

Time after time a branch or frond laden with water bent over me, trailing a wet finger across my cheek or through my hair. It was eery to find so much life in these vegetables. When we reached the clearing, the shower had stopped, leaving everything, including myself, to drip more than ever.

Presently, Bouramie began to lag behind, and I had to call her, ordering her to join me. The open toes of my high-heeled sandals were no help when I had to push aside that last strip of vegetation and a rotting, soggy log that lay across the path, before we came out upon the edge of the Tangerine Pool. A cloud was moving rapidly over the sun, causing all the foliage around the pool to shift and move in giant shadows, and it took careful walking through that slime of dead leaves to approach the pool's edge without slipping into the great chasm.

I had seen it all with my mind's eye so many times on this hurried trip through the fern forest that for a moment I fancied Isobel's body huddled there in the water at the bottom of the pool, but it was only in my imagination. I was enormously relieved when the cloud began to move off the sun and I saw that I had mistaken lighter shadows and the reflection of pale green foliage for the lumpish body. I closed my eyes and gave a little prayer of thanks. The pain in my head was fierce, but I didn't care.

Bouramie, seeing that I did not cry out or make some other disturbance, came forward in a gingerly way.

"Why, there's nothing!" she cried in a disappointed voice.

I laughed at her tone, partly because this was almost in the nature of an anticlimax, and partly, too, because the whole experience of the last few days, along with my headache, made me feel a little hysterical.

"Nothing at all. I'm sorry you are disappointed, Bouramie."

"Oh no. Missus . . . Miss Amber. I only go to think about Miss Isobel and all." She leaned over the pool, and her sandal slipped in the ooze of mud at the edge. I caught her and pulled her back.

"For heaven's sake! Let's not make trouble where there isn't any."

"Surely is a funny place," she murmured, still staring into the waters. "You watch now. It changes lights and shadows all the time. But at sunset . . . there. That's his eye lookin' up at you, and not yet sunset neither. Red as fire!"

"Whose eye?" I asked, walking around to where the

176

ground was more firm before I peered into those murky depths. She was right, though. A gigantic eye glowed up at me, all crimson-orange, burning into my brain. I realized that it was the afternoon sun, casting its reflection just as the cloud floated off its face, but I could see how, to a sensitive mind bred on superstition, that eye could be supernatural, even a devil. I blinked but was aware all the time of its burning, burning, right through my eyelids. I backed away and wandered further around the pool. The eye became bigger as the reflection changed, until the entire pool was ablaze, and even Bouramie's dusky prettiness across the pool had an orange cast to it. The murky water turned from deep green to an ugly dun color, and it was all I could do to look away from that baleful red eye glaring up at me.

I was shaken out of this mesmerism by Bouramie's voice and her pointing hand. "What a funny thing, missus! Right by you, just below the edge. It looks like a toy-thing, for a baby."

I stepped forward carefully and peered over. Long ages ago a fern or other bush had grown over the edge and then been covered by the silt and mud of time, until now, only a bare twig stuck out, directly over the pool. Suspended from this twig was a toy, as Bouramie said. But a toy for grownups, and for one in particular. What had Dr. Torri boasted about his case—that there was no voodoo in it? This was a doll like that one I had in Amber House, which resembled my sister, Ellen. Only this one, as I watched it swing from the twig, was dressed in a blue linen dress like mine. I could see the nylon slip beneath the dress, and on the feet, two badly sewn shoes of black oilcloth, with silly little sticks for high heels. It was *me* I was looking at, Catherine Amber, swinging from that twig. Horribly garroted.

Like Ellen, I'd got my death card.

I began to shake so much I could hardly keep from falling forward, plunging down into that glowing red eye that hypnotized me.

Ellen had known more about voodoo than I did. Yet Ellen had died. What hope was there for me? I was so cold. I was so horribly, unbearably cold and scared!

FIFTEEN

I LOOKED UP and caught Bouramie's eyes across the pool. She had begun to speculate about my danger. I was tarred with the brush of voodoo. I could see it in her face. She was beginning to withdraw from me mentally.

She pointed a shaking arm toward the doll just as the inanimate thing danced in a little breeze, at the end of its "rope."

"Oh, missus!" Bouramie exclaimed, catching her breath. "I see someone once that is like that fetish. Hanged, I mean."

To keep my lips from chattering at my own fears, I managed to say, "Why? Why was he hanged?"

"He'd made trouble for the *ouanga* man. And he had much bad luck after. When he wanted a fetish to save him from bad things, he can not get it anywhere. Not anywhere. After a while . . . he hanged himself. Oh, missus! Tell the *ouanga* man you're sorry. Make it up to him." She seemed very much worked up over my danger, but all the time I could see her shrinking away from me, even at the further side of that chasm.

I was so scared I was furious with the first object I could reach—Bouramie herself. "Why look at me like that?" I almost screamed. "I didn't hurt your *ouanga* man! For all I know, you are in this with him. Who is he, anyway?"

Bouramie had definitely retreated. I could see her shifting her feet backward, away from me and from the chasm. In another moment she would be running.

"How can you ask me, missus? When you've had him to your house, at your own table! I cannot tell. It's bad luck to say the name. You've made him mad at you. Don't you see? You . . . you're lost. Lost!"

"Go away!" I screamed at her, losing my head at this idiocy (and its possible truth). "And don't come back. You hateful little voodoo monster! I believe you got me out here just to see that stupid doll!"

Oh, damn the weather, anyway! It was beginning to sprinkle again. And there was Bouramie, taking my advice, running away toward Amber House for all she was worth, with her skirt pulled handily over her head.

Shaking so that it was difficult to keep from lurching forward, I felt behind me until I found the chair made out of the old hardened lava flow and sat down, huddling there in the falling rain, trying to conquer my shakes before returning to that dreadful house.

What a stupid act, to let Bouramie go without finding out who the voodoo man was and why he had been at my dinner table!

The rain came faster, pelting me on top of the head. To add insult to injury, a fern frond that was spread out near my head carefully leaked water down my neck. I pulled it further over me where it served as a partial umbrella during the downpour. To an unseen observer, I must have looked insane, sitting there shivering in the jungle, with my muddy feet and ruined sandals just missing the rim of the deadly Tangerine Pool, and my eyes staring into the pool's depths. The truth is, I was too scared to stay and too scared to go back to Amber House.

Having nothing better to do, and with rain running down my face in rivulets, I began to cry. I looked hideous and felt worse, hugging myself to keep from freezing with my chills.

From somewhere long ago, I remembered a phrase in French: *"Du calme . . . du calme,"* and I repeated it between chattering teeth. And then I remembered that it had been my mother who had said it, and Mother, the bravest woman I have ever known, had also fled from Amber. So why should I be brave?

I began to feel better. The hollow sound of rain splattering the tops of fern fronds seemed to drum in my ears with a regular, rhythmic sound that made me

179

sleepy. It was the abrupt cease of this sound that aroused me from my stupor. The downpour had done me one favor: it had knocked the horrid hanging doll into the pool, where I watched it sink gradually out of sight. But my annoying thoughts told me, "It's myself I'm watching drown there below me in that slime."

I closed my eyes for an instant, to shake off this absurd hypnosis.

The rain brought in its wake a vaporous, misty fog that settled down over this little clearing formed in large part by the Tangerine Pool, and the fog so thickly shrouded its little world that I became aware of an enormous, weighted silence all about me. I got up, dripping wet, with my clothes soggy and my feet squishing in my sandals as I moved. I stood for a moment staring around the clearing whose loneliness was now emphasized by the fog, and finally I glanced back into the pool.

The recent deluge had left the pool shimmering with water through which streaks of a desolate sky and the ghostly fog were now reflected. The glowing red eye of the sun had been vanquished, and as the water was caught by a sudden, chill breeze, its surface bubbled like gooseflesh rising under the impact of some fresh terror. I looked over the edge, into those depths, and for the first time the light was right so that I caught my own reflection, a pale smudge of a face staring back at me.

Behind my head, in the reflection, I could see the shifting clouds and the vaporous curtain of fog. The fog had become so thick in those few moments that I could almost imagine it had its own solidity behind me, a grey pillar of nothingness, the color of a rotting shroud. I knew, even as I peered into the reflection in the Tangerine Pool, that I could make out this shroud of vapor at closer range if I turned my head, for it must be directly behind me, but after the horrors of last night, the totally irrational appearance of Miss Nell, and then the voodoo doll today, I think it would have been worth my sanity to turn at that instant. I stared at my reflection, hoping against hope that the curious phenomenon behind me would somehow dissolve into fog and rain.

Then, behind me, I heard the little swish-swish of the wind rustling through very thin garments, garments like a shroud. It was close behind me at first, and then more dim, barely audible.

I turned. Silently regarding me from the edge of the jungle was the shrouded figure of Miss Nell. From this distance I could see the thickly wrinkled complexion, blue-white in its color, and the burning eyes. The mouth was pale and bloodless, almost invisible in that ghastly face. The mouth of one long dead. I felt my sandal sliding back toward the edge of the Tangerine Pool as I stared in my silent horror. Another slip like this, and I should be in the pool. I did not feel faint, only frozen with cold and unbelief. The wind blew up, swirling those funereal draperies of hers and churning the misty fog between us, until I realized that Miss Nell had vanished in that last little cyclone of air, and I was alone in the glade again.

I stumbled over to the lava chair and leaned on it with my eyes closed, thinking that the greatest horror had been when I did not know how close she was. She had been standing immediately behind me. Perhaps she had intended to push me into the pool. Was that how Ellen had died? What had stopped this monstrous apparition from pushing me in as well? If it really had been Jessica Nell, of course.

When I could get hold of myself, I stiffened against all my cowardly instincts and walked over to where she had disappeared. Phantoms don't leave tracks. This one had. Either Miss Nell was not really dead or this shrouded ghost was not Miss Nell, for I saw the mark of one of her shoe-heels—the broad imprint that was typical of the comfortable, mannish shoe Miss Nell had always worn.

The apparition had been swallowed up by the jungle, and I could go no further without losing my own way; for there was no definite trail here at the north end of the pool clearing. I had had enough. I was not going to wait until late today to meet Joel and Brett.

I went back around the pool, and when I found the trail to Amber, I began to run. All the time I was running I could hear the wind blowing through my own clothes, and I kept imagining it was the sound of Miss

181

Nell, floating through the grim, stormy air behind me. I do not believe I stopped running until I was back in the Amber garden.

Bouramie and Soochi were hanging bedroom curtains when I rushed by their window to my own room, tore off my soggy clothes and changed quickly with fingers that still shook with my uncontrollable tension. Then I went to the lounge and telephoned.

Joel was not in when I called, and a shipping boy finally answered the telephone.

"Ain't seen Mr. Bingham now for some'ut over an hour, missus. He's out at the docks, I'm fair certain, missus. He's to meet one of the boats. A gentleman's coming in any hour now."

"Any hour." That sounded like an easy life. I told the young man to ask Joel to call me at once, when he came in, and then I sat down beside the phone to wait. It was a gloomy room. I had not liked it the first time I saw it, and now, with the day so wretched, and the road running by the windows so deserted, it was even worse. I tried to think of something else, resting on my knees on the sofa and looking out the front windows. But that didn't help. Across the road the fern forest was under siege from the sharp wind I had encountered at the pool. All the ferns were waving about, with their gaunt arms beckoning to me. It was like a spell put upon me. I had to stop looking at the stupid things.

It seemed forever before the phone rang and Joel, jovial and obliging as ever, said, "Glad to drop by and pick you up. Righto, old girl. Immediately—if not sooner. But what am I to do about your poor chap? He'll be expecting me at the docks. He's due in shortly."

"Let him wait," I said selfishly. After all, Brett hadn't spent the last couple of days with ghosts and murderers and whatnot. "We'll meet him together."

"By the by—" He laughed apologetically. "Is Amber anywhere about? Shouldn't like to risk crossing your Bluebeard friend today of all days. Not by a long chalk. I'm not up to his weight, you know."

"He is out looking for Cousin Isobel."

"What? Not found the old girl yet? Well . . . as you bally Yankees say—'You're the boss.' Be there in a jiff."

Dear Joel! When this was all over, I thought, I would have Joel to think for any peace of mind that was left to me. And to think I had never heard of him before a week ago!

Joel was as good as his word; he must have rushed to Amber, breaking every one of the island's speed laws.

As I was leaving with him, Soochi came out on the steps and said abruptly, "What must I tell Mister Michael, ma'am? He'll be looking for you."

"Tell him I've gone out," I said.

Joel laughed as we drove away. "That won't improve his ferocious temper, I'm afraid."

"I don't intend that it should. I'm sick of these ghosts and voodoo fetishes and all the rest of the horrors that Michael has prepared for me."

"Michael!" He looked startled.

"Well . . . he can't have lived on this island all his life and not known something about these crimes."

Joel piloted the car neatly over a big hole in the road before replying.

"Have you given any thought to that doctor who seems to know so much about the situation? In town there's talk that Torri himself is implicated in the voodoo. Sort of a faith-healing business."

Yes. I could believe that. Dr. Torri knew a great deal, though I didn't suspect him of planting the voodoo doll and faking the ghost of Miss Nell, for, somehow, as I had talked to him, I had believed he was as troubled over the happenings as the rest of us were. They reflected on his people. Then, too, whoever was doing these things to me, and had done things to Miss Nell herself, was attempting to make it look like voodoo. I agreed with Dr. Torri on that, at any rate. I wondered how much David Earle really knew about voodoo.

I said abruptly, "An hour or so ago I saw my own voodoo doll swinging from the Tangerine Pool. Dressed in my clothes, I'll have you know."

"Good Lord!"

"And that isn't all. I saw Miss Nell's ghost. Or what was meant to be her ghost."

"Sticky business all around." He frowned and studied the sky through the windshield. Then he exclaimed, "Old Soufriere's finally blown! That explains

183

the murky sky. We can expect nasty weather for a day or two. Hope it doesn't interfere with the highways. The lava flow, I mean."

"What?" I sat up straight. This probably explained the earthquakes last evening, before Miss Nell's ghost had made its first appearance. "You mean that wicked old volcano is really active? When is the next boat?"

He was surprised. "For where?"

"Anywhere!"

His expression relaxed, and he grinned. He seemed to find my tourist fears amusing. "Happens every few years," he said. "Nothing to alarm you. It's only reached Amber once this century."

"We're more than halfway toward the next century," I reminded him, and he laughed, obviously feeling masculine and superior in his fearlessness.

"I shouldn't worry about that. The lava path will cut across the northeast tip of the island and maybe fizz a little when it rolls into the Atlantic. Nothing to worry about unless you're sunbathing on one of those lava beaches. But that's no matter. Aren't you happy to be seeing your friend Caldwell?"

I was too cross with Michael for getting me into this danger in the first place to work up much enthusiasm for Brett at the moment.

When we were going down the steep hill into Port Anne with the volcano spewing out its fumes far behind us, Joel said slowly, "The talk is that Miss Nell isn't really dead. Sounds pretty daft, but there it is."

His offhand way of saying this made it sound almost logical to me.

"Michael said she was—but of course, we can't trust Michael either. Still, the police and the local doctor examined her . . . didn't they?"

"Oh yes. No question. They swear she was dead."

"*Is* dead, you mean."

He caught himself. "Yes. They swear she is dead."

This gave me more uneasiness. "You mean you've already checked?"

"Quite. Just thought I'd make sure. But it doesn't seem to help, I'm afraid. The natives hereabouts still claim to have seen her since her death. Well, here we are. Let's hope Caldwell hasn't arrived with no one to meet him. He'll think we've let him down frightfully."

184

Joel's hopes were in vain. In front of Cross and Bingham, the imposing old pink, two-story building on the corner of the waterfront and the careenage, Brett Caldwell was striding up and down like a quarterback limbering up for the First Quarter. He looked very good to me—so natural and unmysterious, there in the muggy tropic daylight, his thick black hair gently ruffled by the hot, sulphurous breeze. When he saw me, I was flattered and touched at how quickly he came toward the car; and then, before Joel could do anything but slow down, Brett lifted me out of the car and began to hug me.

"Sugar, you are a sight for sore eyes! I got to counting the minutes last night, since New York. I've missed you, sweet."

He gave me a long, no-doubt-devastating kiss, partly for the benefit of the townspeople who had stopped to watch these crazy Yankees.

"Well, I like that!" he complained as I broke away, but he was soon his amusing self again as Joel came around the car and put out his hand. Brett was effusive and Joel a trifle reserved as I introduced them. Brett excused himself by saying, "Seems like I'm all buddy-buddy with old Joel after the times we've buzzed on the long distance phone. How about that, Joel?"

"Old Joel" agreed politely, beginning to thaw.

By the time the men came out of the building with Brett's luggage, he had begun to accept the enthusiasm of Brett and was reacting with the charming, unobtrusive friendliness that I had liked immediately in him.

"It's all a bit of a bore," he confessed, "having Saint Cloud prove so unhealthy for Miss Amber. But we thought she might need some action around here, if things got any worse."

"How worse?" Brett wanted to know, and Joel and I explained as we drove out of town, over the hill toward the Atlantic coast of the island, to Joel's cottage. Joel and I took turns, each of us with some harrowing detail, and Brett kept looking from one to the other of us as though he couldn't believe his ears.

"You mean this old governess woman may have been what? Buried alive?"

"Heavens, no!" I cried, shivering at the whole sub-

185

ject. "But—it's possible she didn't die at all. At least, that's one theory."

"And then there's the voodoo," put in Joel. "Miss Cathy's being haunted by little dolls that appear to suggest her imminent demise. Jolly good way to scare the poor thing to death, you know."

"Not my Cathy," said Brett stoutly. "Anyway, there's to be no monkey shines now. Papa's here. I'll tear that Bluebeard Amber limb from limb when I get hold of him."

He kept on saying things like that, with some very voluble assists from Joel, who surprised me by his own talkativeness. I was exceedingly glad I hadn't let Brett come immediately to Amber. I could just see the embarrassing, perhaps even dangerous, meeting between him and Michael Amber. I had wanted Brett down here because his presence was some protection in case I needed swift help, but I didn't like the sound of his rugged threats. I wanted his brain, not his brawn.

"How is your aunt?" I asked finally, hoping to change the subject. "And how is dear Unkie?" Not that I cared; the aunt had my hearty dislike, but it seemed the only topic of conversation that wouldn't lead to a parade of force. I wanted to ask, "How is the Southern Belle? Miss Scarlett of nineteen-ten," but I was polite about it.

He was surprised. "Fine, I guess. Haven't seen them for weeks."

"A brilliant lady," Joel put in, while I made silent faces to myself. "Lovely Southern creature, as I recall."

"Yes. Uncle's gone downhill, but the old girl's not hard to take, for fiftyish."

They were on safer ground now and could talk on this subject all day while I figured out how Brett might help me without running into Michael. I had hoped he would come brimful of ideas, but it appeared that his brightest thought was to "knock somebody out." This wouldn't solve anything, and it might result in hurrying the disaster.

They were still talking about dear old Aunt and Uncle when I began to listen again.

"She has your eyes, right enough, old chap," Joel was saying. "Or to be exact . . ."

"I know—I have hers." Brett raised an eyebrow, and I glanced at him, aware, as I had been in San Francisco, just how handsome those black eyes of his were.

"But now, I expect all that lovely blue-black mane of hers is more salt than peppery. It was getting that way, last time I saw her," and Joel sighed as though he had been mad about the woman. It was annoying, to say the least.

Brett grinned. "Yes. She's the only woman I've never heard say she wanted to be a blonde."

Joel lapsed into silence as though thinking of more serious things ahead and looked for the turnoff to his cottage. Brett put his arm around me and squeezed me, but I was growing too nervous to enjoy his touch.

"Isn't there some way we can get to the bottom of what's been happening?" I asked him hopefully.

"Sure. Sure. Give me five minutes alone with . . ."

I groaned. "No. No. I mean—using our brains."

Joel opened his mouth, stopped, then smiled and said nothing. Brett saw his expression.

"I get it. I'm handicapped before I start."

He was sweet about it, at any rate. And there was no getting around the fact that he might be very handy if someone tried to murder me. At least, Brett was capable of using his brawn.

"Speaking of Auntie," put in Brett, although we had got off that subject, "This isn't going to do you any harm in her eyes, hon."

"What?"

"I mean Amber, and all that."

Thanks a lot, I thought, but I merely smiled and pretended to be interested in the little, bumpy road we were on now, heading toward the sea, with the lush vegetation around us thinning out to twisted, stunted thickets through which we could see the white Atlantic rollers not too distant.

Presently, we drove down a small incline in a southerly direction, with the smoky funnel of La Soufriere looming up to the north of us, and Joel stopped the car. We walked through coarse sand to the little walk made of lava rocks which led to the rear of a charming beach cottage. I could see that the cottage fronted on the ocean and, although isolated, would be an ideal spot for a honeymoon or sun bathing or swimming in the surf below the wide veranda.

"Feel as if I ought to carry you over the threshold," Brett announced, and he looked as though he might try it. I laughed at the conversation, and that made Joel prick up his ears, but at that moment he stumbled over a loose rock in the lava walk, and Brett looked back, laughing at his expression.

"Don't look at it as if it's the rock's fault, old boy."

"'Fraid it is," said Joel, although he grinned at the accident. "Never was out of place before."

He unlocked the back door into a tiny entry, and as we walked in, admiring the Cotswold-cottage look of the interior, he went back out to the walk, saying, "Make yourselves at home. Forgot the provisions. We don't want friend Caldwell to starve, you know. Most inhospitable."

"Nice fellow," Brett said, and I agreed.

We heard a loud, hollow sound outside, as though one of the porous lava rocks had fallen upon another, and Brett said, "Good night! He's probably spilled everything."

We hurried outside and saw Joel Bingham standing on the lava walk. Two flat rocks had been shoved aside, leaving a gaping hole in the walk. It was not the gaping hole, however, that made Brett turn away with a startled expression and say to me, "Don't look."

"What do you mean?" He was blocking my way. "What is it? Tell me!"

I shoved him aside and saw what he was trying to hide from me, in the hole uncovered by the boulders . . . the thin, pale fingers curved palm-upward, almost into a claw. I knew with a horrible certainty that it was the graceful, satin-smooth hand of Cousin Isobel.

SIXTEEN

"GOOD GOD!" Brett was saying in a stupefied voice, "Who is it, anyway? What's it doing here?"

As I knelt and scratched away at the rocky sand, my hands were stiff with shock and fright. Joel began to remove other rocks, uncovering more and more, until I saw the back of her neatly coifed head, which had been crushed, and then, when I could again look at her, Joel had turned her face upward and I saw it, pitted by sand and pebbles where it had been pressed hard into the ground.

Joel's self-possession, his absolute calm, unnerved me more than Brett's silly questions.

"Is it?" Joel asked me.

I nodded. My nausea was such that I found it impossible to speak for a few minutes. Cousin Isobel couldn't have been dead too long, possibly overnight, but even this time lapse showed its signs. Her mouth was open, and her eyelids barely parted, enough so we could see that the pupils of her eyes had rolled upward in her death agony, and only the vein-flecked whites glistened now with a horrible life of their own.

. . . Miss Nell at the pool today. Now this. I thought, "I'll leave today! Any minute. Let them have Amber. Let them have the money, the power, the estate. Just leave me my life, my sanity. . . ."

"Well, for Christ's sake, isn't anyone going to tell me anything?" Brett complained. "What the hell is going on? Was this a cemetery, or what?"

As if aroused from sleep and still confused, Joel
189

looked up; he seemed to be staring through Brett and me in an abstracted way, as though he didn't see us. I wondered what he was really looking at in his mind's eye.

I backed away, tried to rise and failed until Brett lifted me to my feet. As he brushed me off, he murmured in a lower voice, "Is it someone you know? I mean—is it a crime, or was it just a—a burial?"

Joel came back to life. "Miss Isobel Amber," he said crisply. "And I think we can rule out—'just a burial.'"

"She left Amber last night in a taxi around eleven or so . . . unless . . ." I suddenly remembered Bouramie's words.

"Well?" Joel prompted me sharply, as though he were not quite so dazed as I supposed him to be.

"The housemaid says she saw Cousin Isobel walking toward the Tangerine Pool later in the evening. But I heard Soochi phoning for a taxi, and I heard it leave Amber."

"Yes, but what in the name of common sense is this woman doing here?" Brett wanted to know, echoing my thoughts. "If it is actually the woman I met in New York. God! What one blow can . . ."

"You asked an interesting question," Joel agreed drily.

Brett tried again to inject some sense into us.

"Hadn't someone better call the police or—or whatever?" he asked. "I mean—not that it's any business of mine. But, what with bodies strewn all over the place and murderers lurking around corners . . . I mean— for Cathy's sake, maybe we ought to get cracking."

Joel Bingham's backbone stiffened. He said in his most crisp British voice, "Precisely!" and leaving Cousin Isobel there, only half-covered and terribly vulnerable to sand and wind, he led us into the cottage. I was still looking back, wondering if I should put a sheet or something over her face, when Joel made a quick, muffled exclamation and added, "Now here's a devil of a note! I forgot. The telephone's· not connected. Well, there's nothing for it but to go . . ."

"Hey! How about that?" Brett interrupted, peering out the window. "A car's turning in here behind yours, old boy. Let's hope it's the police or—oh, God, no! It's Cathy's Bluebeard!"

"What!" I rushed to the window with Joel right behind me. My first reaction had been tremendous relief. Michael always knew how to handle things. But then I remembered Brett's presence, and I began to dread the encounter between them, for they were sure to have opposing ideas on anything, even Cousin Isobel's murder.

"What the deuce!" Joel muttered in my ear. He opened the door and went out on the walk to meet Michael as my cousin got out of his car. I watched Joel neatly avoid the overturned rocks and what lay crumpled up among them.

My heart seemed to be hammering all through my body, and I rested my head against the window pane for an instant. Brett, who had been watching the two men meet at Michael's car, put his hand on my shoulder without speaking.

"How did Michael know?" I asked myself. "How could he possibly know about this place, and what happened, unless he brought her here?"

I was not aware I had whispered this aloud until I felt Brett remove his hand and saw it clench into a fist.

"Probably came back to see how his latest body is cooling off!"

"Don't!"

"Well, Good Lord! If it is true—if he's mixed up in this, he could have killed you!"

I turned from the window, feeling completely spent. "Now you know why I sent for you."

The flippant, easy charm was gone from his face as he stared down at me. He held out his hands to me, offering me the protection I had so desperately been seeking these past few days. "Poor little Sugar. Fighting this rotten business all alone. Well . . . it won't be going on much longer. I'll see to our precious Cousin Michael, and that's a . . ."

"Very impressive, Mr. Caldwell," Michael said, standing in the doorway, while behind him, Joel looked from Brett to me and raised his eyebrows. "You might see to the police, as a beginning."

"Now, look here, Amber!" Brett began, advancing in a state of war. I got between them, wondering at the same time why Joel Bingham did nothing but cross his arms and stand in the doorway watching the two men calmly.

I gave out a banshee shriek, drowning the voices of both men, and although Michael stood there like a stubborn Rock of Gibraltar, not retreating an inch, Brett shrugged, looked at me and smiled sheepishly.

"All right. I'm talking out of turn. But God-Almighty, this fellow has a few questions to answer."

"Be more explicit," Michael ordered him, with icy self-assurance.

I was surprised, and impressed, when Brett did not give up, but answered directly, "For one thing, how did you get over here—at Bingham's place? What are you doing here?"

"Obviously someone has to do something—unless you propose to leave Miss Isobel Amber to the elements," Michael added with heavy-handed irony.

I looked at Joel, ready to help him remove Cousin Isobel while the two men argued, but he shook his head, with a meaning that puzzled me. Then he mouthed the word "evidence," and I shuddered.

Michael went on, "But although I cannot conceive how it could possibly be your business, I came to get my Cousin Catherine." He turned to Joel. "Can you tell how Isobel died? And how long ago?"

As he moved toward the door again, Joel stepped quickly, as though to help him with the body, but I felt that he wanted to be quite sure Michael touched nothing without a witness.

The two men studied that pitiful clump which had so recently annoyed me with its chic and good grooming and cool malice. With more curiosity than feeling (not that I blamed him for that), Brett went and stood over the two men, asking several times, "Anything I can do?"

Michael finally said impatiently, "I passed a cottage on the Cliff Road. Why the devil don't you walk over and call the authorities? Make yourself useful."

Brett nodded and without protest hurried up the road and out of sight.

Michael finished his examination under Joel's watchful eyes. "Well, it's clear she took a heavy blow across

192

the back of the skull," Michael said. "That must have done for her."

"Poor creature," murmured Joel.

I think his comment caught Michael off-guard, for he said more warmly than was his habit, "Yes. A vicious, rotten attack, strong enough to have killed a man, I should imagine." Then, as though his cold, level-headed view came to the fore, "But she *would* put her nose into affairs that didn't concern her! I warned her."

Joel's head went up sharply, and I caught my breath, but I reasoned that Michael's comment was perfectly innocent. He wad warned her repeatedly, in my presence, about her extraoardinary interest in other people's affairs. I wished I could tell Joel Bingham this, for I didn't need supernatural powers to read the suspicions that must be running through his mind.

Suddenly, in the cottage, the phone rang sharply. There seemed nothing odd in this and I watched Joel pass me and go in to pick up the old-fashioned phone. The horror of Cousin Isobel's death was still too much for me to encompass, and Joel Bingham had spoken for a moment or two apparently on matters involving Cross and Bingham, before I realized what was wrong with this scene. I stood there in the doorway prey to so many shocks that I must have revealed them on my face.

Michael stood up from Isobel's corpse and stared at me. "What is it?" he asked.

"Before you came, he said the phone was out of order."

"Oh? Interesting. Everything about Master Bingham grows interesting today. Come along!"

I was amazed. "But Joel said . . ."

"I'm sure it was edifying. Come along." He held out his hand to me, that strong, brown-gold hand looking stronger than ever by its lack of any jewelry. For an instant a thought flitted at the back of my mind. Something about his hand. Then I forgot what had troubled me. His gesture was insistent. Somewhat to my own surprise I obeyed him, following as he strode up the path toward his car. I had the same instinct as most independent modern women. I knew what to do when a masterly male ordered me about. I obeyed.

193

"But Michael, shouldn't we at least stay so they— nobody can falsify the evidence, or whatever people do?"

"I've seen enough, and I've got to get you home where you will be safe under the eyes of someone I can trust." (And whom could *I* trust, I wondered, but I said nothing.) He went on. "Isobel occupied very little part of my life, yet—more, I fancy, than that clerk and your loud-voiced boyfriend. Neither of them can falsify anything without my testimony against them, and I assure you, my testimony will outweigh theirs. There is one small problem remaining."

"Small?" I asked ironically.

"That an Amber should avenge her murder. I have things to do. I'll be busy with the police tonight."

I was glad he was going to handle this part of the terrible affair, for I did not feel physically equipped, being in a pretty shaky state. I knew I should have waited and made our excuses to Joel, waited for the police, but Joel had tricked us anyway, not to mention tricking Brett into trudging up the hill looking for a phone that was not disconnected.

"Nothing ruffles you, does it?" I asked now, not really expecting an answer to my sarcasm. "Not even the fact that I saw Miss Nell's ghost again—out at the pool today."

He made just the nasty (and always quite sound) observation I might have expected of him. "My child, if you hadn't been out at the pool, where you've no business being, you wouldn't have been ruffled by ghosts either."

I made one last effort to behave in the way Joel or Brett would have expected. "But the police? By the time they get there somebody may have—well, may have destroyed Isobel's body."

"Unlikely, unless Bingham is a sorcerer. Before I came after you, I called the police."

"Good heavens, why?"

"Did it ever occur to you that you yourself might have been lying there dead? All right, now, calm yourself; you aren't. But the police will be at Bingham's place now, and probably were there five minutes after you left. That was why I hurried. They would have questioned you, and in the end I couldn't have got you away so quickly."

Suspicious as always, I wondered if this concern for me accounted for his haste. "But won't the police wonder about your own disappearance?"

With that almost arrogant confidence I had noticed so often, Michael said simply, "The authorities know where to reach me."

We drove up onto the highway in silence. There was no arguing with such complete self-belief. Once we had come up from the beach, we could see plainly the plumes of black off to the north, where La Soufriere was still hidden in a cloud of steam, or whatever it is volcanoes emit to inconvenience all living things near them. The air had grown so sulphurous that my eyes watered, and I sneezed. We were driving directly into this shadowed landscape and were hindered as well by the approach of evening over the jungle-bordered road. But Michael seemed to know where he was going, even when his car lights failed to illuminate more than a few feet of the road ahead.

Then I saw that there were small fires far off to the right of us, among the decaying vegetation of the giant fern forest. Little flickers shot up now and then like dying embers. An earth tremor shook the road, and I had to grasp my seat with one hand and the door handle with the other. I began to feel giddy, and I glanced at Michael's impassive face. He recognized my fear and put one hand on mine on the seat for an instant, and I felt its strength, the warmth of its touch. I tried not to think of the coming night in that terrible Amber House, perhaps surrounded by licking tongues of volcanic mud, creeping closer and closer, around the cliff and through the fern forest.

"Yes," he said, reading my thoughts or guessing their direction. "That's the Dillingworth Plantation on your right. There will be difficulties over the crops this year."

"Has the volcano killed anyone today?"

"I doubt it, not at last reports, at any rate. Its just that these little lava spurs are annoying, and they burn out the land. It will be all over by midnight, I should think. Old Soufriere has probably stopped belching already. What you see is just the aftermath."

I changed the subject nervously. "Michael? How did you know I was at the Bingham place?"

"Soochi said you might be."

"Yes, but how did she . . . ?" It was beyond me. "I thought . . ."

He smiled a little to soften his reply. "Never *think*, Cathy. It is not one of your strong points."

I was half pleased at his mastery and half annoyed at his remark, and I sat silent, in a huff.

Michael maneuvered the car around a jog in the road, and we began to see a bumpy little river of lava crossing half the road ahead of us. I wanted to scream but restrained myself, fortunately, and we passed around it on the left side in the British fashion. We could see why it had gone no further across the road; it was cooling. Apparently it was the furthest advance of some spur of lava. There were no fires around now, and we could make out men at work in the fields not far from the road. The rest of the lava flow seemed to have taken a turn toward the sea on the east coast, just as it had two hundred years ago, when it had wiped out the pirate haven. I was relieved for a minute or two, but then I realized that the distant mountain looked as smoke-shrouded as ever.

I said anxiously, "This road is awfully dangerous—or will be later in the evening. There'll be no light at all except the car lights, and they won't do much good. Shouldn't we warn Brett and Joel?"

He peered ahead through the murky twilight that pushed in at us beyond the windshield. "There is a little store in the clearing somewhere around here. I'll see if they have a phone."

"How on earth could Isobel have gone out to Mr. Bingham's?" I asked, talking to myself.

"I rather think she was carried there," Michael said as calmly as he had discussed the dangerous road ahead. "And I shouldn't be at all surprised to learn that she was murdered at Amber."

I pulled my hands together and sat with them clutched tightly, so tightly locked that they began to ache. "Am I to sleep there tonight?" I asked.

"Certainly." Then he smiled that rare and gentle smile which illuminated his face. "David will be there to look out for you. No one will be bashing your head in, if that is what you are worrying about."

This was supposed to relax me, but unfortunately, it failed of its purpose. I wished I could be as sure as Michael was. It was all very well for him to put his trust in David Earle, but I hadn't known David all my life, as he did. For all I knew, David might be the very man who had murdered Cousin Isobel.

We pulled up at the side of the road, under the stretching fingers of a giant fern, and I saw what I took to be only a cane cutter's shack, built up from the ground on high piles, but it was apparently the store Michael had mentioned. While Michael got out and went into the store, I occupied my time with imagining all sorts of terrors hiding in the damp blackness under the shack, among those rotting piles. I could just see the clumps of greenery, ferns and other less familiar growths, and with no effort at all, I could have made out weird faces and horrid phantoms, grinning at me. All the while, the air was full of jumbled odors, sometimes the sulphurous haze, and then a whiff of rotten vegetation, like flowers too long in a vase.

Michael came out very soon and got into the car, starting the motor without a word.

"Did you get them?"

"Yes. Called the Commission, too, to prevent anyone's coming in the opposite direction."

I was relieved. "I'm glad. Brett and Joel could have taken a nasty spill back there and maybe have been killed if they didn't know about that stream of lava."

"Small loss," he said as the car jumped forward.

I stiffened at this inhuman remark, and he laughed.

"All right. I'm sorry. God knows there has been enough death around about lately. You musn't mind what I am saying. I've been trying to unravel something."

"What?"

"The less little girls like you know, Cathy, the better."

I was too stunned by the day's happenings, and by the approaching night, with that accursed volcano still playing about us, to resent his remark. I said nothing more until we reached Amber. As though psychic, David Earle came out on the steps and opened the door

197

for me. I was about to get out when Michael held me back by my arm. I turned and, caught completely off-guard, felt his kiss upon my cheek. Like most women at such a moment, I was completely won over, and as I got out, I looked back quickly, smiling in a perfectly inane way, and got his answering smile.

"David, take good care of her," he called out, and David nodded. David, I noticed, was not amused by any of this.

Michael drove away, and I went in the house with David. I wondered how much I should tell him about Cousin Isobel's death, and I was astonished when he brought up the subject himself.

"Has Michael found out any more about Miss Isobel's murder?"

"What do you know about it?" I asked sharply.

"He called me a few minutes ago."

I couldn't think of a single thing to say to that. Had Michael actually had time to call David Earle and the Commission, as well as to warn Joel about the road, during the brief time we stopped at the store on stilts?

I was going to my room but thought better of it and went, instead, to find Soochi. She and Bouramie were in the dining room arranging flowers on the table. Bouramie looked cowed at the sight of me, remembering, no doubt, our last meeting at the Tangerine Pool today, but I ignored her. Soochi was her usual calm self. It may have been my imagination that she was stiffly on guard.

"Soochi, how did you know I was going to Mr. Bingham's cottage today?"

Her delicate black eyebrows raised in surprise as though she had been expecting quite a different remark. "Me, ma'am?"

"Yes. Why did you tell Mister Michael that I was over at the Bingham cottage?"

This time I knew she was being watchful, choosing her words with care. "Was that what—Mister Michael told you?"

"Certainly. How else would he have known where to look for me?"

Her fingers kept working on the top-heavy hibiscus she was placing in a bowl, and she gave this her attention for a time during which I might have counted five.

When she turned her head and looked at me again, with a sickening, false smile, she said sweetly, "Then if Mister Michael told you so, it must be so. Mustn't it, ma'am?"

"Yes, but *is* it?"

"Oh, but of course! Do not ask me how I knew, ma'am. For you must ask Mister Michael that, too, since he knows so much more than I do."

I felt a fiendish urge to slap her, but I managed to retain enough dignity to walk out of the dining room without further degrading myself or Michael. In my own room I tried to gather whether she had said yes or no, and what it really added up to.

I ate a light dinner alone. David Earle did not come to the table, and yet I had the feeling that he was never far away. Several times in the evening I heard a footstep on the portico outside my window, and once I caught sight of David walking past.

Ever since my arrival home there had been sieges of distant drum beating, somewhere in the fern forest, probably a gathering of Dr. Torri's voodoo friends. Were they beating out the news of Isobel's death or, perhaps, anticipating my own? This drumming, combined with an occasional shake from stubborn Soufriere, gave me a thoroughly unpleasant time. When I saw David walk by I thought: If I knew as much as he does about all this, I would know who was back of it. Michael was mistaken to trust him, or to trust anyone. As for me, I determined to be on my own guard, no matter how protective or otherwise David Earle proved to be tonight. And after tonight I would leave Saint Cloud by first available transportation.

I had not counting on the phone ringing, however. Bouramie came to call me, and before I answered it I made her precede me into the lounge. It was cowardly of me, but I was beyond caring about appearances.

It was Brett calling me, a Brett I had never heard before, his voice tense, keyed up, and furiously angry.

"Good God! Cathy, are you all right? And are you alone?"

"Yes, of course. Why?"

"Did you and Bluebeard come back by the central north-south highway?"

I said we had. I had a horrid premonition of what was coming.

He asked, "Did you have any trouble?"

"Yes. There was some lava, and the road was dangerously rutted in places. . . ."

"Well, for Christ's sake, couldn't you warn a guy? We didn't get away from the police until an hour ago. And there was nothing wrong with Bingham's phone. You could have called us any time. Or let the highway people call us."

"I'm sorry. I thought Michael—I thought we had."

"Well, Cathy, you've got a lot to learn about your precious cousin. After all that hassle with the police, then this had to happen! I was driving, and we damned near cracked our skulls off. Overturned in a foul, stinking ditch."

"But you couldn't have. I mean, it was on the right side. If you were coming from the opposite direction— yes. But . . ."

"I'm an American, remember, sugar? I drive on the right side."

"But Michael tried to—" I began, when he cut me off harshly. "Bingham and I know what Michael tried to do. Sweetie, we know a lot more than he gives us credit for. We know . . . that is, Joel suspects . . . how all these weirdo things happened and why that woman today was murdered. And you've got a pretty fair idea who it is he suspects!"

I don't want to hear any more, I told myself. I want to hang up and not hear the rest. I took the phone and sat down on the wicker couch. I felt myself shaking and held on tightly to the phone. Please . . . please go away and leave me alone, I prayed silently. I don't want to know it if my suspicions are true.

SEVENTEEN

"Cathy . . . Cathy . . . are you there? Can you hear me? What the devil is all that racket I hear?"

"Just the good old voodoo drums. Think nothing of them. I can hear you."

"You scared me to death. You are alone, aren't you? He's not forcing you to talk or anything. Just say 'yes' if he is there listening."

"No. No. No!"

"Thank God. You had me worried. All right. Here's the scoop, hon. Your Bluebeard may have committed those crimes himself. That's how old Joel and I see it."

"No!"

"Is there any conceivable reason why he wouldn't have warned us about that road?"

I fumbled desperately. "Well, there must be—it's obvious he wouldn't have let you take that road if he thought . . ."

"Is it, honey? Stop and think. He knows you sent to the States for me . . ." I started to protest, and he interrupted, very much the masterly fellow, exactly as I had always wanted him to be, but not at the expense of Michael Amber. "No, listen. You know as well as I do, you may be next to get it in the neck. We're going to take you out of there, and fast! If they want to make you an heiress, let them do it long-distance. Let 'em translate it all into dollars. You're getting out of that hole tomorrow morning."

My first reaction was overwhelming relief. I longed to get out of this mouldy mausoleum with its wall of damp, grasping ferns and its ghosts who prowled at midnight—and sometimes in broad daylight! But—to leave Michael without knowing whether he was innocent or guilty? He would be so angry, and I couldn't blame him. He had left David Earle to guard me, and now I would prove I didn't trust him or his efforts to protect me. Suppose, though, that Michael *was* back of all these horrors?

Those idiotic drums in the fern forest occasionally seemed to recede momentarily, and just as I was hoping they had stopped, they would roar up again, a tantalizing sound that made me want to scream. Even as I silently cursed the superstitions of the field workers, the whole house trembled under the smouldering rage of La Soufriere and I had to grip the telephone and hold on tightly to keep from crying out. Not content with that, I began to imagine noises out in the hall beyond the lounge that had nothing to do with the creaking of the old house under the repeated earth shocks. To my overwrought imagination, these were the sounds of prowlers creeping over the wooden floors—very near the open door of the lounge.

Brett was right. I had had enough. "Well then, I'm with you."

"That's my girl," Brett commended me, not guessing the state of my nerves. "I'll borrow a jalopy from old Joel and pick you up as early as possible. What time?"

I stopped to sneeze before replying. I had begun to notice the faint, acrid odor of sulphur seeping into the house, just an added reminder of our proximity to the volcanic monster. I didn't want to stay here a moment longer than I had to. I only hoped I'd still be alive tomorrow.

"How about eight o'clock? We can eat in town and take one of Joel Bingham's company boats over to Charlotte Amalie."

"And catch the plane from there. Fine. I'll have to have Joel give me directions. I'll be out in front of your place around eight."

"No, wait!" I had a sudden thought. "You might not be able to handle things if David Earle should be around. I mean . . . if he is working for Michael. He has connections. He might try to use force."

"Sugar, I didn't spend four years in college cram-

202

ming ancient Greek. How do you think State made the Sugar Bowl that year? Old Yours Truly."

Even in my present state of shudders, I couldn't help smiling at this bravado.

"Brett, dear all-American, you're not on the football field now. You just might be tackling a half-dozen murderers. Get some help, for goodness sake."

"Fine. I'll take old Joel along. Not much of a tackle, but a hell of a talker. I'll let him keep them occupied while I carry off my little sugar. What say?"

"Good. I'll be waiting at eight o'clock." Joel Bingham was level-headed. He wouldn't let Brett come off half-cocked. Then I remembered. Brett was already hanging up when I cried out to him.

"No, Brett. Wait! I don't trust Joel. What about his telephone today?"

"What about it?" He sounded a little impatient at this latest vagary of mine. I hardly blamed him.

"He said it was disconnected. But it rang while I was there."

"Oh, that. Puzzled me, too. But there's nothing to it, hon. He told the power people to disconnect it and they didn't. Perfectly simple. Much more simple than your Michael's not warning us. Explain that away!" he ended in triumph.

He was right. I still couldn't think of one good reason why Michael should have lied to me about that. And yet he had. I had asked him the direct question, and he had lied.

I was torn between two loyalties—my old friendship with Brett and my new infatuation with my cousin. I couldn't help liking Brett and feeling responsible for him in a tender sort of way, and I felt that he might be endangering himself, coming alone as he planned, or with only Joel Bingham, a slim and doubtful buckler. On the other hand, I couldn't very well stay here to be murdered, and I should certainly be the next after Cousin Isobel. I began to think of ways to bolster Brett's position, but no matter whom I called in, it would be someone who owed allegiance to Michael Amber, and I would be running an even greater risk of giving Michael more help.

"Oh, Brett, do be careful! When you come tomorrow, park up the road, not directly in front of the house. I'll walk up there and wait for you. And for heaven's sake, come from the direction of town, not the way you did this evening. I don't want you dumped into a ditch again, on my account."

"Thanks for the warning, hon. A little late, but that's beside the point. I'll be there."

"I wish it were over."

He chuckled and said expressively, "If you want the truth, so do I!"

I laughed at his lack of heroism, but I wished very much that it were this time tomorrow evening, with everything neatly solved and the guilty party someone totally strange to me. Nevertheless, I wanted no harm to come to Brett. He was sometimes a great deal more human than my austere and dominating Cousin Michael. I began to wonder if, in some odd way, I liked Brett as well as I liked my cousin, but differently. With a protective feeling. But I would not spoil him by telling him now.

Never in a million years would anyone imagine Brett Caldwell capable of doing something really heroic. And I doubted if Joel Bingham was any better prepared. If Michael really were guilty, I was reasonably certain that neither Brett nor Joel, nor the two together, could outsmart him, and I was absolutely sure I couldn't.

Meanwhile, to keep me company, there were the damnable voodoo drums, the annoying, nose-tickling smell of sulphur and burning wood, and one tiny, defiant shake from the volcanic goddess as I set the phone back in place. What with the racket of the drums and the worry over whether my departure tomorrow morning would be disputed by force, I left the lounge with a roaring, throbbing headache and immediately stumbled over David Earle, down on his knees in the dark of the hallway.

"What on earth!"

He got up, brushing off the knees of his white dungarees, apologizing for my near spill, but in no way discomposed, as if he spent half his time crawling around on dark floors.

"Beg pardon, Miss Cathy. Hope you didn't hurt yourself. Mister Michael lost a ring this morning when he was washing up. Thought it might have rolled out of the door and . . . into a corner."

Not believing a word of this, I said caustically, "You'd have better luck with a few lights on. Unless you like being bitten by spiders and whatnot."

Behind the overseer my bedroom door stood ajar, and the single shaft of light from my room made his unexpected smile curiously unnerving to me, for like the Cheshire cat's, it was the only thing I could make out in his darkly handsome face.

"You needn't be afraid of spiders, Miss Cathy. They won't hurt you here."

I ignored this and started to pass him, but my head was aching abominably and I exclaimed, half to myself, "Why is heaven's name are they drumming at this hour?"

He stopped grinning. There was a breathless little hush between us, as though in attacking those drums I had attacked him and his people. I became aware that his shadowed eyes were intent, not upon the direction of the drumbeat, but upon me.

"It's a kind of lodge meeting, Miss Cathy. They don't mean any harm. It's like Doctor Torri says. It lets go of a lot of their problems, just having a little fun at those meetings. Even Miss Ellen used to go. Said it was as good as visiting a psychiatrist any day. They don't believe it above half."

He needn't soothe me as if I were a child. He must have got the trick from Michael, and Michael was the only one from whom I enjoyed it.

"I heard the same drumbeat today, Mr. Earle. I know what it means—that someone has died."

I opened my bedroom door, thinking I had certainly got in the last word, but I had underestimated David Earle, whose deep voice came out of the darkness behind me.

"No, ma'am. This one means someone is *about* to die."

I slammed the door upon what I took to be a decidedly misplaced humor and set a chair up under the doorknob. If David Earle were to be my guardian tonight, I had one wish—to be protected from my protector!

"Lost a ring" indeed! The man must think I was a complete fool. Obviously he had been trying to overhear my telephone conversation. I attempted to remem-

205

ber if I had said anything that he might find useful. He had undoubtedly heard my arrangements for meeting Brett tomorrow. That was something to worry about.

I got ready for bed and lay down with every nerve on the alert for something—I didn't know what. The normal sounds of the household died away, but not those unearthly night noises, each of which was magnified out of all sense by my nerves. The creaking boards of the floor were something I was prepared for, as I faced the prospect of a night of earth tremors. But then—what of that light, brushing sound . . . as though someone passed my door, or even listened there briefly, with garments brushing the wooden panel? And the peculiar liveliness of the garden, where the sighing breeze managed to sound like the distant babble of light, eery voices. . . .

Gradually, sleep overpowered me in spite of myself. Even the distant drums seemed muffled. There were no more earthquakes. I closed my eyes and slept.

Several times I awakened with the feeling that some slight sound had aroused me, either inside my room or very close outside. Once I sat up and looked out the window. Under the shadow of the portico, David Earle was just moving quietly away, like some furtive night prowler.

Would we be able to slip by him in the morning? I knew he would call Michael if he thought he needed help. I dreaded leaving without a word to Michael, but when I thought of that, I was equally afraid of departing under his eyes and witnessing a nasty quarrel and perhaps even violence between him and Brett.

But the hands of my little travel clock on the old-fashioned bureau moved on inexorably.

Shortly after three A.M., I was sure I heard a hand stealthily trying my garden door. With a sudden start that gave me a severe case of nervous indigestion, I sat straight up in bed, and almost before I could concentrate on the danger, I sprang out of bed and ran to the door. Let Miss Nell be standing there! I dared her to. I snapped the lock noisily and opened the door, peering out. There was a drugged stillness over the dark garden that one notices only in the dead of night. Then a large, dark hand closed on my shoulder from the portico shadows.

"Go inside!" David Earle ordered me. I could not see his face, but I recognized his mastery in that command. "Stay there. Don't come out until after sunrise. You hear me?"

Trembling, wondering at his authority, I obeyed, but when I was inside my room again I got hold of myself and slammed the door to let him know I wasn't the scared child he thought me. Shaking with anger, I forgot my fear, and presently, I slept.

It was after five when I awakened again, this time to the sharp buzz of the telephone in the lounge, and I got up apprehensively, sneezing at the heavy, sulphurous air and wondering, as one always does, what calamity caused someone to call Amber House at this unearthly hour. I threw off the bed covers and slipped my feet into the first shoes they found handy, a pair of thong sandals whose spiked heels were far too high for this time of day. Then I went to the window and looked out at the garden. It was already visible in the daylight, with the big, too-heavy heads of the blood-red hibiscus and unidentifiable blue flowers beginning to perk up, to face me across the lawn and portico, watchful as ever, some of them nodding like wise old gossips in the murky dawn.

Even though I was waiting for it, I was jarred by the sharp knock on my door. Soochi was in the hall. She had a shawl over her head, hiding her turban, the way she looked when she went marketing in the morning. She stepped into the room with me, pushing me aside. Her slanting eyes glittered in an odd way. They had lost all the serene calculating look that had used to unnerve me, and she seemed unable to control them. What had upset this cool, insolent creature?

"Please, they say there is no time. We are to hurry. La Soufriere is angry. Pack a few things, please. We must leave."

"What? The volcano? You mean this house is actually in danger?" It was incredible. Besides, Michael had said the threat was all but over.

She saw me staring at her as though she had gone crazy, which, as a matter of fact, I began to suspect, and she shook her head. I had felt no quakes for hours, but the air was thick and mephitic, making me cough,

207

and the sound of my own coughing did much to convince me of what she was saying.

"Quick! My mother died from La Soufriere. There was a panic among the field hands many years ago, and they rushed in here. She was knocked down and trampled. The lava did not kill anyone, but the panic did. And this time the lava path is closer. Come!" She started picking up my things—scattered clothing, my makeup case . . . Her slender, sallow fingers trembled, and she kept dropping things. I began to help her.

"Who was that on the phone?"

"Doctor Torri. He is at the Volcanic Institute. There is a new—what they call—plug blown, on the south slope. This has not happened in two hundred years. The highway to Port Anne is pocked with lava tongues. We go the other way, across the Shore Road. We must carry things. As few as possible, he says."

I hurriedly put on lingerie and a sundress and then a knitted stole, and in ten minutes I was ready to join her as she carried my makeup case, weighted with odds and ends she had picked up, into the hall. I could see Bouramie in the distance just leaving the front veranda. She headed up the road as she usually did early in the morning on shopping errands, but she was hurrying a little faster today, I thought. I started toward the front of the house, but as I passed the lounge the phone rang again and I answered it. Soochi stood nervously in the hall looking first toward the road in front of the house, and then at the garden in back, which must have seemed a haven against the sort of panic in which her mother had been killed.

It was Brett calling again. He sounded more than a little uneasy. "Hon, have you heard the news?"

"Yes, yes. We're leaving now."

He took a big breath. His nervousness was contagious, and I wished that in this crisis he could borrow some of that courage he had evinced last night on the phone.

"Look, sugar, I can't get over the highway. I guess they told you. I'm going to meet you same place as planned, but I'm taking the long shore road around the south end of the island and I'll bring up somewhere along the East Shore Road. That's like I said . . . beyond the fern forest back of Amber. Got it?"

"No, wait! We can't go through the forest! It isn't even light yet."

"Sugar, we've got no choice, old Joel says. He says it's that or nothing. He's driving me. He says for you to come straight along the forest path from Amber to the Shore Road. It'll take us about an hour and . . ." He stopped. My heart almost stopped at the same time. What had happened to him? Then I recognized the faint sounds as he took his hands off the mouthpiece of the phone. There was a murmur in the background. To my great relief, Brett's voice came back to me. "Okay. Okay. . . . That's what I said. Hon, Joel says we'll be there in an hour and fifteen minutes, providing the whole damned island doesn't blow all to hell. It'll take you a little less time to get through the jungle. Just wait on the road for us."

"All right." I didn't like it, but I didn't like being toasted crisply here at Amber either. "We'll wait." I was about to hang up when he called my name. This time his voice warmed me as I had hoped it would when he first spoke.

"Cathy, hon, take care of yourself. Don't let anyone at Amber know unless you can trust them."

"I have to," I said, speaking as low as possible. "I don't want her—anyone running to warn David Earle that I'm leaving."

"No, no, for God's sake! That's all we need, having that guy around. Well, promise me you won't stray off the path. No side ventures. It's a hell of a thing to ask you, but Joel says it's perfectly safe."

Thanks a lot, Mr. Bingham, I thought silently. It might be perfectly safe to good old Joel, but in a place where I had already seen one ghost in broad daylight, I wondered if I would see more than ghosts at this hour of the morning. For the first time, I was relieved that Soochi was accompanying me.

"How serious is it, Brett? The volcano, I mean."

"Who knows? It's just a precaution. But I want no part of it. And we've got to get you out of Amber anyway, so this is as quick a way as I know of. We'll be moving so fast they won't have time to work up anything against you. Besides, the volcano business will keep them all occupied. Now, take care of yourself, hon. See you in a little over an hour." He made a sound which I took to be the blowing of a kiss, but it hardly served to calm me. When I put the phone back and glanced at the doorway, Soochi was watching me like a serpent hypnotized into immobility.

I said, "We are going through the fern forest to the Shore Road." And then, being doubly cautious, I added, "You go before me."

For the first time since the volcanic confusion arose, I saw the flicker of a smile cross her lips. Then it was gone and she was alert and tense again.

"Yes, ma'am."

I wondered if she would try to tell David Earle of our intentions, once she got out of my sight, so I did not let her do so. I could thank the old volcano for one thing. It provided me with a way of escaping from this house without the overseer's knowledge, and it would prevent any scene between Brett and Michael, such as I had envisioned all night. I began to think better of the jungle path and its ghostly dangers. At the same time, as I followed Soochi out to the garden, I was mentally framing a letter to Michael, explaining how I felt so unsafe and had returned to San Francisco, and—just to be quite sure—enclosing my address. He would hardly come clear to San Francisco just to kill me. On the other hand, he might come there if he had been at all sincere in his feeling for me. There was always the possibility that he was innocent, and in that case, I didn't want to break off every tie with him, only those dangerous ties which bound me to Amber.

The little cat, Soochi, saw me looking quickly over my shoulder, so obviously trying to avoid anyone who might report my departure to David Earle, and she stopped and said to me with something of her old insolence, "Mr. Earle is down the highway with the road menders. Should we tell him we are taking the jungle path?"

"No," I replied coolly, trying not to let her make me nervous. "Don't bother on my account."

Shrouded in the thick, smoky fog at dawn, the garden and the fern forest beyond waved before my eyes like a damp and desolate primeval swamp. Now, on the

210

verge of escape, I hesitated. I would much prefer leaving Amber by the highway. But there was David Earle to consider. Suppose he stopped me. What then? He had been forceful enough in the night when I had merely stuck my head out, with no intention of leaving my room. And what had he said about staying inside until after sunrise? It would not be sunrise for another half-hour. Anything could happen in the meantime. And Brett and Joel would wait in vain, perhaps risking their own safety, if I didn't make the rendezvous. I could not risk failing to meet them. It would have to be the jungle path. But I made up my mind to get through that in record time, not stopping for a dozen ghostly Miss Nells.

As though she guessed my dilemma, Soochi dragged her sandalled feet, scuffed at the lawn underfoot, and set down my makeup case, while she swung a small overnight bag of her own from her other hand. She, who had been so excited ten or fifteen minutes ago, was now the picture of nonchalance, once it had been decided that we should get out of Amber House. Her whole attitude was a challenge to my courage, and I picked up the carpetbag that contained a few other hastily packed garments and prepared to follow her. She began to walk rapidly, yet preserving the grace that had always seemed so eerily reptilian to me. I kept my eyes on the bright pattern of her shawl, wondering why it interested me, but it was a beacon light to follow in this tangled morass.

As I hurried after her, past the boundary marking the end of the Amber garden, I was at once tightly surrounded and enclosed by the greedy giant ferns, and I glanced through a single opening to the north and saw the crown of La Soufriere appear for an instant against a dirty brown sky. It looked harmless enough. I would not have guessed it could cause me to rush through a dangerous jungle in the foggy dawn. My high-heeled shoes sank deeply into the spongy earth, so I removed them, and in a very short time my bare feet were muddy and cold. It had been stupid of me not to come prepared. I must have been more than usually panicked. The thought angered me, and I slowed down, choosing my path with care. This caused Soochi to vanish ahead of me where the path twisted around an enormous piece of vegetation that looked as though a dozen tree trunks were laced together by entangling vines. I was just about to call to her when she stuck her head around the huge, wet and mouldy tree trunk and stared at me, her oblique eyes unblinking and inhuman in their total lack of expression.

I was beginning to find myself a trifle out of breath, and that, combined with my irrational dislike of Soochi, made me demand crossly,

"What are you looking at?"

"Me, Miss Cathy? I thought I saw Mister David. That's all."

Before I could control my instinctive reaction I jumped nervously. My foot, spinning around so I could look back along the path, trod down twigs and fern fronds that were half-sunk in the slimy ooze formed by the nightly rains. Tiny jungle insects, a part and color of the scene, rustled off into the covering forest. I was furious with myself for having yielded to this cowardly fear, reminding myself that I would very soon be out of this possible danger.

I saw nothing, of course, except the long fern fronds still swaying from my swift passage, but dimly, swallowed up in the immense congestion of the forest, I heard David Earle's voice call, "Back here, the rest of you! To the house!"

I was tremendously relieved.

More faintly now, the overseer said, "I'll go with . . ." Whether I was to be the object of this search, I could not hear, for his voice was blotted out by the quick flutter of a scarlet-breasted jungle bird winging up above the tree tops, perhaps frightened by the distant voices. It flew straight up into the sky, which had begun to take on more of the hue of daylight so that the smoky grey-brown color was gradually becoming a dirty orange. It hurt my eyes, and I stared toward Soochi, squinting a little.

She laughed. There was no reason for it, and the queer, mirthless sound might well have been made by the strange bird that took wing.

Coming toward her I challenged directly, "I know you hate me, Soochi. I don't really care. But just tell me why. I'm curious."

I was pushing foliage out of our way as we moved.

212

What she would have said if the ground underfoot hadn't shaken suddenly from a little earth tremor, I have no idea. But the quake made her rock a moment uncertainly, and she reached out, grabbing my arm to steady herself.

She seemed to find fresh amusement in this, and to my astonishment she half-whispered in a melodramatic voice quite unlike her usual tones, "Sister! You lend me your arm. How like a sister, dear Miss Cathy! Not so high-and-mighty is my Sister Cathy when we are alone with La Soufriere. It was different with my Sister Ellen. She it was who leaned on me!" Her fingers tightened in the flesh of my arm, and the sudden twinge made me snap the wet fern frond so hard it broke off in our faces, showering us with water. It would have been ludicrous but for Soochi's tinkling metallic laughter.

"You think I am joking? Oh no, Miss Cathy. Your precious, arrogant mama left Papa Richard when she learned who my father was."

The curious thing is, I believed her instantly, without the slightest proof. I was very calm. Even my steps slowed, and I made a great effort to see exactly where I was going on this treacherous little path.

"Your mother worked at Amber? That would be after the death of Ellen's mother?"

Soochi hesitated. I wondered if she were thinking up some lies, but either the nearness of danger from the volcano or the failure of her inventive powers made her say abruptly, "The marriage lines—they mean so much to you people. But you are the aliens here. Here the marriage lines are not so good as loving, the way my mother loved Mister Richard. She died before your precious Miss Catherine married Mister Richard. And Papa Richard promised me—over her grave—that I would have half of Amber. The rest for Miss Ellen, who did not know that the stupid, funny little Soochi was her sister. That is how it was." She jerked her hand away from me in a sudden, unexpected fury. "But you lie . . . all of you! As Mister Richard lied to me. It is the way with you."

The conclusion I drew was ghastly. "So you tried to frighten me and the others into panic and death! And then to kill . . ." I stared at her, conscious of a creeping horror that this monstrous creature must have destroyed her own father, her own sister . . . her cousin . . . yet who could guess what another would have done in her place, a servant in her father's house? Cut out of all inheritance, cut out even by a woman like myself who had to be brought thousands of miles to this place which had been her familiar home since birth.

At my accusation she burst out sharply, "The rest— the terror—yes. But not the death. I helped to push that hideous old Miss Nell out into Mister Michael's car. But she was dead before the car struck. Dead for hours. We—we frightened her to death, with the ghost of Miss Ellen. But that was because she was weak. The killing . . . that was my husband's idea. My own man. With the marriage lines. All proper and legal."

"Who . . . ?"

Something loud and sharp, like the breaking of a gigantic tree branch, cut the heavy air somewhere in the jungle behind us.

"These crimes were your husband's idea?"

"Of course. I told him who my father was. And my father's promise. He said he would marry me and help me to take what was mine. I have Papa Richard's letters to me . . . his feeling for his 'love daughter' as he called me."

"Oh, no!" I whispered, sickened. There were two of them in it.

"Oh, yes," she mimicked me. "My man and me, we were married on Haiti. So they would not know here. But Ellen saw us. To keep her quiet, he made love to her. But she knew it was wrong. It was amusing . . . very funny, Miss Cathy. I used to laugh to see her leave Amber all solemn and proper. And to know she would look like a harlot when she met . . . my husband. She thought it pleased him for her to look so."

"And so you killed her."

She shrugged, said almost in her old emotionless voice, "Not me. It was him, my man."

"You monster!"

"You do not hear me," she said as if trying to reason with a child. "My husband is the one with the brain to think of these things. Not me. He killed them. I would . . . never think to do things the way he does. He is very smart!"

"I'm sure he must be!"

Her face crumpled into a sort of emotion, like her look this morning when she had told me of the volcano, and she added a curious postscript to her horrifying confession, "There have been so many deaths. Too many. I am glad it is almost over."

"Who is your husband?" I cut in quickly, when we both heard David Earle's voice, so close he seemed almost within sight of us.

Soochi's eyes widened. She was in a panic. "NO, NO! Quick! There is enough killing. No more!"

As I started to run, she pulled at my arm. "Not any more. There is enough. You understand? This way."

"Is David Earle the one?" I demanded, scrambling breathlessly after her into the fern jungle and away from the path.

"Yes, yes. But we have had enough. You go away, leave Amber if I show you how?"

I was in no condition to speak, but she apparently took my silence and numb terror for an assent. Her lithe and sinuous body made a way for us in some mysterious fashion so that not more than a minute passed before we were completely swallowed up in the dripping forest, so tightly locked in that without Soochi I should never have been able to recognize which growths would let us pass and which were impregnable.

By turning away from the path we avoided the clearing where Dr. Torri's Voodoo Lodge Meetings (as I thought of them) took place, and where our pursuer certainly would have seen us. I was conscious of the great physical effort we were making but at the same time my mind was full of the horror of my sister, Ellen's, miserable life, her love for that scoundrel David Earle and her death at his hands. Again I was running, running, through the dreadful brown mist, knowing all the time that I ran toward the Tangerine Pool, which was death, as in my nightmare. I knew that we would be approaching the pool at any moment, from the steep and muddy west side. When Soochi parted the ferns ahead of us, I suddenly made out the lava chair which was on the opposite side of the pool from where we would come out.

At the same time, a blinding orange light pierced the entire scene, and I had to cover my eyes from its intensity. Soochi slowed now and carefully made her way to the muddy little ledge above the pool. Half-blinded, I followed her, putting one foot forward cautiously until we came out of the thicket and stood on the brink, feeling the mud and slime yield under us, inexorably drawing us to the lip of the pool. Staring downward, I could see now that this glaring orange light, reflected up from the Tangerine Pool, was the sunrise. The hideous evil eye that had bothered me yesterday was twice as frightful today, so blinding that I could see nothing around the pool itself, only the glare. I shoved my hands over my eyes, and at the same instant was assailed from the side by a sudden shove of such force that I slid out to the edge of the pool and was barely able to keep from plunging into the very pupil of that horrible orange eye. It was Soochi behind me, her red-lipped smile gleaming over her white teeth.

I thought of poor Brett and Joel waiting patiently fifteen minutes away, Brett with his big football muscles so capable of handling this little devil at my side, and without realizing the absurdity of the cry, I screamed at the top of my lungs:

"Brett! Brett! Help me!" as if my voice would carry clear to the end of the fern forest where he and Joel waited for me.

Dropping her shawl, Soochi came at me again, but this time I was prepared, and even though I was still partially blinded and saw her in a blaze of orange glare, I managed to sidestep as swiftly as ever Brett had done on the gridiron. She caught herself just in time, wavering an instant. Then she licked her lips, grinning at something behind me . . . something I could not see.

"Well then," she said to that Thing behind me, "you are almost late."

Without daring to look back and leave myself open to another of Soochi's attacks, I stepped gingerly around her shawl. I knew now why it had bothered me. I had already seen a torn scrap of it here at the pool, where Ellen had died. Small wonder that she had been forced to steal the scrap from my room.

I withdrew very slowly, one step at a time, half-expecting to see the ghost of Miss Nell when I turned.

216

And in a sense, a play-acting sense, it was. For now, at last, I could see the full face of my enemy, the face so long hidden in the depth of my nightmare . . . the face I had run from all my life and yet had never really known before.

EIGHTEEN

I RECOGNIZED THE stance the ghostly Miss Nell had
taken yesterday, the flat-footed lean, monolithic pose
when her "ghost" had frightened me nearly to death.
With the addition of heavy powder and makeup to
simulate her wrinkles and papery skin, some veiling
and Miss Nell's clothes, this could have been she. But
this was a man, in a brown suede jacket, staring at me
without the powdery wrinkles and draperies that he
must have used as Miss Nell. And a moment ago he had
stood there—no doubt with this same endearing smile,
for he had great charm—and watched Soochi try to
murder me.

"You really did call me, you know," Brett said in his
warm voice.

I felt the dry harshness in my throat so it was hard
to get a word out. "Why me?" I croaked.

He shrugged. "You were just unlucky enough to be
the next heir, sugar. It's been a long campaign. A long,
tiresome deal. If you knew how long, you'd see my side
of it."

I could have laughed at Soochi, this incredible half-
sister of mine, thinking of her trust in Brett. He might
be her husband, but it was Amber he wanted. He could
not help thinking of it as his own. "My side of it," he
had said. "My Amber," he had meant.

He wasn't excited like Soochi. Somehow, in spite of
the monstrous thing he said, he managed to be reasona-
ble and sympathetic in pleading his cause. "I met Soo-

chi on Haiti three years ago . . . a long time to wait. Each time we thought—now we've come to the last of the Ambers. . . . Soochi will be the next heir . . . and each time, there was one more." He took a step toward me. I moved back, aware always of Soochi behind me, and keeping out of her reach.

"Sugar, I liked you from the beginning. You weren't like your sister—like that ghastly Ellen. Making love to her, meeting her secretly over on Haiti, all the tiresome, disgusting mess! First she was prim and prissy. Then she was God-awful in black satin and pearls."

"Why was it necessary to make love to her?" I asked finally, trying to make time . . . prolong this . . . hoping against hope that someone would know, would come. What about Joel Bingham? Where was he? "Why couldn't you just kill her? Why kill her soul first?"

Soochi laughed. "That one! He thought he could drive her mad with wanting him, so she would seem to have killed herself. But not she. No. She was tougher than we bargained for. In the end we had to . . ."

"To do what you intend to do to me, is that it?"

I did not mind about that animal Soochi. That she was my sister was a mere accident of biology. I felt no kinship to her, and I had never expected anything except her hatred. But Brett! That easy, delightful friend, so accommodating, so stupid and innocent! And to think I had been afraid that Michael might hurt him!

"They will know this time it was you," I bluffed, hoping to gain a minute and run for it.

Brett opened his fist. A heavy signet lay in the palm of his hand. I remembered seeing it on Michael's hand so often.

"Poor old Bluebeard! In his struggle to drown you, he lost his ring. Soochi tells me his friend Earle was searching for it last night. Damned shame. And we all liked our terrible-tempered Bluebeard; didn't we?"

I ignored that. "Where is Joel Bingham?" I asked, hoping to get them both occupied with defending themselves, so I might run . . . and run . . . and run. . . .

Brett moved again, this time coming slowly around the pool as I retreated. My body felt as though it had become numb and boneless. Even now I could scarcely believe what he had told me. His limpid black eyes looked so innocent, so straightforward, so frank. Only the orange glow of the rising sun behind him reminded me of the lie that was his face.

"Good God, Cathy! Do you still believe that hogwash? Old Joel's where he should be, snug in his waterfront office. What's he got to do with it? Come now, be sensible. It isn't going to hurt if you don't struggle. With Ellen it was over in a minute. Soochi!"

Just as she reached for me I swung my fist around and belted her hard across the eyes. She slipped on a muddy fern frond and went sprawling. I hoped she would roll into the pool, but no such luck! Meanwhile, I got to the path and began to run. Brett reached the spot a second after me, and his flailing arm grazed me and missed.

Ahead of me the fern forest opened just enough for me to rush through. I ran . . . faster . . . faster . . . suffocating . . . always just a hand's width, it seemed, ahead of Brett. I was back in the nightmare of my childhood, breathless . . . trapped . . . only now I knew at last the face of the danger. A dear face, one I had known and trusted.

I was too confused, too tired, to think anything through, except that Michael was not guilty. Michael must have warned Joel and Brett about the highway after all. Everything I had believed was a lie. I had been looking into a mirror in which the image was reversed. But even as I ran, I kept asking myself, "How? How? How?"

How could Brett have been in San Francisco and also here at the same time? How could he make the long-distance phone calls . . . hundreds of details . . . . . . how? What about his aunt and uncle in South Carolina?

I was so tired . . . deathly tired. . . .

I felt Brett's hands seize me around the waist, and I was lifted high up off the path and swung around, kicking, screaming . . . carried back over the path toward the pool. Soochi came running toward us; she reached up and clawed my face. I tried to bite her, to bite Brett's bare hands. . . . There was a roaring ball of flame in my face, and I saw that I was being held just above the Tangerine Pool. I mustered up all my waning strength and wriggled partly free from Brett just as I heard a terrible cracking sound and found myself free, hovering back and forth on the pool's muddy crust. I was blinded by the round, orange globe of the sunrise. Suddenly I felt myself gripped around the wrists.

"It's all right. It's all right now. . . ." Michael's voice soothed me with its strength, its mastery, its tenderness. He pulled me against him, and I felt the comfort of his absolute and iron control of everything. How clever he was, how like a god, I thought comfortably, getting my breath back and staring sleepily at his arms with their golden color, their warm, powerful, muscular look. (Nothing like Brett. I'd never have escaped from Michael's arms as I had escaped from Brett! I thought of this with an odd satisfaction.) I looked around me, but just a little, as my neck seemed very stiff. I must have twisted it in the scuffle. Then, I wished I had not looked. I saw something lying a few feet from me, at the edge of the pool. It was Brett's body, graceless, slack, all twisted in a horrible way, his handsome head hanging downward over the pool. David Earle was examining him.

Over my head, Michael said, "Well?"

"I'm afraid I hit him too hard," David murmured. "He seems to be dead. By the way, here's that ring you lost yesterday."

The drums had been right last night. They had been beating for someone who was about to die. I had not guessed it would be Bret Caldwell.

If I closed my eyes, I thought, it would all go away. I would awaken from my old nightmare and find myself still in San Francisco, thousands of miles from this bloodshed and greed and cruelty.

Michael seemed to understand, for he drew my face against his chest gently, with the palm of his hand, and said over my head to David Earle, "You had better find Soochi. She's somewhere around here. I saw her as we came up."

But the overseer, it seemed, had thought of everything.

"No need. Bingham will run into her. She took the path back to the house."

"Clever fellow, that Bingham," said Michael.

221

I remembered our great danger and tried to sit up but was firmly held in place.

"The volcano—the lava is coming!"

Michael's voice soothed even while it chided me. "You never take my word for anything, do you? I told you old Soufriere was no danger to Amber. The lava flow stopped late yesterday. The old girl will be quiet again in due time."

"But Soochi thought . . . and Brett thought. . . ."

"I'm afraid you've been listening to some very odd people. Just listen to me. And don't think!"

It was very comfortable advice.

I didn't ever want to talk about it again or to hear the whys and wherefores, but I could not escape; for even if Michael wished to spare me, there was good old Joel Bingham, exceedingly proud of his detective work, as he explained that afternoon when he assured me, correctly, that I would feel much more "the thing" over a spot of tea. I looked at Michael, hoping he would change the subject, but he and David were discussing the coming trial of Soochi, and I received the full brunt of Joel's Holmesian deductions. Even so, I preferred suffering his cockiness to dwelling on the probable fate of the woman who had been, by blood only, my sister. For I still could feel nothing for her—no sympathy, not even hatred. She was still a stranger, incomprehensible to me.

"I expect anyone else would have reasoned the same," Joel began modestly, but there was a most immodest swagger in the way he sat there waving his tea cup. "You see, I'd never met old Brett, but I had met his aunt and uncle. So I took him at face value. Never would have thought twice about those trunk calls he made to me, supposedly from California and parts north. Except that the female States operator had a very familiar voice. Then, I got to thinking when I heard your housekeeper's voice. Devilishly like the voice of the trunk operator. Suppose, I thought, suppose old Brett weren't in the States at all, but right here in Saint Cloud, using Soochi to fake the trunk calls."

I remembered something that fitted his theory. "And, of course, when he called me, it was always Soochi who told me it was a long-distance call."

"Precisely. After that, it was a mere question of 'why?' You remember yesterday afternoon when we drove out to my cottage? I mentioned his aunt's resemblance to Brett—particularly the eyes, dark and black?"

I didn't but said I did.

"Well then," he finished triumphantly, waving drops of tea over me. "Mrs. Caldwell's eyes are blue. He'd never even seen his supposed aunt. He was a born cluffer."

Heavens! I thought. No wonder Brett was upset when I called his "aunt" and asked her about Brett. How relieved he had been when he found I had learned nothing from her that would betray him! I remembered distinctly his relief, yet it had not seemed important at the moment.

"But suppose the Caldwells came to Saint Cloud themselves?"

Joel shook his head. "Unlikely. I haven't seen them in nine or ten years. Both in their sixties. And apparently our Brett kept tabs on where the real Brett was."

"Yes," I said. "In Canada, his aunt thought."

"Risky," Michael agreed. "But that is what makes murderers, I imagine. They lack that element most of us guard so well—a sense of the risk."

I could see that Joel didn't like having his role played down. He put in quickly, before anyone else could speak, "That's why I faked it about my phone being off and sending old Brett to phone the police. I didn't want him hanging about Miss Isobel's body destroying evidence. The cheek of the fellow! Killing and burying her on my property."

"I'm afraid he killed her where he found her, and unless Soochi talks, we may never know where that was," said Michael. "But she would play detective. Prowling about as she did, she undoubtedly saw him at Amber that night, got suspicious of a man who had no business within a thousand miles of the place, and—was either killed at Amber or at Joel's place. Curious place for Caldwell to hide, by the way."

Joel said airily, "'Fraid that's my doing. I mentioned it to him on the phone several times. Said I never went there during the week." He nodded sagely.

"Bloody awful show! But you know, I can't for the life of me see why it was necessary for him to have the Southern-Aristocrat relations."

Michael looked up from his whisky and soda and took my hand. "I think I can answer that," he said. "Caldwell . . . which is obviously not his name . . . was a better detective than we were. He and Soochi counted on her inheritance at Ellen's death. When that failed, he traced Cathy's mother from New Orleans to San Francisco. He knew he had to bring Cathy to our attention somehow and soon, so she could be—be eliminated . . . after she had inherited. I rather imagine he knew we would tumble to Cathy sooner or later, and he preferred that it be sooner. So he persuaded Cathy to run that ad which we read. Once Cathy arrived at Amber, though, our murderous friend ran into some sticky problems. First Miss Nell, and later Isobel, tumbled to what was going on. Miss Nell may have suspected the identity of Ellen's secret love."

I said abruptly, "You didn't kill Miss Nell. They killed her—or scared her to death—and pushed her body in front of the car. That's why she appeared to head right into the lights."

I was a little annoyed to see that Michael knew all this, but he patted my hand in a very sweet way, all the same.

"Yes. They told me at the morgue that she'd been dead some hours before my car struck her."

There was a little silence. In spite of the cockiness of the three men, who all seemed to act as if the matter were not the least mysterious and they had been in on the secret all along, I couldn't help feeling that they were nearly as shaky as I was. The silence made me uncomfortable. I half expected to see Miss Nell's ghost come floating out on the portico at any moment, and to forestall this, I said brightly, "I just can't see how I could have been so wrong about Brett. I always thought he was so—so delightfully nothing. Why, I thought he was . . ."

Michael interrupted me, giving me one of his rare and beautiful smiles and warning me, "You're thinking again."

So I had been. I pretended to stop at once. Why tell a man *everything* you do?